Trigger John's Son

Books by Tom Robinson

BUTTONS

MR. RED SQUIRREL

Books by Robert McCloskey

LENTIL

MAKE WAY FOR DUCKLINGS

HOMER PRICE

BLUEBERRIES FOR SAL

CENTERBURG TALES

ONE MORNING IN MAINE

TIME OF WONDER

BURT DOW: DEEP-WATER MAN

Trigger John's Son

BY TOM ROBINSON

Illustrated by Robert McCloskey

New York · The Viking Press

COPYRIGHT 1934 BY TOM ROBINSON

COPYRIGHT 1949 BY ROBERT MCCLOSKEY AND TOM ROBINSON

FIRST PUBLISHED BY THE VIKING PRESS IN NOVEMBER 1934

ILLUSTRATED EDITION PUBLISHED IN SEPTEMBER 1949

PUBLISHED IN CANADA

BY THE MACMILLAN COMPANY OF CANADA LIMITED

EIGHTH PRINTING OCTOBER 1966

FIC 1. TRIGGER JOHN'S SON

PRINTED IN THE UNITED STATES OF AMERICA

BY THE VAIL-BALLOU PRESS, INC., BINGHAMTON, N. Y.

CONTENTS

6 CONTENTS

Trigger John's Son

I. THE JOURNEY

Trigger John's son busied himself with searching in his duffel
bag for a thing that wasn't there. He knew it wasn't there and
if it had been he didn't want to find it. He was just avoiding the
attention of the conductor who was punching tickets down the

aisle. The conductor would call him "Sonny" and pat his shoulder and try to cheer him up. Trigger didn't need cheering up and if he did he wanted to do it himself when he got around to it. The conductor had been cheering him up ever since the train left Philadelphia five or six hours before. Trigger had stood the strain pretty well, but after a while it got to be just too much. So for the past hour or two he had been asleep or busy when the conductor passed by his seat.

Trigger was tired of conductors. He had been in charge of one after another for the last two days. He hated being in charge of anyone, especially with nothing to show for it but a ticket and a baggage check. Not that Trigger had any baggage. He was just his own baggage. The minister who had arranged everything had insisted that Trigger should be checked. "Because," said he to himself (as Trigger figured it out), "if the boy loses his ticket he can still travel as baggage." He even had to promise the minister that he would not throw the check away or untie it from his shirt and put it in his pocket. The only thing he could do was to keep his coat on when every other man in the car had his coat off. That made him hot, but it concealed the check. He supposed it was all because he was small for his age and had red hair and a freckled face and they thought he didn't know anything. But it was humiliating.

It was even more humiliating to have everybody else in the coach notice the conductor cheering him up and start cheering him too.

"What's your name, Sonny?"

"Trigger."

"Trigger what?"

"Trigger John's son."

"Oh! Then your name is Johnson?"

"Yes, sir. Yes, ma'am."

"Where'd you come from?"

"Calais, Maine."

"Where you goin'?"

"Beechwood, Pennsylvania."

"Never heard tell of that place."

"It's not a very big place, I guess."

Then would come a variety of comment: "Well, it may not be so bad." "You'll get there right side up, I expect." "Keep smiling." "Be good to the place and the place will be good to you." "Keep a stiff upper lip." "Every road has an end." And so on. The only interest in any of these conversations was to wait and see what the advice would be. Trigger knew it would be cheerful, but it was sometimes amusing to hear how.

The train slowed down and stopped. The brakeman stuck his head in the door and called out, "Williamsport!" He helped some of the passengers off and then came back in the coach and sat down with Trigger.

"By rights, I oughta stay outside, but I guess nobody'll notice. If they do I can say I was in here to answer questions. That'll be true enough if you go ahead and ask me some."

Trigger rather liked the brakeman because the brakeman just talked to him. He began his questions:

"How big is this place?"

"Well, I never counted. Don't stop here long enough. I run through to Lock Haven. It's bigger'n Lock Haven and not as big as Philadelphia."

"Is it big enough to get lost in?"

"That depends on how much you don't know about it. What you want to get lost for?"

"I was just wondering about it."

"Well, you might try."

Trigger shifted his line of inquiry. "How far is it to Beech-wood?"

"Three hours' run, about."

"Will it be dark when we get there?"

"Not naturally, unless there's an eclipse or a thunder storm. Get there at five-forty. Not dark for a couple hours after that. Why?"

"I was just wondering."

"Somebody gonna meet you?"

"Yes." It did not seem to afford Trigger any pleasure, and the brakeman looked at him questioningly, but before he could frame a question Trigger asked another.

"That's a freight train, isn't it?" He nodded toward a line of box cars standing on the next track.

"Looks like it," said the brakeman. "Why?"

"Just wondering."

"It's on a siding there, waiting for us to pull out. After that it'll hitch up its breeches and trail along after us."

"Does it go to Beechwood, too?"

"Goes through there, I reckon."

"Stop there?"

"Mebbe, mebbe not. Guess yes, because it's just a string of empties and more'n likely it'll drop one or more at about every station between here and Erie. Why? No, don't tell me. I know. You're just wondering. I expect you'll wonder yourself into being president." He grinned at Trigger and Trigger grinned back. "Well, I'll get out and let the stationmaster see me. See you later."

Trigger surveyed the freight train, as much as he could see of it, with a contemplative eye. From his seat he could read the signs on four box cars: "Maine Central," "P.R.R.," "Rock Island," "Canadian Pacific." Moving across the aisle he could read four more: "N.Y.N.H.&H.," "B.&O.," and two more with "P.R.R." Trigger knew them all. He was a specialist in freight cars, had a list a mile long and was prepared to swear that no representative of any railroad had ever come to Calais and got away without his seeing it. He was not surprised that no new railroad met his eye. But his present interest was in a train that moved and not in a string of box cars. For Trigger had a problem and his mind was occupied with ways and means.

He was an orphan who had lived as a public charge for several years, boarded and lodged from house to house. His latest residence had been with the Methodist minister. Here he had come to the attention of Miss Clarissa Barlow, an elderly spinster who had money and the prestige that goes with it, especially in a small place.

In Beechwood, Pennsylvania, Miss Clarissa had a niece whose only child had died. She and her husband had decided to adopt a boy. What more natural than to bring them and Trigger together?

The town of Calais raised no objection. Miss Clarissa compensated the minister for his loss of a needed boarder and Trigger found himself on the way to a new home.

But there was an unfortunate side to the arrangement, or so Trigger thought. His adoption was subject to the inspection and approval of himself by his prospective parents. If they liked him, well and good; if not, no harm was done and he had merely enjoyed a vacation from the minister and had the benefit of travel. "But how," thought Trigger, "if they like me but I don't like them?" Not that he was oversanguine about himself. He knew that he was not a beauty and he had doubts about his manners and customs. Still, he considered the arrangement unfair.

Living here and there as one or another family needed his

board money, was one thing. If he did not like any particular place it was only a matter of making himself more trouble than he was worth. There was nothing permanent about it. But the adoption business was different. If they took him he was tied for good. All very well for them, they had a choice in the matter; but how about him? Trigger suspected that they would say it was for his own good; he'd had much experience in doing things for his own good of which he could not see the benefit. He made up his mind in this matter of adoption to size up his proposed parents before they had a chance to size up him.

The first step was to see them first. The thing that had been troubling him was how he could do this if he arrived checked and ticketed on schedule time and was met, as he would be, at the station. The freight train appealed to him as a solution of his difficulty.

He drew the strings tight around the mouth of his duffel bag, which he tucked like a huge sausage under his arm, and made his way casually to the door of the coach. Here his luck went out for the moment. The conductor, watch in hand, was waiting at the foot of the steps to signal his train to start. He saw Trigger before he could duck back.

"Where you bound, Sonny?"

Trigger was used to emergencies. "I'm headed up to the smoking car."

"In the name of all, why? Do you smoke?"

"No, sir, not usual. But I like the smell of it."

"Get back to your seat, young man."

Trigger tried a different lead. "There's a woman in there that's begun to pump me for all she's worth. I don't want to talk about me and she's making me do it. Please let me go along up to the smoking car!"

The brakeman was about to object, but Trigger looked at

him, man to man, and when he spoke he said something else:
"What's the harm?"

The conductor relented. "Well, don't go through the train.
Get down here and run along where I can see you. It's the
second car, the one back of the baggage car." Then he became
jovial: "Beat it. I'll hold the train."

Trigger beat it. He climbed the steps of the smoking car,
crossed the platform, vaulted the guard-gate, and was down
the other side in an instant. He heard the distant "All aboard!"
and the train began to move. Running in the direction of the
moving train, Trigger scouted the freight until he came to a
box car with an open door. He threw his bag into the car and
climbed in after it, dodging from sight just as the end of the
passenger train swung by him.

II. A DRAWN BATTLE

When Trigger opened his eyes the next morning he did not
know where he was. Then he remembered—he had hidden in
a pile of straw in the corner, he had held his breath to bursting
as a trainman had glanced inside for a possible tramp; he remembered the jolt and jar of the starting train, and his supper

taken from the canvas bag. The last thing he remembered was watching the stars as they passed the crack in the doorway before he fell asleep.

Then his mind switched to the future. He imagined himself getting the better of his prospective parents by seeing them first, finding that he liked them, and allowing himself to be adopted on his own terms.

But it was really the present that he was concerned about.

His car was at a standstill, probably on a siding, for it was close against the wooden wall of what appeared to be a freight shed. It was painted red, or had been, for the paint was now scaly and crumbly. Trigger took this as a good omen. Red was his favorite color. It was early morning as he could tell from the light that seeped in and this also was good, for morning is the right time to start a new adventure. And the birds were singing as they do in early morning. He heard robins and sparrows and in several directions the noisy clatter of gathering groups of cawing crows.

Where he was he did not know, but it was certainly a place not larger than a village, for though robins and sparrows frequented sizable towns, crows were seen in big places only when they flew over. The crows he heard were holding caucus and there must be fields or pastures near by.

Trigger crawled from his hole in the straw and tiptoed to the door to see what he could see. He stuck his red head out and glanced quickly left and right. To the left three or four hundred yards away was a wooden station. The station would have a name and when he chose he could go and learn it and then by reference to his time table find out exactly where he was. In the other direction the track curved to the right, buttressed by a thickly wooded mountain side, and between it and the track he made out the back yards and sheds of widely spaced

wooden houses that must front upon a street. He could not see
more on account of the shed.

His car was the only one on the siding: he and it must have
been dropped sometime in the night. As he withdrew from the
door he caught a faint odor of leather and sniffed several times
in an attempt to place it. He concluded that it was merely his
nose's recollection of the shoe factory in Calais, which the shed
somehow resembled.

For breakfast he ate the big slab of fruit cake that Miss
Clarissa had contributed to his larder and which he had saved
to the last. He relished it hugely, recalling the spicy fragrance
that emanated from parlor closets where down-East house-
wives stored their dainties. The last crumb found and swallowed, he sighed with satisfaction and turned his attention to
the business of the day.

First he considered the Smiths. They would have been looking for him the night before. He was not concerned with any
worry they might have been put to but rather with what their
worry might lead them to do. He did not want to be run down,
not yet. Clearly they would look for him in Williamsport. For
hadn't he asked the brakeman about getting lost there? And
even if the brakeman had kept this to himself, the conductor
would have missed him shortly after they left the place. Probably there had been a lot of telegraphing. He could see the
city being combed by detectives on the lookout for a redhead
with a freckled face and a canvas duffel bag that looked like a
big sausage. Anyhow, they hardly could be searching for him
here—he himself did not know where he was.

Being lost bothered him not at all. He had been lost before
or at least he had made believe being lost. It was difficult to be
really lost in Calais where he knew every alley and by-pass of
the town and every shed and cellar and empty hogshead. But

making believe was just as good and when he was young he could make believe to a frightening degree. Now that he was older he had to get really lost to experience the delights of it. Well, he was lost and that was all to the good. The next step was to go to the railroad station and read the sign and after that to study his time table.

He picked up his bag and prepared to leave. The sound of boys' voices in shrill dispute brought him up short at the doorway. The voices came from the freight shed. Now Trigger noticed two huge doors in the wall of the shed. As he looked, there came the thump of bars being removed and the doors swung slowly inward. Trigger ducked from sight. There followed him a belch of hot air laden with the heavy odor of leather and a man's voice saying:

"Here's the hides now and there's the car. You can load the one with the other, while I go get breakfast."

Another and younger voice, equally Irish, asked, "And where's the five dollars?"

"What five dollars?" in tones of pained wonder.

There was a pause ending with a grunt of disgust and then the younger voice said, "Come on, boys. Let's get along to the tannery; we can get it there and no fuss at all. We're fools and old women to think Pat Mullen would do a straight piece of business." A shuffling of feet followed, to be interrupted by the older voice in mock anger:

"You're a fine bunch of bums, Dude Quinlan, you and your gang, not to know a joke when you rub noses with it. Come on now, was it five dollars the bargain was?"

"You know biggety well it was five dollars," said Dude.

"How would I be remembering a trifle like that, then?"

"Trifle, is it? A trifle to put both your eyes out, Pat Mullen."

"I'm concerned with large affairs," said Pat Mullen.

"Humph! Come along, boys."

"Wait a bit then. What's makin' you so sure it was five dollars? You might misremember the amount your own self."

"I might but I don't. Isn't it half the price of the catcher's mitt and mask that Tubby Roach is holding for us at his drug store till we bring the money? We pay half and Castle Garden pays half, and we're playing this afternoon to see which nine gets the mitt and mask. You can ask Tubby if you think I'm lying on the price."

"You might be makin' a bit besides."

"What would we want with more than we need? Do you think we're like Mrs. Hennessey's old sow that eats all she can hold and then lies on what's left in the trough to keep the other pigs from getting it?"

"Well, you're just in a hurry to lose your money if you ask me, Dude Quinlan, for Castle Garden can beat Goosetown any day including Sunday."

The entire gang replied to this gibe, "Castle Garden beat Goosetown? Never!"

"They'll wipe up the ground with you," jeered the older man.

"That's a nice way for you to talk, Pat Mullen. Go back on your own race and country like that—and take sides with Swedes and Norwegians!"

"What I mean is, I've not got the five dollars with me. I left it to home."

"Then none of us will see it, nor you, Pat Mullen, not if you give it once to your old woman."

"You're wrong about that, me boy. It's home fast enough, but I know where it is and the old woman don't. It's under the clock in the parlor."

Much relief followed this remark and Dude concluded the

conference with, "Get along home and get it then and not a hide do we move till you're back with the money."

Trigger paid scant attention to the last of this argument. "Castle Garden" and "Goosetown" had sent him to his time table to discover where he was. He found no such places listed among the stations and concluded that they must be local sections of the place, like Harbourtown or Milltown in Calais.

He was disappointed, but forgot it quickly in renewed attention to Dude Quinlan and his gang.

Pat Mullen had departed for his five dollars and breakfast and the question before the gang was what to do until he came back. They agreed on marbles at Dude's suggestion. This, Trigger supposed, would take the gang away from the shed, since marbles was a game properly played on the ground. But he was wrong, for the game presently began on the plank floor of the shed. Relying on the boys' interest in the game, Trigger slid forward and peeked from the door.

The game he watched was different from any that he knew. There was no circle enclosing marbles with several boys shooting at them from a given distance. Instead, Dude squatted behind a short piece of board held on edge against the floor and the other boys, six of them, were shooting their marbles at the board, or so at first it seemed. It looked queer to Trigger and he decided it would bear closer inspection. He now noticed that the bottom of the board was cut by little arches and that the shooting consisted in an effort to send the marbles through the arches. When it succeeded, as once or twice it did, Dude added a second marble and returned the two for "keeps." When it failed, as usual, Dude put the loser's marble in his pocket and grinned an Irish grin.

Trigger became excited, for clearly this was gambling. His

hand went down the side of his bag to a certain spot and without much feeling around brought to light a little chamois pouch. From this he took his store of marbles, a dozen alleys and one glassy (only one glassy, but a big beauty, his pride and joy), and slipped them loose into his pocket. Thus armed he stood openly, but unnoticed, in the doorway of his car and studied the game, for Trigger believed in understanding a game before he entered it.

Two things he noticed: the boys had to shoot across the joints in the plank floor instead of parallel with them, and when, in spite of this handicap, a marble went truly toward an opening, a swift, almost imperceptible movement of Dude's hand sometimes brought the board into position to stop it. Trigger grinned and wondered if the other boys didn't see this or were afraid to say so.

Trigger leaped the gap between the car and the shed and took a casual place among the group, one hand in his pocket rattling his marbles. A momentary stare greeted his advent but the game went on without interruption until Dude had cleaned out his gang. Then, still squatting, he surveyed the intruder coldly.

"You got some stakes, feller?" he asked.

"I got a little loose change," said Trigger, drawing a handful of marbles, including the glassy, into view.

"Wanta lose them?" asked Dude. His eyes and the eyes of all the others were fastened on the glassy.

"This glassy's worth a couple o' dozen alleys." Trigger made the statement and it was recognized as some sort of challenge.

"Let's see it," said Dude. The glassy passed from hand to hand.

"Guess so," admitted Dude. "Got a mate to it?"

"You betcha and then some," lied Trigger.

"Let's look at it."

"What's the use of making your mouth water for nothing? Let me see you win this one first."

"Shoot," agreed Dude with a noncommittal expression.

"Got a glassy?" asked Trigger.

"Lots of 'em, but I don't carry 'em around with me."

"How many alleys you got?" Dude counted out twenty-six. "Tell you what I'll do. I'll shoot five times; if I make three of them I get the whole caboodle, if I don't, you get the glassy."

"And the alleys you've got there besides?"

"I said the glassy." Trigger was a good shot with a marble, but he had no intention of risking his whole stake and besides he considered that he had made a fair offer. The other boys thought so too, as Dude could see.

"All right!" he said.

"Only I don't shoot across the cracks in the floor."

Dude became belligerent. "Oh, you don't, don't you? The rest of the gang did."

"That's their business."

"Suit yourself!" said Dude, getting to his feet.

"You afraid, Dude?" asked one of the gang.

"Afraid of what?"

"Losing," suggested Trigger.

Dude reconsidered his position. "See here," he began. "It's only an eight-foot shot across the cracks, but it's twice as far if you shoot with 'em."

"It's too far," Trigger said.

"Well, it's twelve anyhow."

"That's all right," agreed Trigger.

Dude changed his position, squatted, and put his board into place. "Shoot!" he said.

"Some other fellow holds the board," Trigger said.

"Ain't you trusting me, feller?" demanded Dude.

"Yes," grinned Trigger, "just like your yellow dog with the seat of my breeches."

Dude dropped his board, got up, and weaved forward, a snarl on his face, as he thrust it within an inch of Trigger's. "You're a dirty liar!" he shouted.

Trigger stood his ground. "I saw you move the board, didn't I?" They glared at each other. "Ask some of these guys if you don't believe me," Trigger said.

Dude studied the faces of his gang and decided not to ask. "We'll settle that later," he said. Then he added, half apologetically, "Takes a steady hand to hold that board in place. I don't trust nobody's hand as much as mine and mine may slip some onct in a while, when I get excited."

"There's a loose plank over there," said Trigger, pointing. "You can hold it with that."

"You can't hold it straight with that," said Dude.

"I'll show you."

"Show me then!"

Trigger, helped by several of the gang, put the board in position and held it in place by resting one end of the plank on the upper edge. "That all right?" he asked.

"Suit yourself," said Dude sullenly. He was thoroughly disgruntled because he couldn't help seeing that several members of his gang were siding against him. He paced off a long twelve feet. "Shoot!" he said.

Trigger knelt on one knee and shot amid perfect silence. His first marble missed, but it gave him the range and the resistance of the wood floor. He changed his position slightly. The next three marbles went straight through the middle one of the five little arches.

A shout went up in which even Dude joined. But when Trigger gathered up his winnings and stowed them in his leather pouch, now filled to bursting, Dude sobered down at once. There was another score to settle.

Dude swaggered over to Trigger. "You gotta take your boots off," he announced.

"What for?" asked Trigger.

"You called me a liar, didn't you?"

"You want to fight?"

"Scared?"

"Not so you'd notice it."

"Then take off your boots and put up your dukes."

Trigger undid his shoes and threw them aside. His stockings followed, to leave him barefoot, like Dude. He wasn't mad yet, not mad enough to have any chance in a fight, so he got as mad as he could throwing his extra things off. He got so mad that when he ripped off his coat, he forgot all about his baggage tag and when he stood up to Dude, whose only preparation had been the dropping of the half of a suspender from his shoulder, there was the tag in full view.

"Lookit!" shouted one of the gang.

"He's tagged!" shrieked another.

"Came in by express." "Marked Perishable." "C.O.D." "Gee! Handle with care!"

These gibes from all directions at once were the one thing needed to rouse Trigger's rage to the fighting point. He jerked off the offending tag, a piece of his shirt and the button with it, and thrust it into his pocket.

"Come on, you!" he challenged.

"There ain't nothing barred," shouted one.

"It's a free-for-all," yelled another.

But the two fighters paid no attention. They were circling

around, fists up, feet moving rapid and catlike. Superficially, at least, they were evenly matched. About the same height and weight, they were also both tough and wiry. Dude's clothes cumbered him less in weight, a black cloth shirt open at the neck and what remained of a pair of blue overalls shortened unequally in the legs. Trigger's store clothes were heavy, and a red undergarment was plainly visible through the new gap in his shirt front. But the extra weight was somewhat offset by the closer fit, which afforded fewer handholds than Dude's more flimsy garments. Both were hatless and their hair, one's carrot red, the other's bristly black, was long enough to grasp.

The initial set-to was mostly a measuring of each other's speed in foot and tongue work. The circles increased and diminished in size as the battling language, augmented from the ringside, waxed or waned. Presently each began to save his breath and with the saving there came an approach to the real encounter.

Dude rushed with a broad Irish whoop and landed a blow on Trigger's right shoulder. But the shoulder bent forward to meet the blow, and Trigger's right foot, thrust expertly behind Dude's, sent Dude in an awkward dive to the floor. On his feet again in a second, Dude rushed once more and this time for a clinch; but Trigger was bent backward at the waist and Dude's arms were not long enough to lock themselves behind him. Meanwhile, Trigger's arms were around Dude's neck, bending it slowly downward. Dude quickly changed his tactics, thrust his head between Trigger's legs and heaved upward with all his might. Trigger went up and then slid down Dude's back, pushed his legs from under him, and both boys went to the mat together, backs first and Trigger underneath. Here for a moment they lay entangled and

locked together, breathing hard. First one, then the other
tried to free himself; it was a double hold for both and looked
for a moment like a draw. After several futile struggles both
stayed quiet, panting and exhausted.

Then came an inspiration from the side lines: "Leggo your
holt and start it again, Indian fashion."

Breathlessly they agreed. Dude released, slid over, and the
two lay side by side and end for end, waiting.

"I'll count three and then let 'er go," the prompting voice
shouted. "One—two—three—go!"

Instantly two right legs rose into the air and locked firmly
with a jolt; but neither boy could roll the other over. They
strained and panted. Presently they were unable to hold the
strained position. Their legs relaxed and, as if by mutual consent, drooped to an amicable wobble. The fighters swung
slowly around, facing each other. Then they both began to
laugh.

"Say," said Dude, "you can fight, can't you?" Then he
rose on an elbow and announced in surprised tones, "I don't
believe I'm mad any more. Are you then?"

"I wasn't much anyhow. I had to work it up," said Trigger. They grinned at each other sheepishly and got up.

"Another washout," one of the onlookers remarked in mild
disgust.

"What's your name?" asked Dude.

"Trigger John's son."

"Johnson?"

"John's son. Father's name was Trigger John and I'm his
son, that's all."

This sounded reasonable to Dude, so he continued, "Where
you from?"

"Calais, Maine."

"Gee! That's way down East, ain't it?"

"Right."

"Where you going?"

"Beechwood."

"Beechwood!" was the general exclamation, and Dude added, "Why, that's this here place, feller!"

Trigger looked surprised, but at once became nonchalant. "Well, then, here's where I'm going. Know a man and his wife by the name of Smith?"

"There's a whole flock of Smiths round here."

"This Smith's a deacon."

"Oh, I know him! He's all right."

"Oh," said Trigger. Then in an effort to change the subject, "Do you all go to church?"

"Naw," said Dude in disgust, "not that church. But I watch 'em through the window sometimes." Then he reconsidered and, turning to one of the boys, said, "Except Dutch here. He's a Methodist."

"I ain't no Methodist neither," denied Dutch. "I don't never go to Sunday school, and I don't never go to holy communion."

"Well, you go to the Christmas tree," Dude reminded him.

"That's for the present. You get a bag of candy."

"And you go to church suppers too," another boy said, a little angrily.

"Well, you get food there," defended Dutch.

"And you go to camp meeting when they have it, down at Sinnamahoning."

"That's fun," Dutch said with gusto.

"Anyhow, Dutch belongs to our gang. Dutch is all right."

"Oh, sure, Dutch is all right." Several members came to his defense.

"Wanta join this gang?" Dude demanded of Trigger.

"What kind of a gang is it?"

"It's a tough gang." Dude was firm. "It's the only real tough gang in this place. The gang up at Castle Garden thinks it's tough but it's not noways near as tough as our gang."

Everyone agreed to this.

"Sure, I'll join," Trigger said after due consideration.

"We'll initiate you tonight up at the Lodge."

"Where's the Lodge?" Trigger began feeling around for a temporary residence.

"Goosetown, where'd you suppose?"

"Can you stay there without being seen?"

"Not in daytime you can't. But it's safe enough at night. What you asking that for? You've got to go and live with the Smiths, ain't you?"

Trigger decided suddenly to take the gang into his confidence and enlist their help. He told his story to a gaping crowd which presently became enthusiastic. The first and most important point being secrecy, it became at once necessary to conduct Trigger to some isolated spot, where he could wait until the gang had finished loading the hides into the car and were free to hold a powwow and confab.

Dude appointed Dutch to guide Trigger down along the creek and up the mountain side, this being the route freest from observation, to the slippery elm tree, a little distance out of the village. There Trigger could remain in relative safely until the gang arrived.

It was now time for Pat Mullen to return with the five-dollar bill, and introductions, interchange of views and ideas, together with other necessary formalities, would have to wait. Without any ceremony, Trigger and Dutch, carrying the duffel bag between them, were sped on their secret mission.

III. THE GOOSETOWN GANG

Woodruff's General Store stands in the northwest angle between Main and Middle Streets, and it was in the red shed at
the rear of the store that the fight took place.

It was still early and Dutch had little fear of being seen
as he led Trigger down Middle Street, across Main Street,
and down over the bank to the edge of the creek below. Here
they turned east. Trigger had put on his shoes, but he took
them off again because it was much more satisfactory to walk

in the shallow water than on the bank. They waded half a mile downstream. Here the mountain rose steeply to the north.

"We turn into the woods here and climb," Dutch said.

Trigger sat on the bank and slipped on his shoes. As he rose he glanced across the creek toward a shallow farm.

"Who's that over there?" he asked.

"That's Cy Perkins," said Dutch. "Make believe not to see him. He's everybody's enemy. Some say he hates himself. That's a double-barrel shotgun he's got and it's loaded two ways. One barrel's shot for woodchuck and the other's pepper and salt for us boys."

Trigger nodded and immediately became interested in the creek. "What's the name of this brook?"

"Ain't no name to it. We call it just the Crick."

"Got a regular river at Calais and a ten-foot tide. What kind of fish do you get out of it?"

"There's black bass if you know how to catch 'em, but mostly it's suckers and mullets."

"What bait do you use?"

"Don't use bait. We snare 'em from the railroad bridge and the horse-and-team bridge up above. Come on. I gotta get you hid and get back or Dude'll say I been sojering."

They fought their way through a fringe of alders up onto the track, which was just notched into the hill, across this and up the wooded mountain side. They came presently to a dirt road notched in like the track.

"This road takes you to Sinnamahoning. After that it goes to Renova and Lock Haven and points east. You must 'a' come through them coming here."

"Don't know; I was asleep."

"The slippery elm tree is just beyond here in a kind of little gully."

They followed the road east a few hundred yards until they came to an indentation in the mountain. Up this they went and arrived in a few moments at an open-faced camp built of dead tree-trunks, its sloping roof covered with mud and sods.

"This is the lookout," Dutch explained.

"What d'you look out for?"

"We look out to see that none o' the other boys but our gang gets to the slippery elm tree. Nobody but us knows about it, but we stand guard over it just the same when we're here. Dude has it fixed for hour watches, first one and then t'other, you know."

"Sure I know. Where's the tree?"

"You stay here. You can't monkey with that tree yet, not till you're a regular member in good standing."

"When'll you be back?"

"We'll all come in a bunch. I expect we'll vote to hook-jack t'day so's to get you settled. S'long."

"S'long," and Dutch was off.

Trigger hid his bag under a clump of spruces and started off in search of wood that was fit to make into a bow and arrow. He had learned the art from the Indian who had taught him how to make a paddle and to paddle a bark canoe. He looked for ash, but the only thing he could find was hickory. He did not know the wood, but an examination of its qualities assured him that it had the makings. He climbed the tree, laboriously hacked off a small limb with his jack-knife, carried it back to the camp and went to work on it.

The making of a good bow takes time and skill and Trigger was a long way from through when a distant halloo announced the approaching gang. He hid the partly shaped bow with his duffel bag, returned to the lookout, and was busy doing nothing when the gang hove in sight, Dude Quinlan in the lead.

They came up the hill panting, strung out one after the other, Trigger thought, like the wooden blocks on the float line of a fisherman's net.

Dude was winded from haste but he announced at once between gasps, "The first business is the interduction of our new member."

"He's not a member yet, Dude," said Dutch. "He's not elected."

"He ain't, ain't he?" said Dude. "We'll vote on it. All in favor, signify, 'Yes.' "

"Yes," came a shout from all.

"Contrary minded, 'No!' Now's your chance, Dutch."

"I voted 'Yes,' didn't I? What's eating you? I just wanted things to be done regular and in order."

"We're too busy to stumble around over carrot seed. We got to find out what to do with Trigger here and do it quick. We got to practice before we match bats with those Castle Garden navvies, or we'll never win that mask and mitt." He turned to Trigger. "Trigger John's son, stand up."

Trigger was already standing, but he sat down and stood up again and saluted, like the customs officer at the bridge at Calais.

Dude continued, "You are now a member in good standing and belong to the Goosetown gang. We can't swear you in yet 'cause the symbols are under the floor at the Lodge. And we can't get you there by daylight without being seen. The first business of this powwow and confab is interduction." He turned to the loosely grouped gang. "You men line up here."

They lined up and Dude placed himself at the head.

"I'm Dude Quinlan. I'm first because I organized this gang. And besides nobody has been able to lick me yet."

Dude then stepped out of line and took Trigger by the arm, presenting him to the others in order.

"This is Bud. He's a Dutchman like Dutch here but only on his father's side. His mother's Irish. He's slow as molasses in January, but he can stay under water up at the swimming hole longer than anybody else. He's just too lazy to come up once he gets down, but no matter." Bud grinned.

"This is Mike Hennessey, Mickey for short. He's good behind the bat, and we want the mitt and mask for him. Mostly the mask, because he can ketch bare-handed if he has to and he's got one broken nose already.

"You've sorta met Dutch here. All his folks come from Dutchyland. We have him to object to everything like he did to your election. He plays shortstop.

"I forgot to say I'm the pitcher of this team and I can throw a out-shoot that'll miss any bat in Castle Garden. You'll see.

"Oh, and Bud there holds down first base and that's just what he does do. He has to. If he moved a foot away and you threw a ball at him he'd never get back to it.

"This is Jim. He works for a living and can't show up very often. He gets off for a ball game. Jim plays third base and, take it from Dude, he eats 'em up.

"There's two more men in this gang. Skinny Muldoon, because he's skinny, and Socks Donovan on account of his clothes. Socks is second base and Skinny covers back field. They didn't dare play hooky for fear their folks would see where Herbie thrashed them when they went to bed."

"Who's Herbie?" asked Trigger.

"Herbie's principal up at the High School. He's no good to anybody except girls."

"Haven't you got a full nine?"

"Nope, don't need 'em. Skinny can get anywhere to a fly before it gets there. I expect he'll make the Philadelphia Athletics in a year or two. If you wasn't living under cover you could get out there and help him. Can you bat?"

"Sure, I can bat."

"Well, I'll strike you out one of these days just to prove it on you."

Dude now initiated Trigger into the mystery of the secret handshake, and everyone shook hands with him. After that Jim had to go off to work.

"Now," said Dude, "the next thing we have to do is to take Trigger up and show him the slippery elm tree." He started off, then turned back.

"Bud, you can stay here at the lookout. You'd rather do that anyhow. And mind you don't go to sleep. If you hear anyone, whistle 'Yankee Doodle.' And if Bud whistles, you fellows scatter quick and take cover. And grab a rock and when you see the whites of his eyes let drive and shoot to kill. C'mon."

Dude led the way farther up the gully and then turned abruptly right up one side a little and stopped.

"Where's the tree?" asked Trigger.

"Take off your blinders," said Dude. "There she is."

It wasn't much of a tree to look at. Trigger had expected nothing less than a giant oak, but this tree was quite small and rather skinny. Dude sensed the disappointment and began to explain, if not to apologize.

"She's not so big but she's mighty important. There's no other slippery elm tree anywheres around. Guess we stunted her a little peeling the bark off, but we don't do that now. We just each of us has one bit o' strip each summer now till she begins to grow. You can cut yourself a piece, because chewing the bark is part of the 'nitiation. And all you other fellows keep off, see?"

Trigger went up to the tree. "I don't see any bark gone anywhere."

"That's because you're a greenhorn. We take the bark off the root."

Dude got down on his knees and dug some earth away carefully. When a part of the root was uncovered, Trigger could see where little squares had been cut away.

"Got a knife?" asked Dude. "If you ain't I'll lend you mine. It's got a broken blade that's just the ticket to cut bark with."

"I got a knife of my own," said Trigger. He took it out and proceeded to cut at the root.

"Be careful not to cut the tree and let the blood out," cautioned Dutch.

"Aw, shut up, Dutch," said Dude. "I guess he knows what he's up to."

"Do I chew it?" asked Trigger.

"Of course, you chew it. And you have to chew it right here in front of everybody. And be sure not to spit it out. You have to swallow the spit."

Trigger chewed. "It's not so bad, but it don't taste much like the lozenges you get at the drug store."

"Of course not, they're just flavored with perfumery. This is the real taste. Like it?"

"It'll do," said Trigger, swallowing, "but I won't steal any more."

"You betcha won't. If you do there's a penalty."

"What's the penalty?"

"Never you mind what, but there is one. You'll get to like it after a while and then's when you'll have to be careful and resist temptation. Only remember you're being watched. And anyhow I'd rather have a chew of navy plug, but the other fellows, except Mickey, don't chew. They don't dast."

There was some grumbling over this but Dude paid no attention. "Do you chew, Trigger?"

"I don't like it."

"Funny thing, but almost most Protestants can't chew."

"How you know I'm a Protestant?"

"It's the way you look, I guess. Ain't you?"

"Mebbe I am and mebbe I'm not. I don't go to church except when I'm made to by someone I live with."

"You live with the deacon's wife and you'll go all righty."

"I expect so," agreed Trigger gloomily.

"Now we got to go back to the lookout and decide about you," said Dude.

On the way back Trigger renewed the subject of chewing. "I chewed once, but it made me sick and I didn't like the taste of it anyway, so I never wanted to chew again. There's a fellow in Calais chews a black plug, he calls it fruit cake. I had some off of that."

"That black is just because it's stuck together with molasses," Dude informed him. "If you're really going to chew you want to get aholt of navy plug."

"Anyhow, all I do now is smoke."

"That's something," said Dude.

When they reached the lookout they found Bud asleep. Dude kicked him. He got up and wanted to fight, but Dude said he didn't have to defend his honor wasting time on him and besides they were busy. "I 'spect I'll have to fight the whole gang over again now me and you just had a draw battle," he told Trigger. This also apparently was mere waste of time.

"The question is, where is Trigger going to hide out till he can learn enough about George Smith and Mrs. Smith to know if he wants to adopt them? Motions is in order."

"I thought we'd decided," began Dutch.

"Hold your horses, Dutch," Dude interrupted. "We talked things over, but it ain't right to decide without Trigger." He turned to Trigger. "You can't go up around Castle Garden. Everyone up there's enemies. They'd make you join up with them and you couldn't do that 'cause you're already joined up with us. And if you didn't they'd crowd you and mebbe kill you. And you can't go to Goosetown for old Mrs. Hennessey lives there. She don't never leave her window where the geraniums grow, but she knows all about everything that's going on. She's Mickey's grandmother, but it ain't his fault. The only place to hide in town is under the shed back of the General Store and that would be mighty uncomfortable."

"Can't I stay here?"

"There's bears here and snakes."

"I'm not afraid of bears. Are the snakes poison?"

"You betcha! Rattlers and copperheads both."

"Don't have poison snakes back in Calais," said Trigger.

"That's like Ireland, ain't it?" said Dude proudly. "But there's snakes here and you gotta get acquainted with the ways of snakes, specially copperheads, before you go among 'em."

Trigger looked around.

"Oh, they ain't right here this minute. They're out on the rocks sunning themselves. And if there was one you wouldn't dast kill it 'cause its mate would follow you and sting you."

"What's the place you all settled on?" asked Trigger, changing the subject.

"There's just one place that's safe. That's the old Englishman's up back of Weed's house, north part of town. There's a ravine there and he has a shack a quarter mile up that. He's a friend of ours and you can stay there and only go out nights."

"Will he let me?"

"He will if I ask him. He mends chairs and umbrellas and things for folks and we get them for him and take them back again. He isn't lame or halt or anything but he's seen better days and he don't go around much."

"Well, that sounds all right," agreed Trigger.

"Then that's settled," said Dude. "We'll go right along over. But we gotta go up the mountain side through the woods, so's not to be seen going through town over along the road yonder. And we got to go single file and careful."

Dude set off up the gully back of the lookout and the rest followed carefully at short intervals behind him. Trigger got his duffel bag and partly made bow, and trailed along in the rear.

IV. THE OLD ENGLISHMAN

Dude led them half a mile uphill and then half a mile downhill along a trail that was an inverted V laid on the mountain
side. Trigger couldn't figure out why they hadn't just gone
round the mountain and saved the climb. But he supposed the

reason was something he ought to know and he wasn't going to betray his ignorance by asking questions. It is doubtful if he would have noticed the climb but for the duffel bag, which got pretty heavy by the time Dude called a halt.

"The shack's just beyond," Dude said. "This old Englishman now, he's a queer guy and you got to handle him right. First place, you don't wanta go and call him the old Englishman; we only call him that behind his back. When we speak to him to his face we call him Mr. England. It's not his name, but because that's where he came from.

"Second place, you don't wanta say nothin' to him anyhow 'less he says something to you. What I mean, he's a quiet sort of feller and you don't wanta hurry him with the talk. May look funny-like just at first, but when you been with him a while it's all right and you don't mind if he don't say nothin'." He took a deep breath. "Whole thing is, you just keep a weather eye on yours truly and if you do what I do, things'll go slick as grease and by and by you'll be acquainted. C'mon."

The gang got under way without troubling to fall in line and presently came out of the woods into a small clearing in a notch that ran up and down the mountain side. A dry brook bed ran down the middle of it on its way to the village just visible below and the clearing climbed the hill in irregular patches on either side of the brook bed.

"There's water in this brook in the spring when the snow melts off the mountain," Dude explained. Then, in a whisper, he added, pointing, "Lookit! There he is now."

Trigger looked up along the line of the brook and saw a rough and ready shack built into the side hill. In front of it was a man washing clothes in a round wooden washtub placed on a bench.

"Hullo-o-o!" Dude called, explaining to Trigger, "That's sort of a knock on his door to let him know who's comin'. He knows everybody he hears like he does birds and things."

The group trailed up to the place in a huddle and then spread out and around, all very much at home.

"Goosetown come to make you a call, Mr. England!" Dude said.

The old man had turned his face toward them as they approached. He acknowledged Dude's greeting by bowing his head deliberately two or three times and a smile that began with his first bow and ended with the last one, came and went. He didn't say a word; only gazed vaguely in the boys' direction. Trigger thought he looked like a cross between Santa Claus he had seen on a Christmas card and a picture of Andrew Carnegie in the sixth-grade geography—both very pleasing. For the man's ruddy face was enclosed in a rumple of wavy white hair and beard, and his smile was a cordial welcome. Even his clothes were friendly, like old slippers: a soft flannel shirt that had once been orange tucked into a pair of rusty green corduroys and the legs of these in turn tucked into the tops of high leather boots. His suspenders, a faded black, had been thrown from his shoulders for ease in working and hung in loops around his hips. He was short in stature, almost squatty, not fat, but round and pleasing.

He was scrubbing his clothes on a home-made washboard and he continued with the operation, pausing only with one hand which rested for a moment on the side of the tub and then slipped back into the suds to keep pace with its fellow. His motions were quiet and unhurried and his whole body moved rhythmically with the movement of his arms.

"See how easy he does it!" Dude whispered, adding, "You oughta see my old woman for a difference." The old man

turned to them smiling, then back to his tub; the two boys watched, fascinated.

"He makes his own soap too," said Dude. "We fetch him the suet from the slaughter house when Boney Remick butchers a critter and he tries it out. Water's hard out of that spring of his but that soap he makes softens it. And look at the suds and bubbles."

Trigger had noticed the soap bubbles rapidly forming and
bursting and their colors as they flashed in the sunlight. He
wished he had a new clay pipe to dip in the soapy water and
blow bubbles of his own.

After a while Dude said, "C'mon away a while, Trigger.

Mr. England's busy and he won't wanta talk till he gets his washing on the line."

Dude led the way around the hut to the rear. The first thing Trigger saw was a long run fenced in with chicken wire and a young fox in it, running up and down. Bud and Dutch squatted on the ground in front of it, watching the fox.

"Oh, a fox!" Trigger said, glad to show that he knew a fox when he saw one.

"You betcha," Dude agreed.

"His name's Freddy," said Bud.

"Freddy Fox England," Dutch elaborated.

Dude began at once on the history of Freddy the Fox. "The old Englishman found him when he was a pup. He was making circles round his ma that was caught in a trap and died. The old Englishman never set the trap—he never kills nothing except snakes—but he stumbled on it accidental. Well, when he sees Freddy there running round barking and whimpering, he makes up to him—almost anything will make friends with the old man—and Freddy makes up to the old Englishman. And the old Englishman gathers him up and totes him home in a bag and brings him up on a bottle. But he's big now so the old Englishman figures he can take care of himself and he's gonna let him loose on his birthday some day."

"When's his birthday?"

"Every Friday's his birthday because it's a Friday the old Englishman finds him and brings him home."

"Why doesn't he keep him, I wonder?"

"Because he's growed up now, and when a fox is growed, he don't like it to be kept in. You can see how he keeps running back and forth. He's always on the move like that. You can't really tame a fox, not ever."

"It's a red fox," Trigger said.

"All foxes is red," Bud assured him.

"I saw a silver gray once," Trigger told them.

"Huh!" jeered Dude to that. And then, "C'mon, got something else to show you if he's to home." He led the way up the gully, coming presently to a dead tree and Mickey sitting at the base of it, whittling.

"Lookit!" said Dude.

Trigger looked. Pretty well up in the tree and going higher was a ball of something; it scratched and slipped, but struggled on awkwardly. "It's—why, I do declare, it's a porcupine!"

"You know a lot, don't you?" Dude said, but rather admiringly. "But I suppose there's porcupines other places as well's here. His name is Billyus."

"What?"

"Billyus. B-I-L-U-S, Billyus. We call him that 'count of his always acting like he had a bellyache."

"What's he up the tree for?"

"Nobody knows. Not even the old Englishman."

"When does he come down?"

"Soon's he gets up. And when he gets down he goes up again. Jest up and then down and nobody knows the reason. Don't know hisself, if you ask me. He's got the tree all wore out. What he'll do when it's wore out complete I don't know."

"Doesn't live there, does he?"

"No. It's just at times. When he's here he goes up and down but when he ain't here nobody knows where he is."

"Don't you ever follow him up?"

"Nope," Dude admitted, a bit ashamed. "You see, th' old Englishman says if he knows we know where he lives, then he'll think he's gotta move and it's a whole lot o' trouble for a porcupine to move. He's so all-fired slow getting whatever he does done."

After this explanation, Dude hunted up a fine pine stick, sat down, took out his knife, and began to whittle. Trigger did the same. All three were busy and silent for a long time. Finally Trigger said, "Why don't you whittle something?"

Dude looked at him compassionately. Mickey said, "We are whittlin' something."

"What?"

"Shavings."

"Oh!" said Trigger. He noticed for the first time that the other two had been whittling a very special kind of shavings. Instead of cutting each shaving off the block of wood, as he was doing, they cut each one nearly off and left it there; then they cut another and then another and so on until they had six or eight, each curling up behind the other. Then they split off the lot of them so Mickey and Dude each had in front of him a pile of shavings that looked like a lot of little fans, but Trigger had only a litter of single shavings.

"What you make 'em like that for?" Trigger asked.

"That's the way to do it," said Dude. "These things you've whittled off ain't nothing at all but slivers. There's ways of using a knife and there's ways not to use it. Besides, these of ourn are good to kindle a fire with. When we come to see the old Englishman and he ain't ready to talk, we gets us a chunk of pine and makes these kindlings for him. What you got a knife for, anyhow?"

Before Trigger would answer that question he had to defend himself, so he said, "Back in Calais they don't make shavings to make a fire with. They just pick up a lot of dry twigs. They're a good kind of tinder and when you put a match to them they burn quick and plenty. Back there when they take out a knife they take it out to make something with." He stopped short.

"What?" Mickey fell into the trap, while Dude maintained a sturdy silence.

"Boats and canoes and paddles and bows and arrows and things," answered Trigger.

"Bows and arrows! Is that what you hunt Injuns with?" asked Mickey.

"No! Not Indians. It's Indians that show you how to make them. It would be pretty low down to hunt the folks that showed you with the very things they showed you how to make, wouldn't it?"

"I reckon it would," agreed Mickey.

"What do you hunt for, then?"

"Rabbits and foxes and pheasants and squirrels."

"What kind of squirrels?"

"Red squirrels, of course! There's no other kind, 'cept chipmunks and they're red too."

"Huh!" said Mickey.

"There's other kinds of squirrels here," Dude bragged.

"What other kinds?"

"Gray squirrels and black ones, mostly; but I saw a white squirrel onct," Dude went on bragging.

"Golly!" exclaimed Trigger in spite of himself. Then he changed the conversation: "What you hunt with, if you don't use a bow?"

"We use slingshots," Dude said emphatically, as if slingshots were the only real weapon.

Dude waited a while for Trigger to ask about slingshots, but when he didn't Dude stuck his hand in his shirt and pulled one out. "That's a slingshot!" he said, not without some show of importance.

"I've heard about 'em," Trigger said. Then he took the thing from Dude and examined it in an offhand way. "Looks like it's not strong enough to kill much with," and he handed it back.

"Say!" exclaimed Dude. "That there slingshot is so strong I don't never dare shoot at a target or a barn with it for fear it'll go clean through the boards and kill somebody that's inside."

"The kind of wood's the important thing in a bow," explained Trigger. "Ought to be ash. And of course the catgut's important too. Some fellows use a string and wax it, but catgut's what they ought to use. Catgut's what the Indians use and I guess they know."

"Well, it's the 'lastic bands that's important in a slingshot. If that's good and strong with a good stretch and give to it you can kill a bear." Dude entered his defense.

"I'll find out about it some time, p'raps," was Trigger's disposal of the subject.

"And I'll look into the bow 'n' arrow business sometime and see what's in it," concluded Dude. "Guess we better go on back now. Like as not the old Englishman has got his wash up by now."

Mickey and Dude gathered up their shavings, Trigger kicked his pile apart so they wouldn't look like accumulated evidence against him, and the three boys started back, collecting Bud and Dutch from the fox's run on the way.

The old Englishman had got his clothes hung up. They found him sitting on his log doorstep smoking a corncob pipe.

"This is a new member of the gang, Mr. England," Dude introduced Trigger, and the old man beamed a welcome. "His name's Trigger John's son. That is, his Pa's name was Trigger John and this here Trigger is his son. He come in this morning or last night sometime on the freight and got sidetracked alongside the shed back of the General Store. He come from a place called Callus, back in Maine som'mers. He's an orphan. He's looking around for a Pa and Ma and he's expecting t' find 'em right here in this town. But he ain't got nowhere to put up while he's lookin' round. An' he don't wanta be seen much. An' us fellers figgered on how you'd sorta let 'im be here till he sorta got the lay of the land and knew what he wanted t' do."

Dude delivered his speech with a good deal of feeling and anyone could see that he was anxious to win his point; but all the other boys, except Trigger, who was nervous, occupied themselves with paying no attention to what was going on.

The old Englishman kept right on smoking, but he didn't say a word or even look in Trigger's direction for a long time. Then he took his pipe out of his mouth, knocked the ashes out of the bowl and stood up.

"Let me hear you say something, young man," he said.

Trigger did not know what to say but finally decided to say, "I don't know what to say."

The old Englishman smiled slowly, looking vaguely in Trigger's direction. "That's enough," he answered gently; then he turned toward Dude. "We'll have to get him a place to sleep on besides the floor. My bunk is only just big enough for me. If you boys will scatter up the gully to that swale and cut me some saplings, Trigger and I will get a frame ready to lay them on."

With a whoop that was a command, Dude led the gang at high speed around the shack and out of sight, leaving Trigger alone with the old Englishman who sat down again, refilled and relighted his pipe, and then fell into a brown study. Trigger was afraid he was going to question him. Whenever he went to live with a new family, the first thing the family did was ask questions. He had told what he knew of his family history so many times that he knew the lesson by heart. It was a long story, because he had learned from experience that people never were satisfied with a plain unvarnished tale and he had been obliged to invent and include innumerable fictitious details before he had achieved the final edition of his life history. The old man's face was turned away from him, he appeared to be lost in thought and Trigger studied him closely if surreptitiously. There was nothing in the wrinkled, kindly countenance to excite fear; on the contrary, it had a benign and gentle look, inviting confidence, but without curiosity, and Trigger began eventually to revise his tale down to the brevity of true facts in preparation for his spoken answer.

But the old man had no intention of asking questions, as Trigger soon found out. "Are you there, my boy?"

"Yes, sir."

"I've been thinking where to build the bunk. It isn't like a bed that you can move about. Where you build it, there it stays, so you want to think and put it in the right place to start with. I have it: at the northwest corner with your feet to the south."

"Yes, sir."

"We must get that frame set before the boys come back."

"Yes, sir."

The old man was looking toward Trigger, but his eyes moved around him vaguely and when they settled, as sometimes, on Trigger's they looked through him and beyond. Trigger suddenly got the idea that the old Englishman was blind. That would account for his never leaving his shack to go into the village, for the boys' bringing him the things he worked on. Besides, he knew a man in Calais who was blind and that man looked at you vaguely too and moved slowly and was good natured and smiling. But that man's eyes were clouded and the

old Englishman's eyes were blue like the sky and keen as a
sailor's. Of course, the boys hadn't said the old man was blind
but that didn't mean anything. He must find out for himself
and then, whatever he found out, keep still about it.

"There's some cordwood over there." The old man pointed
in the general direction of a pile of wood that had not yet been
cut into stove lengths. "Are you pretty strong?"

"Yes, sir." Trigger moved closer. The old Englishman ran
his hand over him lightly and Trigger knew he was finding
out how big he was. "You're not very big."

"No, sir. I'm small for my age, folks say. But I'm strong. I
can carry any of those logs if you want."

"We must pick out the right logs; right in size and right
in kind of wood. Bugs get into some kinds of wood. Of
course, there are bugs under the bark in most any kind of log,
but these bugs stay there, it's where they live. What we want
to pick out is a kind of bark that will keep out the foreign bugs,
the bugs that don't belong there by rights. You know about
that?"

"Yes, sir. Fir and spruce'll keep out the bedbugs."

"That's right, so'll hemlock," smiled the old man. "You
fetch along a couple of hemlock sticks, pretty good size, and
three little ones to tuck alongside of them to keep them from
rolling. I'll just step inside and clear out that corner."

"Yes, sir."

The old Englishman had a space cleared by the time Trigger had carried in the five short logs. He got down and sniffed
at the logs and felt them over to make sure the branches had
been cut off close to the trunk. Then, with Trigger's help, he
put them in position. He put the biggest log against the north
wall with one end of it tight against the west wall. Then he
paced off about six feet and put the second biggest log at this

point, sticking out perpendicularly from the west wall. Then he wedged the three smaller logs against the sides of the big ones and tried the big ones with his feet to make sure they would stay in place.

"I don't use nails or spikes or even wooden pegs unless I have to," he said. Then he went back to his doorstep and lighted his pipe. Trigger could not help seeing that the inside of the hut was just one big room with a general air of neatness and order, but he didn't want to look things over on purpose until he was invited to, so he followed the old man out and sat down beside him.

Presently the gang came back on the run carrying a load of saplings, which they dropped to the ground. Dude took some to the old man for inspection and Trigger noticed that Dude didn't say anything until the old man had one in his hand and could tell by the feeling if it was right.

"That's a pretty fair average sample, Mr. England," he said. "We got a dozen seven or eight feet long and a whole caboodle shorter ones."

"It's alder," Mr. England said.

"Yes, sir," Dude agreed.

"Now then, we'll show Trigger how to make a spring for his bed. Two of you and Trigger are enough for that. Let the rest take my ax and hatchet and get along up the hillside and cut some hemlock boughs and fir and balsam for a mattress."

Dutch and Mickey at a gesture from Dude disappeared inside for a moment, came out again with the ax and hatchet and were up the hill and out of sight among the trees in less time than it takes to tell it.

The old Englishman took his pipe from his mouth and gave directions: "Lay out the long ones on the ground, about a foot apart with all the butts pointing the same way."

Dude performed this operation himself while Mr. England smoked placidly and Bud and Trigger looked on. "Done, Mr. England," Dude said, and again Trigger noticed that it was a cue to the old man.

Mr. England removed his pipe: "Trigger, you get at one end and—" he paused.

"That's Bud there," Dude said instantly.

"Of course, it's Bud. You, Bud, you stand at the other end. And, Dude, you weave the small saplings into the ones you've laid out on the ground."

"I put down all twelve and these short saps aren't long enough to go way across."

"Eight of the long ones will be enough."

Dude kicked the extras to one side and set to work weaving the smaller, more flexible saplings in and out across the eight larger ones, while Trigger at one end and Bud at the other held the long ones in place. It was a long operation, for the saplings were bulky, easily got out of place, and had to be adjusted and readjusted. Several of the short ones broke and had to be withdrawn and replaced. Finally it was done. The boys stood up, breathed freely, and surveyed the finished job.

"Now then," said Mr. England, recognizing the conclusion by the sounds, "push the long saplings as close together as they'll go."

The three boys managed to close them up until the outside saplings had been shoved from the original seven to only about four feet apart, and the intermediate ones had been more or less regularly spaced in between. Then again the boys sweated and puffed and panted.

"Now cut off the ends even all round," the old man said.

"There's no hatchet, but my old hunting knife will do it."

Dude seemed to know where this was kept, for he went inside and got it.

"Here, Trigger, you and Bud hold the darn thing on the chopping block and I'll knife off the ends," he commanded.

The two boys lifted the crude spring onto the block, turned it around and moved it along until Dude had clipped off all the irregular ends. The result was a rectangular, flexible, self-supporting framework approximately four feet wide by six or six and a half feet long.

"Now put it in on the frame," the old man directed and contentedly resumed his smoking.

The boys carried the spring into the hut and placed it on the logs that were already in position.

"You put the butts up against the north wall?" asked Mr. England as the boys came out.

"Yes, sir," said Dude.

Then everyone sat down and smoked. The old Englishman shaved some tobacco from a plug, tamped it slowly into the bowl of his pipe, lighted it, and sort of dozed off. Dude and Bud took cigar butts out of their pockets and puffed at them. Trigger, not to be outdone, hunted up some dry mullein leaves and rolled them up in a fragment of newspaper into a clumsy cigarette. When Dude and Bud saw this, they looked at each other and then expressed their disgust by spitting. Trigger just grinned and told them:

"Back in Calais none of the boys smoke cigar butts after they get out of grammar school."

"They feed mullein to babies round here," said Dude.

"It's the difference in places," Trigger answered calmly.

After a while Dutch and Mickey came back, puffing and blowing under a load of hemlock and balsam boughs, and then everyone went to work building a mattress on Trigger's bed. Mr. England just nodded to Dude as if he had confidence in him and Dude took charge.

The big hemlock branches were placed first, up and down the bed. All the butts were tucked down under the cross bars of the spring, and lapped over one another as shingles are put on a roof. Then came a layer of smaller boughs and then another of still smaller ones of balsam. And so on. The last layer of all was just the tops of the balsam which Dude clipped off with his knife and sort of sprinkled over the bed. The finished mattress was at least sixteen inches deep and when Trigger, following Dude's suggestion, stretched out on it, he said it was as soft as a rabbit. The old Englishman came in and nodded his approval slowly between puffs. Then the gang went outdoors and practiced a new cheer that consisted of a flock of "Goosetowns!" After which they were off in a rush to get ready for the baseball game, leaving Trigger and Mr. England sitting on the doorstep.

V. TRIGGER'S STORY

The old Englishman smoked for a long time without saying
a word; he smoked till his pipe went out and then kept right
on smoking without any smoke. He kept still so long that Trigger began to get nervous and wonder what was up. At last
the old man took his pipe out of his mouth and said:

"I've heard of you, young man."

The way he said "young man," friendly enough but firm,
made Trigger sense that there was something wrong somewhere. He hastily went over in his mind some of the incidents
of his past and wondered if the old man ever could have been
in Calais. He thought he'd better clear up the uncertainty, so
he asked.

"No, I've never been there."

"Then it must of been some other redhead you've been hearing about, 'cause I've never been any place but Calais."

"Heard about you right in this spot. Last night, it was. After the up train came in. Seems you were expected to be on that train, but you weren't."

"No, sir," said Trigger weakly.

"The man that went to meet you came up here afterward and told me. He comes up here sometimes and brings newspapers and things. He's head clerk down at the General Store and he gets papers the drummers leave around when they drop in to sell him some new stock. His place is right down yonder, so it's not far out of his way to come up here sometimes on his way home to supper. His name's George Smith."

"No—not Deacon Smith?" Trigger asked in a weak voice.

"Yes, Deacon Smith."

Trigger's heart went up to his mouth and his stomach turned over. It was clear enough what was on the old man's mind: he was figuring out what he was going to do about turning Trigger over to the authorities as represented by George Smith. For a minute Trigger was sick all over and he felt as weak as water. Then he scared himself half to death thinking about getting caught. He looked vaguely around him, making sudden desperate plans of escape, and half rose from the doorstep as if to take to his heels immediately.

"Trouble with running away is, you never get much of a lead on yourself." It was as if the old Englishman read his mind.

Trigger lost his fear and suddenly got mad. It was just as if a trap had been set for him all covered up with leaves and branches and he'd walked right into it. He felt like a rabbit when it runs into a snare and gets jerked up into the air and

hangs there dangling frantically. But Trigger was no rabbit.
He'd show George Smith and he'd show this old man that
smiled and looked friendly and was just a mean trapper.

Then he realized, in spite of his burning brain, that Mr.
England was speaking again.

"As I was saying, there are two sides to most things, sometimes more than two. I heard George Smith's side. I'd be glad
to listen to yours."

This sounded reasonable to Trigger and the way it was
said had a kind of sympathetic ring to it. It was something in
an unfair world to hear a man say that a boy might have something to say for himself and still more to have the man willing to listen to it. Trigger was about to open up when it occurred to him that the old man might just be stalling for time
until the Smith person should come. But Mr. England seemed
to feel this doubt, for he said, "There's all day to talk things
over, because George Smith has to keep store and can't ever
leave till about six o'clock."

Trigger quieted down. After a while he began to talk. "I
never had any regular home after Pop died," he said, choking
a little. "Pop and I got on first rate. We never had much, but
we always had a good time with what we had. I don't remember
my mother much but I liked her too, near as I can remember.
She used to make cookies for me, sugar cookies. Pop used to go
hunting and set traps and trade with the Indians. That's where
his name came from. Trigger John. I guess the Indians gave
him that name and then other folks took it up. We had a camp
near Calais, something like this one, only our camp was made
of logs mostly, except the roof and that had log rafters. We
had a garden in summer, not very big. Ground was full of
rocks and stumps and Pop had a durned hard time whenever
he made it bigger. We raised turnips 'n' cabbage for winter

and some potatoes, not much; but what he really liked raising
was his tomatoes. Pop's tomatoes were prize tomatoes. He'd
pick 'em just as they showed yellow and before the weather
started rotting them and put 'em in blankets in the bureau
drawers to ripen. He used to say tomatoes riped best in the
dark. He'd handle 'em over pretty often, too, and turn 'em
around on the blankets." Trigger had got to the place where
he had to tell about the death of his father and this stopped him.
He decided he didn't have to say anything about that, anyhow.
He just went on from there. "I lived with some folks, name
of Martin, a while at first. They lived down river apiece. They
had a lot of kids and the kids sided against me pretty often. I
could of stood that. Then one day Sam Martin twitted me
about Pop, and I got mad and licked him. He was bigger'n me
a good sight too. Then the old man thought he'd lick me, so
I ran off back to town. They told the town board or something, I reckon it was the Board of Health, that they wouldn't
have me round any more. So the board advertised me and then
I went to live at the Hunter place. That was upriver a ways.
There were just two of them, pretty old, and they said I was too
stirring for them.

"Next I was put out on the Bay road, sorta in the country.
Mr. Nesmiths's place, that was. There were quite a few fellers round and it was pretty good fun. We had a gang.
Trouble was, we snooped around where we hadn't any business and we found out—well, we found out things about
some of the old folks, some things they did. And they said I
was bad and a ringleader, and so I was sent out to Medi-
bemps. That's a lake where you can get a fair catch of pickerel
or black bass. I spent too much time fishing, I guess. Anyhow,
the people around reported me in town that I didn't go to
school enough. The Hills didn't care themselves, I was with

the Hills then, but the neighbors said the Hills were shiftless.

"After that I was with a family called Miller—that was right in town. I had to go to school there, because there was a truant officer, and he was a mean man. Pop was educated and he'd taught me a bit, so I knew more than the grades they put me in and didn't have to study much. You know how it is when you don't have to do a thing you're made to do. Teacher made me sit with a girl, first one and then another. But I didn't mind that enough to make me enough better to satisfy anybody. They didn't switch you there like they did in other places where I'd been to school. There they used a ruler and my hands got so blistered the teacher had to quit on me for fear he'd break the blisters and infect me.

"I hadn't been very regular to church and when the Methodist minister wanted my board money they jumped at it. He kept me in church at one thing or another most of every Sunday. I got not to mind that. They treated me right. Had the same food they had and as much as I wanted almost always. And they got me some clothes and paid for 'em themselves, not new, but no holes in the pockets. Then old Miss Clarissa Barlow got her eye on me and nothing would do but I had to come up here to be looked over and see wouldn't I do for an adopted son."

Trigger was surprised at the brevity of his own story— usually it ran on for at least an hour. He didn't know whether it was because he felt mad enough to tell the bare truth or whether he wanted to get through and get to the real point at issue. He didn't know how the old Englishman took it, the only thing he noticed was that he kept up his puffing, faster and faster, and that it didn't seem to make any difference whether the pipe was lighted or not. Then Trigger began to think how he could make the old man understand how he

felt about being adopted on a one-sided basis and thinking
made him mad again. Why should he tell the old man anything, anyhow? It wasn't his business. He got so mad he sweated
his collar and his neck swelled till it nearly burst. And the
madder he got the less he could say anything; all the words
that came into his head came from somewhere besides the
dictionary, and he didn't like to swear. His Pop used to tell
him that nobody swore that knew anything; it wasn't wicked,
particularly, but it betrayed a fellow's ignorance and once a
fellow did that other folks could take advantage of him. He
would have run off then and there, only he was hungry; and
the thing he did do was cry. The tears just welled out like a
baby's. . . . He didn't ask for them and he couldn't keep them
back. They came so fast he got shaking mad and then he began
to sob and he was so ashamed he didn't ever want to look himself in the face again.

"What we need is something to eat," the old man said without paying any attention at all to Trigger; and he got up and
went inside pretty quickly for a blind man. After a while Trigger stopped crying and the sobs settled down to just a few
leftover lumps in his throat and he went inside too.

Mr. England had built a quick wood fire of cones and
shavings and some dry pine. Then he took some grease and
melted it in a skillet and sliced up some cold boiled potatoes
in the hot grease. After that he got four big trout out of a
bucket of water and put them in with the potatoes. The smell
was so good that Trigger forgot his troubles and could hardly
wait till everything was ready and dished up on a couple of
tin pie-plates.

"You put three fish on my plate."

"Three for luck."

Trigger wanted luck by any means whatever so he was bound

to eat all three fish, which he did, except for heads and tails.

They did up the dishes after scraping the orts into the fire and burning them and then went back to the doorstep.

"I see what you mean," Mr. England began, just as if they'd been talking all the time. "Trouble with me is I'm in a quandary. I never did learn how to keep one ear shut while the other was open, and I heard George Smith talk with the other ear. He's sort of made up his mind he's going to have a son to play round with. And he's afraid something's happened to the son and that makes him feel pretty uneasy."

Trigger got suspicious and interrupted hastily: "It's not fair to work on my feelings."

"It would be a mean trick to do that," the old Englishman agreed. "What I mean is this: George Smith isn't a bit like the folks you've been telling about; he's human. You'd like George Smith, even if he didn't like you."

This turned the business wrong side out for Trigger. He said, "Of course, he mightn't like me well enough to—to—" It died out.

"The only way for folks to find out if they don't like each other is to meet and get acquainted."

Trigger was still suspicious. "He's got a wife, hasn't he?"

"Yes."

"What's she like?"

"I never have seen her."

"Anyhow, there's two of them."

"They live together, that's right."

They both kept still for some time. Then the old man said, "Of course, this is your business. I'm not expecting to betray any secrets, but I feel as though it wasn't just being square with George Smith to let him go on being uneasy when there's no call for it. Here's how it looks to me. I can't show you to

him, because you say no. But I never promised not to show
him to you. Suppose when he drops around next, you cover
up where he can't see you and you look him over. Then you
can come out or stay hid as you like."

"That's fair enough, I guess," Trigger said doubtfully.

Mr. England spent most of the afternoon reseating some
old chairs, and Trigger lazily looked on. It was a good way
to get acquainted. Trigger had not been let so luxuriously alone
since his father died, and the more he was let alone the better
he liked the old man for doing it. Twice he was startled: two
men went up the mountain, following the brook bed, and he
ducked from sight in sudden fear of George Smith. There was
not much talk; nevertheless, at the end of several hours Trigger
had learned quite a lot. He was sure of one thing: the old man
was blind. The work on the chairs proved that. It had been
done with sure and skillful fingers, but without the help of
eyes. Besides, and most mysteriously, Trigger discovered that
he had a pretty good picture of George Smith, whom he began
to like in spite of himself.

Yet George Smith was much on his mind and kept him in
sight of quick hiding-places the whole day. Then, too, he had
flashes of suspicion when he thought the old man might be
putting up some job on him and at times he became very uneasy
like the fox in the run back of the shack. He would circle round
the place, darting quick glances hither and yon and looking
behind stumps and piles of wood, and juniper bushes, and the
like. These short trips enabled Trigger to get a pretty good
idea of his immediate surroundings. And, taking things by
and large, the day went off pleasantly and the uneasy spots
didn't count much alongside of the easy ones.

Dude and Mickey came up in the late afternoon about six
o'clock. Mickey had the mask under his arm, and he was

wearing the catcher's mitt, but didn't look particularly happy, Trigger thought. Neither did Dude. Not much like the return of the conquering heroes. The rest of the gang didn't turn up at all.

Dude was so glum that Trigger, even with his eye on the mask and mitt, couldn't get excited and was just matter-of-fact. "You won the game, didn't you?" he asked.

"Naw!" answered Dude.

"You're not telling me Castle Garden won!" Trigger exclaimed.

"Not on your tintype!" Mickey said.

"A tie?" asked Trigger.

Mickey looked at Dude, and Dude spat viciously. "There wasn't any game!" he growled.

"Oh!" Trigger looked from Dude to Mickey, and pointed to the mask and mitt. "How come?"

"We matched for who keeps them till the game comes off," Mickey explained.

Dude went cockeyed all of a sudden. He ground his heel into a tuft of grass, and then jumped on it and dug into it with both heels.

"Who you jumping on, Dude?" Trigger was very calm but curious.

Dude began to cuss the tuft of grass: "You low-livered, black-bearded, cross-grained son of a dirty stinky dead skunk!" he cursed, all the time digging in with his heels. "You snake-eyed, yellow-bellied rat! You long-haired girlchaser! You sissy! Sissy, sissy, sissy!" And every time he said "Sissy," he stamped it in. When he stopped for breath, Trigger suggested:

"Count ten, Dude, and forget it!"

That made Dude worse than ever. He reared up and went on cussing and spitting and digging in and telling the world what he was going to do to somebody when he got him alone.

"Who's he talking to?" Trigger asked Mickey, after he got tired of watching Dude.

"Herbie Lord," Mickey answered, with a lip-wide grin. "He checked up on why all of us hooked-jack this morning and found out about the game and sent Daddy Coleman, the constable, up to stop it and bring us all back to school. He was waiting for us there. He switched the gang, except Skinny and Socks. He made everybody write 'Truant' a hundred times on the blackboard. Who cares! It's having to call off the game that Dude's fussing about."

"I'll get even with him, if it's the last thing I do!" Dude sputtered. He gave the grass a final dig and then went and sat on the doorstep in the mad sulks.

Mr. England came to the door. He pretended he hadn't heard, and said to come in and get supper. He had it all ready —baked corn and tomatoes.

After supper, Mickey said none of the gang felt like having any initiation that night, because, the way things had gone, nobody would have any fun. Then he and Dude left.

Trigger was so sleepy that he went to bed at sundown **and** slept like a log.

VI. TALK OF THE TOWN

Trigger was hardly out of bed the next morning before Dude turned up. He said Trigger's being lost had got out in the town and everybody was telling George Smith what he ought to do about it.

Dude had had a busy evening. He had been to the General Store and the Post Office and the Commercial House lobby. He had even listened in at a meeting of the Women's Aid at the church. The women had their sewing in their laps but they weren't sewing, they were talking about the danger of adopting a child. They said such a child was bound to turn out bad,

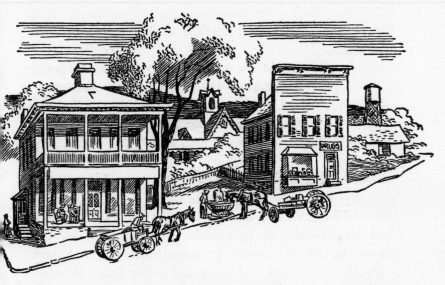

and that Trigger's only getting lost was letting the Smiths down easy. Mrs. Locke said the whole thing was the Lord's will and they let it go at that for a while, but Dude said you could see they were going to start up again and that "like as not they were there yet running on like a waterfall."

Then he told about the excitement at the General Store —that's where George Smith was, so everybody that wanted to tell George Smith what to do had to go there. That meant about everybody in town. George Smith was so busy listening that he didn't have time to wait on customers. Every so often old Woodruff would come out from behind his wire cage and tell George that Mrs. So-and-So wanted a half-pound of this and that and then he'd go back and slam the gate behind him and sit down and look like a thunder cloud.

Most everybody thought George Smith ought to go to Williamsport on the morning train to see if he could get a trace of Trigger. George Smith told them he was thinking of going way back to Philadelphia to get traces of Trigger there and follow them back so by the time he got to Williamsport he'd know what a trace looked like, and be able to tell one when he saw it.

Daddy Coleman said that wasn't necessary because the police at Williamsport would have all the well-known traces together on file at the jail and George Smith could find them right there. George Smith was doubtful because he wasn't sure you could trust the police to find out anything except what wasn't very important.

Daddy Coleman flared up at that and lit into George Smith in defense of the law, but they pulled him off and somebody threatened to lock him into his own jail for disorderly conduct and disturbing the peace. After that he quieted down in his corner, but he wouldn't go home because he said there might be trouble and he'd be needed and he knew his duty.

Every now and then someone suggested that George Smith send a telegram. George Smith said he would only he couldn't afford to pay for any more, but he'd send it if somebody else wanted to pay for it. So about half the town got busy writing out telegrams on wrapping paper and as soon as one was ready, George Smith told someone to take it to the telegraph office and send it. He said he didn't care how many were sent nor who they were sent to as long as he didn't have to pay for them.

Joe Jackson tried to get George Smith to let him print an advertisement and George was to pay for it. George said that as Joe was the editor of the *Beechwood Gazette* he ought to know Trigger's getting lost was news and that he'd have to print it if he wanted his paper to be up-to-date. He said Joe could print it in the "Lost and Found" column; he could print he was found, too, but in the same paper, because Trigger'd be found before the next issue came out. That made Joe hot,

but George Smith said if he felt that way about it, he needn't print anything. The whole county was printing the news, anyhow, and before Joe got his paper out the thing wouldn't even be news. Joe said he'd print George Smith's own picture and shame the devil and George told him to go ahead and do it.

After a while Daddy Coleman got an idea. He said if George Smith would pay his fare and keep he'd make an official trip to Williamsport himself and look up Trigger. George Smith said he ought to have made that offer before, but it was too late now. Now all the police were on the search. He said they were working from Calais and Philadelphia on one side and from Erie and Emporium on the other and he reckoned they would close in on Trigger right about Beechwood.

All he was worried about was how to feed so many million policeman, because Mr. Woodruff refused to buy in a new

stock of cheese. They kept it up until eleven o'clock. Dude
said George Smith didn't go home till after that and when
he did he found his wife crying about Trigger being lost. He
told her it would help her to blow her nose, and she did. Dude
followed George Smith and heard them.

Mr. England said he thought Dude was stretching things
a little, but Dude swore he was just telling the truth. Trigger said it didn't look to him as if George Smith was crying very much because the boy didn't turn up, and the old
Englishman said that George Smith was not the kind of person
to cry over spilled milk.

Trigger looked at the old man suspiciously.

"George Smith hasn't been around, has he, Mr. England?"

The old man hesitated a moment and then admitted, "Yes,
he has. Now, don't think I have betrayed you, young man!
I have not betrayed you. What came about, came about by
accident." The old man spoke wearily as if appearances were
against him, and there was small hope that Trigger would look
beyond them. He lighted his pipe and began to smoke slowly.
Presently he said, "George Smith paid a visit to me unexpect-
edly. He entered the house before I could prevent him. He
saw the new bunk and you lying upon it. He went over and
looked at you.

" 'Who's this?' said he.

" 'A young boy,' said I, 'a stranger.'

" 'He has red hair,' said he.

"It was true; I said, 'Yes.'

" 'And freckles.'

" 'Yes.'

" 'The freckles are big freckles and sort of splashed on.'

"I had to agree, because I was not in a position to dispute.

" 'And he's got a pug nose!'

" 'Yes.' "

Trigger burst out, "How do you know I've got red hair and freckles and a pug nose?"

"Shut up," Dude said.

"I'm sorry," said Trigger.

Mr. England didn't seem to notice, and he went on, "I know many things for other reasons than because I see them."

Trigger was ashamed to have said anything even indirectly about the old man's blindness; but he couldn't help being angry. Luck just hadn't been with him. "What happened?" he demanded sullenly.

"Nothing happened," the old Englishman said. "George Smith never pries like most folks."

"But he knew!" Trigger half sobbed in his vexation.

"I expect he knew. He said you reminded him of someone he ought to know but didn't. He said he hoped to get acquainted some day."

"Then he's not coming to take me away?" Trigger asked.

"He is not like that. I expect he's the only man in the county that knows you can't make a person like you by force, and I guess he'd like you to like him. He's got a funny streak in him and that goes with wisdom."

"There's no fun in it now," Trigger said to Dude. "It's like getting the teacher to let you play hooky."

The three of them had breakfast together. The old man had a pan of cold cornmeal mush which he sliced and fried and served with molasses. Dude said it was licking good, but Trigger was blue and might as well have been eating sawdust. After breakfast Dude said Trigger could be initiated that night; then he went off, saying he was going to surprise Herbie (the Principal) by being early and immaculate all day, so he wouldn't be kept after school.

VII. A DAY IN THE WOODS

Mr. England got out some more chairs and went to work on them. He didn't say any more to Trigger and Trigger didn't say any more to him. Trigger just looked on: he thought the old man was as quick and sure as Chief Red Feather shaping a paddle, but he didn't tell him, because he was still feeling resentful. He knew the old man was not really to blame for what had happened, but he wanted to blame somebody or something, and Mr. England was there. The trouble with blaming him was that it made Trigger feel lonely. He went out on the doorstep and whittled aimlessly. Then he went around the hut to look at the fox; the fox was there going up and down. Trigger got cross at the fox because the fox made him think of himself; up and down, back and forth, and all the while in a cage and couldn't get out.

He went on to see if the porcupine was in the tree. He was, going up and down like the fox, only slowly and awkwardly and slipping back and scratching. Trigger asked the porcupine what he thought he was doing except wearing out the tree-trunk, but the porcupine didn't pay any attention—just kept on going up and down, down and up. Just like himself, thought Trigger—and the fox, both of them caught, only the darn-fool porcupine caught himself.

Then Trigger thought of the old Englishman. Being blind was being caught too and pretty badly caught. The fox could see what held him and the porcupine was stupid; but the old man couldn't see and wasn't stupid and wasn't any more to blame than the fox or the porcupine. It was tough. Trigger went back and told Mr. England he was sorry he'd been mean and Mr. England looked up and smiled all over his face. That made Trigger feel like crying, but it made him feel pleasant too and the loneliness oozed away and he decided that he felt like an exploring expedition.

He couldn't go down to the town, but he could go up the mountain. Real mountains were new to him—there were nothing but hills around Calais. He started off, following the dry brook bed. It was a gradual slope at first and easy climbing; there was a trail alongside of the brook so you didn't have to walk on the rocks unless you wanted. Trigger wanted to as long as he didn't have to, though it was hazardous footing and once in a while a stone rolled under his feet and he sat down without meaning to.

After a while the side of the mountain got pretty steep and Trigger was glad enough to take the trail and stick to it. He felt as fresh as a daisy and pretty kinky in his legs so he hop-scotched part of the time, which was better than mere climbing. He also tried going up backward but not very successfully, and it was hard on the insteps.

When he got into the deep wood and well away from civilization he began to look for unseen enemies; several times he saw savages and wished he had a bow and quiver of arrows,

or even one of Dude's slingshots, but the best he could do was
sneak up as near as possible and let drive with a good-sized
rock. He almost always got his man and scalped him and covered him with brush. He saw several rabbits and some
partridges, and once a young red fox slipped across the trail
in front of him. He wondered what other animals might be
lurking in these strange woods. It would be awkward to come
face to face with a panther or a tiger, but he thought he was
man enough to look out for himself.

He began to break branches and blaze saplings with his knife
so that he could follow his own track back if he got lost or
forgot about the trail under his feet, and several times he got
stones from the brook bed and built cairns to mark the route.
Before long he was pretty hot, because the June sun got at
his back sometimes through the trees, and when he came to a
little clearing or what had once been a clearing he sat down
and looked around.

The valley that made the brook bed dished into the side
of the mountain at this point, and there was a little pond in
the middle of the dish with alders and blackberry bushes growing up around it. The water was still and black, but it looked
fresh and Trigger decided the brook must run in and out of it
underground. He got up and moved nearer. Several mud turtles
that had been sitting on a slimy log sunning themselves went
kerchunk into the pool out of sight. He noticed some small birds
fussing around among the branches and identified one as a
lady wren, a friend of his of long standing. He couldn't see
that the birds here were different from the ones he knew around
Calais. The trees were of the same kind, too, mostly, though
he had trouble with the hemlock which was certainly not
spruce though it resembled spruce somewhat. He'd taken
note of the trees only incidentally while keeping a sharp look-

out for slippery elm. He thought it would be a lark to have a slippery elm tree of his own, then tell Dude and the gang he had it and let them hunt for it and not be able to find it.

He thought this might be a good place to laze round a while. He looked the ground over, spotted an outcropping of ledge up the mountain from the pool, and started for that. It was drenched in sunlight, but he had cooled off somewhat now so he wouldn't mind that and besides it ought to be a good lookout. He made his way round the pool looking for the trail and to his surprise was unable to find it. He went all the way round again, fighting his way through the encircling shrubbery. Then he made up his mind that the path he'd been following went just to the pool and no farther—anyhow, he was bound for the ledges and that's where he was going, trail or no trail. He was most careful to mark his route with broken twigs as he went, for now he was not just imagining that he might get lost. He was pretty well acquainted with woods and he knew that getting lost was no trick at all, but a shameful trick it would be to a regular woodsman like him.

The ledge was higher than it had looked from the pool, but the face of it was broken up into seams and crevices and cracks which made good climbing. He might have gone around, for the huge boulder stuck out like a nose from the mountain side, but that was a girl's way. He gave himself a start by going up an old tree and out along a limb that reached to the face of the stone. Here he set his foot in a convenient crack and began to mount. It was slow going even for Trigger's agile legs and by the time he reached the first shelf he was tuckered. He stopped to rest and shake the sweat beads from his forehead. Then placing his two hands on the edge he began to draw himself up.

Breast high along the shelf he came to a sudden stop. He found himself staring at what looked like a couple of dead limbs. They didn't look just right. Instinctively he knew they were not limbs, at all, but snakes, larger snakes than he had ever seen before. They were stretched at full length asleep. In a moment they began to move, first one and then the other; their straightness broke up into a series of gentle curves; the curves became loops and the loops became coils and then Trigger was staring into two pairs of beady bright eyes and watching the quick forked tongues dart out and in. Then he was aware of a low buzz and he knew that he was face to face with a couple of rattlers for the first time in his life. There was no movement except the blur of the vibrating tails; they were as still as they had been when he first saw them, but Trigger knew that they were coiled to strike. He was frightened but fascinated and could not have moved to save his life. He was as silent, as immovable as the snakes themselves. Luckily for him! After a few seconds the rattling dimmed and ceased, the snakes uncoiled by imperceptible degrees, made off at increasing speed, and disappeared in a crevice of the boulder. Trigger drew himself up and fell forward on the shelf, exhausted and trembling.

His recovery was rapid; he had no desire to remain longer than necessary on the boulder, let alone lie there and rest, but having set out to climb the mountain, he proceeded to advance. He climbed the rest of the cliff with great circumspection. Arrived at the top, he crossed the broad face of rock and began climbing again with considerable haste in spite of watery knees, for the picture of the coiled snakes was vivid in his mind and the boulder was no longer a desirable spot. Indeed, his uneasiness was so great that he had gone some distance before he realized that he was not following a path and that he had failed to mark his own track. He looked back. The lay of the land seemed clear enough for a regular woodsman

like him; he felt that it would be an unnecessary precaution to
go back to the ledge and that it was safe enough to go on, mark-
ing his progress from where he stood. He found a sizable stick
for a weapon and proceeded with his climb.

The valley had now flattened out. He no longer had any
indentation in the mountain side to mark direction, so he pre-
served a straight line by keeping each third blaze in line with
the preceding two. It was tedious work and took his attention
from other things more interesting and he had not gone very
far before he got tired. He looked around for a safe place to
stop and standing still he found his knees were still trembling.
He was ashamed to have frightened knees after the scare had
gone from his mind, but he decided he needed a rest. He found
a clump of pine trees, made sure there were no dead but suspicious limbs in the immediate vicinity and lay down, stretching out luxuriously on the bed of pine needles. Before he knew
it he was sound asleep.

When he woke the sun had swung around the mountain
and was so low in the west that he thought it had already set.
Dampness had begun to fall and he felt stiff and chill. He
jumped up and shook himself vigorously. Seizing an overhead branch, he skinned the cat three times for luck and then
looked about for the broken twigs and stone piles that marked
his trail. He set off at a good pace down the mountain, for he
knew only too well that the blazes to guide him would help
very little if darkness overtook him before he made the pool
and the path from it to the village. He had no fear, only a
sense of necessary speed and an aggravating hole in his stomach.

Here and there were patches of crumbled stone and in
crossing one of these he got a pebble in his shoe. It settled to
an uncomfortable spot and he sat down to take it out. This
done he was suddenly conscious of something or someone

apparently following him. He looked around just as a young black bear emerged from the nearest clump of underbrush. Trigger and the bear saw each other at the same instant and both boy and bear looked more astonished than frightened. Trigger jumped to his feet, the bear turned tail, and they set off at a run in opposite directions. By the time Trigger reached the boulder, skirted it, and stood once more at the pool, he was laughing. He thought the bear's astonishment and flight was the funniest thing he ever had seen and then he wondered if the bear had any thoughts on the matter and if so how Trigger's speedy retreat looked to him.

Once more in the path, Trigger resumed a more dignified gait. He didn't care now whether the sun was down or not. A trail was a tunnel and he could find his way through a tunnel day or night. He even paused to discover that the porcupine had ceased his activities for the day and to call a greeting to the uneasy fox. By this time his breathing was normal and when he rounded the end of the old Englishman's hut he was walking carelessly as if he had just been to the spring for a bucket of water.

VIII. THE INITIATION

Yet Trigger was glad enough to be back and gladder to find Dude and Mickey waiting for him. He had been alone long enough. There was no fuss made over him as though a lost lamb had returned and Trigger wondered if he had been missed at all. But he was given supper, which the old man had kept warming on the stove. By that time it was dark and Dude and Mickey were in a hurry to leave.

"C'mon, Trigger," Dude said, and the three got under way.

Trigger saw little of the town. There were no street lamps and no moon and the boys' feet found their way without help from their eyes. They went downhill a short distance, crossed back of the village, and again downhill into what Trigger learned was Goosetown, seat of the mighty.

"That's the tannery," Dude said as they trailed along Indian file round a big low bulk of blackness against a blacker background. Presently they came into a settlement of small huts and cottages with here and there a light gleaming from a window. Dude led a zigzag course among them, making diagonally toward the creek. Here on the edge of the creek they all but bumped into a tiny shack.

"This is the Lodge," Dude whispered.

"It's dark enough," said Trigger.

"Hist!" signaled Dude; then he said to Trigger, "The windows are blindfolded, but there's a lamp inside."

A door opened slowly and Trigger was pushed in. There was a dim light from a rusty tin lantern hanging on the wall.

The place appeared to be empty, but Trigger noticed a blanket stretched across one corner and he thought he knew what was behind that blanket.

"We oughta blindfold you, by rights," Dude said, "but we won't if you shut your eyes and face the wall and swear on oath not to turn round till we give the word."

"All right," agreed Trigger and did as he was told.

"Count two hundred by fives and then turn around. If you count wrong or stop you gotta begin all over again."

Trigger counted without difficulty, for he was not the person to lose his head under unusual circumstances. When he turned round the blanket had been put aside and he found himself facing seven sheet-clad figures, with holes for eyes cut in the sheets. He stared and the eyes stared. Trigger was on the alert for anything that might happen from a squirt gun to a rough and tumble, but nothing happened. He relaxed a little and looked around. The walls were unplastered bare studs with nothing on them. But on the floor in front of the center of the group was a wooden box. Trigger could read "SOAP," even in the dim light. A black cloth covered something which lay on top of the box.

A sepulchral voice said, "Step to the front, and take the cover off'n the symbols."

Trigger removed the cloth with a quick jerk and at once stepped back out of easy range of any possible contrivance. Then he looked and in spite of himself, gasped. He was gazing at a cow's skull resting on its nose and looking back at him with fiery eyes that glowed ominously. In front of it was placed a shinbone with the cloven hoof attached. The white-sheeted figures took on weird shapes and the large shadows back of them assumed strange forms that moved and mingled with each other slowly. Trigger, for all his resolution, was scared,

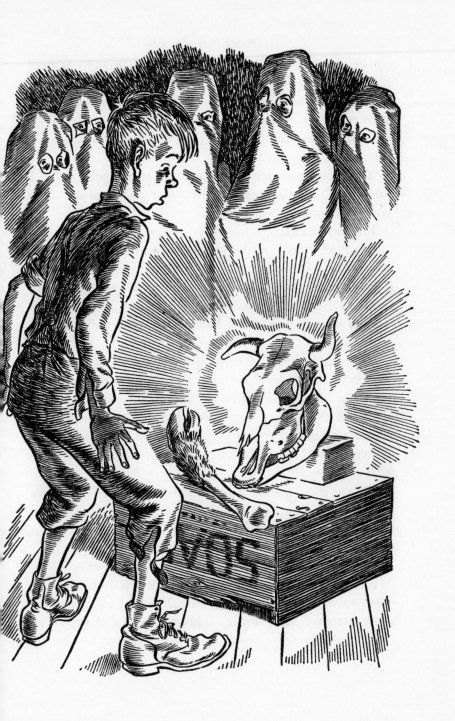

but he clenched his fists and gritted his teeth and remained
silent and immovable like the skull in front of him.

A rather disappointed voice said, "You can shriek if you
want to; it'll be all right."

"I don't have to shriek!" Trigger answered between his
teeth.

"Oh, hell!" someone said sourly. Then at once came the
command, "Turn around again and shut your eyes and don't
you dast to open them."

Trigger obeyed.

"It's all right to turn around now," the voice said, and Trigger turned quickly, still on guard. Things were just as they
had been, but all the terror and glamour had gone. The skull
was now just a dead skull, for the light had been removed
and the sheeted figures had become almost dingy and quite
unimpressive.

The voice spoke again, grandiloquently: "Take up the shinbone in your right hand and place the hoof of the beast on the
top of the head of the critter and attend."

Trigger did this and waited and the voice continued, "You
are now to take the oath of allegiance to the brotherhood
known as the Goosetown Gang. Are you ready?"

"Yes, I'm ready."

"Repeat these words: 'I hereby solemnly . . .'" the voice
paused and Trigger repeated the words. Then the voice continued, " 'pledge and promise . . .'"

"Pledge and promise . . ." repeated Trigger.

"To be true to the prescriptions of . . ." Trigger repeated,
". . . the rules and regulations . . . set down in the book of
deeds to be . . . done and followed and . . . to come to
the assistance . . . of any . . . brother in time of need . . .

especially . . . when attacked . . . by the muckers from Castle Garden. . . . So help me . . . Pumpernickel!"

Somebody objected, "He didn't look at Pumpernickel when he said that!"

"Look at Pumpernickel and say it again," the voice commanded.

"Say what?" asked Trigger.

"So help me Pumpernickel."

"Who's Pumpernickel?"

"That's the name of the cow's skull, dumbbell."

"So help me Pumpernickel," said Trigger to Pumpernickel, looking at Pumpernickel.

"Now bend the knee before him and bow down your head too."

Trigger bent and bowed and was struck sharply on the head. "Rise, Sir Trigger!" said the voice.

Then everyone threw off his sheet and there was general rejoicing.

Socks Donovan and Skinny Muldoon were there, and Trigger met them for the first time. He found out that he wouldn't be seeing them very often, because they both had to leave school the next day and go to work.

"Anyhow," Dude said, "they can get off for the ball game."

"Now I gotta cut for home," Mickey said. "Grandmother saw me go out and she'll be in her window till I get back and the quicker I get back the less she'll lick me. So long."

That broke up the meeting. Dude put the skull and shinbone under a loose board in the floor and conducted Trigger back to the old Englishman's.

IX. GEORGE SMITH

After the initiation at the Lodge the gang had nothing more
to hold meetings about. Trigger didn't see much of them for
several days. He spent several evenings wandering round town
seeing what he could see. This mostly was such sights
as presented themselves through lighted windows when the
shades were not pulled down. The windows that claimed his
attention most often were those in the house of George Smith:
through them he studied the family life of his prospective
parents. The windows were usually open, so he could hear
as well as see. He liked George Smith, whom he found out to
be a humorous gawky man, tall and spare, who soft-soaped
his wife a good deal as if she were ill and needed looking after.

He would tell her all the funny things customers at the store had done and said during the day. Sometimes he would tickle her in the ribs or chuck her under the chin; she would sputter and protest and tell him he was a silly thing and would never grow up, but Trigger could see she liked it. He helped her with the meals and with the dishes. Once in a while he would drop a dish and break it on purpose when her back was turned. She would fly into a fury and George Smith would act sorry and get forgiven. This always happened, Trigger noticed, when they had been talking about a boy who had died or gone away and when Mrs. Smith looked as if she were getting ready to cry.

After that she would talk about Trigger and she would fret and worry over where he could be and George Smith would tell her he had a line on Trigger and that he would turn up before long. This always made Trigger feel guilty, but he made up his mind he wouldn't turn up right away because he couldn't tell whether he would like living with Mrs. Smith or not.

One evening he found Mrs. Smith alone. Supper was over and George Smith was nowhere around and she was fussing about doing nothing in particular, acting as if she had to do something to keep from doing something else. At last she sat down in a straight-backed chair, threw her apron over her head and began to cry. Trigger could not rid himself of the feeling that it was his fault. He tried to tell himself that women cried about everything and nothing and for no reason at all, but the guilty feeling remained. If someone had been there, Trigger would have been able to convince himself that it was just "woman's wiles," but it bothered him to see her crying all by herself with no one to see her do it. So he strode off in the dark, muttering to himself.

When he arrived at the shack, prepared to steal in noise-lessly to bed (for the old man had usually preceded him), he was astonished to find the place lighted, and upon going nearer to discover George Smith and another man inside with Mr. England. The stranger was talking:

"I don't want you to get your hopes up; but if you'll come along to the hotel with me where I've got all my tools to work with, I can get a good look at your eyes, and then I can tell you for sure."

Mr. England didn't say a word, but he got up and put on his hat and he and the stranger started off down to the village, arm in arm. George Smith remained inside. Trigger never knew why he did it, but as soon as the two men were out of hearing, he stepped boldly into the cabin. He just looked at George Smith and George Smith looked at him and both were very sober. Trigger expected to ask what was happening to Mr. England, but instead of that he said:

"Mrs. Smith is crying."

George Smith just kept on looking at Trigger for a long while very soberly. Then he said:

"I expect that's because she's alone over there."

"I expect that's it," Trigger said. Then he sat down and looked at the stove and George Smith looked at the stove too. Trigger got a pine stick and began to whittle shavings. After a while he got another pine stick and handed it to George Smith and George Smith began to whittle shavings too. When they had quite a pile, Trigger said:

"Why don't you say something?"

"It's your turn," said George Smith.

Trigger got red in the face because he knew what George Smith meant.

"My name's Trigger," he said finally.

"My name's George Smith."

"I come from Calais," Trigger struggled on.

"That so?" was George Smith's noncommittal reply. Trigger tried again:

"I came in a box car."

"That so?"

There was another long silence, then Trigger said, "I sorta wanted to look things over."

"Seen anything of interest?"

Trigger burst out: "It's not fair to get adopted without knowing who's adopting you!"

"That's right enough," agreed George Smith, and Trigger was suddenly aware that George Smith understood everything and had just been lying low while Trigger decided what to do.

Trigger shifted around uneasily, lost his nerve and recovered it, and said at last, "I'll come over to your house if you want me to."

"I'll come for you tomorrow on my way home to supper." George Smith spoke so quickly and eagerly that Trigger changed the subject so he wouldn't get a lump in his throat.

"What's that man doing to Mr. England?" he asked.

"He's looking at his eyes. He says he doesn't think his bad sight is forever. He says he thinks there's something growing over the inside of them. Calls it cataracts. Says if that's so, the cataracts can be removed and when they're removed the old man can see again, good as new. He can't say for sure till he's looked at him with some instruments he's got at the Commercial House."

"How come he didn't tell the old man that before?"

"He just came to town today. He's one of these traveling fellows. His business isn't just in one place but all over the lot. There's a dentist comes here like that too, only he comes regular once a month and stays a couple of days. The Episcopal preacher's like that, too, only he shows up every other Sunday. You see, there isn't enough business for any of those fellows to keep them here all the time. This eye chap is new; he never did come here before."

"How does he get to the inside of the eye without hurting him?"

"He don't do it himself, because he isn't a surgeon, but he knows another eye doctor who can do it. That one is in Baltimore somewhere."

"Will he be coming here?"

"No, the old man'll have to go to him—if he can get there."

"Why can't he get there?"

"Costs money to get to Baltimore."

"Oh!" said Trigger; he considered the weather a while, then probed in a different direction: "Should think it would hurt pretty bad to have your eyes cut into."

"Well, I don't know. Anyhow, it's better to take the advice of a fellow that knows what he's talking about, than it is to go blind all your life."

"How much would it cost for him to go to Baltimore?"

"A hundred dollars, about."

Trigger took the news stolidly.

"Haven't got it, have you?" added George Smith.

Trigger shook his head solemnly.

"Well, don't try to steal it from me; I haven't got it. If I had . . ." He stopped short and looked grave. Trigger knew what he was going to say.

After a while George Smith said he must be getting home. "I've got some good news to tell Myrtle." He looked at Trigger questioningly. "Haven't I?"

"I guess so," Trigger said dubiously.

"I'll drop round tomorrow afternoon, won't I?"

Trigger swallowed two or three lumps and nodded, adding, "I'll be here."

It looked for a moment as if they might shake hands, but they both were embarrassed and made a fumble of it and George Smith went off awkwardly, with Trigger's eyes following him out into the dark.

He thought for some time about George Smith and Mrs. Smith and about the prospect of living with them; then his mind drifted to the old Englishman.

He didn't have to wait for the report from the eye doctor; he knew that the old man could be cured. But how was he to get to Baltimore? A hundred dollars was a lot of money. He considered begging around the town. Ministers begged for this and that, but ministers were different. He had begged for a nickel now and then in Calais and he thought he could make a go of it. But he reflected that he was now going to live with the Smiths and he was certain that Mrs. Smith and perhaps even George Smith would not approve of begging. Other ideas came into his head, but after considering them one by one, he discarded them in favor of just a general resolution to get the money somehow.

He hunted up a pencil and paper and with much difficulty wrote out his resolution. Then he started out hatless to round up the gang for action. He had found out just where they lived in his nightly explorations. He began with Dude. He was asleep, but a few pebbles brought Dude to the window, and, presently, down the grapevine to his side.

"I wanta get a meeting right away."

"You?" Dude was on the alert to defend his prestige.

"Anyone can call a meeting, can't they?"

"Yes," Dude agreed cautiously. "It's part of the articles. But there has to be a notice."

"Well, I'm giving the notice."

"A day's notice, maybe two days'; I don't remember exactly."

"Except in an emergency," said Trigger.

"What's an emergency?"

"This is," Trigger said fiercely.

"But everyone's gone to bed."

"No matter. Get them up. All we need's a majority."

Dude was stubborn and felt injured in some way which he couldn't put his finger on, but he gave in at last. They got Mickey almost from under the nose of his grandmother, and woke Bud who was sitting up to mind the baby while his mother was out calling. He left the baby to look after himself under the pretext of the call of duty and the four made their way to the Lodge and lighted the lantern.

Trigger insisted on getting out the cow's skull and shinbone, "Because this resolution's got to be done right."

They lighted a candle in the skull and then Trigger told them about the old Englishman and the eye doctor, adding, "How do you fellows feel about this? Is it up to us to raise that hundred dollars or isn't it?"

"How we gonna do it?" asked Dude.

"I don't know. The question is are we resolved to do it. The main thing is to have the intention to do a thing. If you have the intention, the 'how' of it comes later. The main thing is have we got this intention or are we just cowards that don't dare face a thing just because we can't see it?"

They agreed they were not cowards.

"Listen to this, then," said Trigger. He got out his paper and read: "Resolved to get one hundred dollars for the old man to get to Baltimore with to have his eyes fixed so he can see. Attest our hands and seals. And everybody agrees to do anything he can to get money and not to spend a cent of it on himself or his mother or father or grandmother or anything that is his till the hundred is raised."

Trigger looked up and saw three glum faces.

Mickey spoke first: "That doesn't mean I can't eat the gumdrops I get when my grandmother gives me a nickel to get them for her, does it?"

"Does she give them to you?" Trigger asked severely.

"Sometimes she does," Mickey admitted.

"You can eat them if she gives them to you; but you can't pinch any," Trigger said.

"I'd like to spend a cent on three licorice shoe-lacings once in a while. Is that out?" Dude was struggling for his rights.

"Of course, it's out," said Trigger. "Doesn't it say so in the resolve?"

"We haven't signed it yet," Mickey said.

"I've signed it," Trigger said.

This brought Dude back to his sense of dignity. "What the blazes you sign it first for? Who do you think is leader of this gang, anyhow?"

"Aw, I left the top place for you," said Trigger. "Don't get sore."

"Who's sore?" said Dude, and indeed this tribute on Trigger's part had made him instantly good-natured.

Seeing them hesitate, Trigger issued his challenge again. "You mean you're afraid to sign up?"

"Who's afraid?" said Dude. He signed with the pencil Trigger gave him and Mickey signed afterward. Then they turned to Bud and found him asleep. They woke him up and he signed without being at all sure what he was doing.

"You can get the rest to sign in the morning," Trigger said, handing the paper to Dude.

"Who can?" But Dude took the paper.

"You can," repeated Trigger. "You're the boss of this gang, aren't you?"

"Sure, I'm the boss."

"Well then!" concluded Trigger. Dude put the paper in his pocket.

They put out the candle and hid the skull and shinbone under the loose board and Dude was just about to blow out the lantern when he happened to think:

"Who's gonna keep the money?"

"The treasury," said Trigger.

"We haven't any treasury."

"We'll elect a treasury then. If we're having money around, we have to have a treasury to keep it."

"I'll be treasury," said Dude.

"You're president already," said Trigger.

"Mickey there can be treasury," said Dude.

"No, I can't," said Mickey. "I never can hide anything so my grandmother don't find it."

"How about Bud?" suggested Dude.

"I could hide it down the well," Bud said.

"Look here, Dude!" said Trigger firmly. "You let me be the treasury. I'm about ready to go and live with George Smith, and I'll do it now, because I could give the money to George Smith to keep for us and he could put it in the safe down at the store."

This was too good an argument for Dude's head at that time of night, so Trigger was elected treasurer. But Dude was cranky about it, as could be seen by the way he blew out the lantern.

Trigger got back to the shack just as the old man was going to bed, and he was not in the least astonished to learn that the eyes could be fixed if they could be got to Baltimore.

"But how'll I get the money to get to Baltimore?" the old man said aloud to himself.

"Don't you worry," said Trigger; "it's all settled."

The old man laughed a good-natured doubt, but Trigger didn't mind. He knew the money would be raised even though he couldn't help wishing he knew how.

X. MRS. GEORGE SMITH

Mrs. Smith was sitting in a rocking chair on the front porch and making it go pretty fast, when Trigger and George Smith came up.

"Here he is, Mother," said George Smith with a flourish.

"How d'ye do, little boy!" said Mrs. Smith. "Took you a long while to get here after you got to town."

"Now, Mother, remember we're not saying anything about that. There's only one question before the house and that is, do we adopt him or don't we adopt him?"

Mrs. Smith led the way inside. She made Trigger sit down in a chair near the window. She put two other chairs facing

him and she and George Smith sat down in them and looked
at Trigger. Trigger was embarrassed and got red in the face.
He was afraid Mrs. Smith was counting the freckles. After
a while she said almost fiercely:

"He's got red hair!"

"Well, you knew that beforehand," said George Smith, trying to be gruff.

Suddenly Mrs. Smith threw her apron over her head and
began to cry. George Smith looked as if he wanted to do something but didn't know what it was.

"C'mon, Trigger!" he said at last and led Trigger out
through the kitchen to a shed. "This is the wood shed. See
that pile of kindlings?"

"Yes, sir."

"See that blue chalk mark right at the top of the pile?"

"Yes, sir."

"Well, that pile has to be kept up to that mark. That's going
to be your job from now on. Can you split kindlings?"

"I guess so."

"Guess so? Don't you know? How'd you get your kindlings back in Calais?"

"Picked them up mostly, at the shingle mill and lumber yard
and along the bank of the river where the tide left them."

"Well, we have to split them here and you've got to do it."
He grinned when he said that; so Trigger wasn't afraid to
say:

"I haven't been adopted yet."

They both grinned at this and George Smith said, "I forgot that. Let's go back in the house and try again." He started
back but stopped at the door and looked uncomfortable. "It's
like this . . . Well, we had a boy once. He died. He had red
hair. You know how women are. C'mon!" He stumbled over

the doorsill and then kicked it. After that they went into the house. Mrs. Smith was sitting as before, but wasn't crying now. Trigger and George Smith sat down again and the examination went on.

"Anything else the matter with him?" asked George Smith finally.

"I think he looks real nice," she said. She got up and patted Trigger's shoulder stiffly and added, "And I think his freckles are real cute."

Trigger choked once, he was so relieved about the freckles. George Smith looked surprised, then he blew his nose and went out into the kitchen. When Mrs. Smith and Trigger followed a moment later they found him eating sausages with his fingers out of the frying pan.

"You're eating the little boy's supper," she said, rather provoked.

"I didn't know what I was doing," he said and went out to the shed.

Then a noise broke out. Trigger knew what it was, because Dude had warned him. But Mrs. Smith didn't know and went to the window to find out.

"Goodness gracious!" she exclaimed. "Every child in town is out there and got something to make a noise with. It's just like a serenade!"

"Back in Calais they call it a shivaree," said Trigger.

"Nobody's got married," she said.

"You don't always have to have somebody get married."

"What can it be, then?"

"I guess it's me!" Trigger was quite modest about it, but he knew that he was just being welcomed to his new home. Suddenly Mrs. Smith knew it, too. She smiled and was pleased, but wouldn't admit it.

"I declare, if this town doesn't know everything about everybody. A body can't breathe that somebody doesn't sneeze!
What is it they want?"

"I expect it's something to eat," Trigger volunteered.

"Oh!" Mrs. Smith said. She bustled into the pantry and came back with a big basket of cookies. She gave a handful to Trigger. Then she called her husband and told him to take the basket out and distribute the cookies. An extra burst of tin-horn and dishpan music greeted him; but after that things quieted down.

When George Smith came back he said he'd made a speech and that it was listened to as long as the cookies lasted and that he was going to write to his congressman and tell him to carry a cookie basket when he went to make a speech.

After supper the lamp was lighted in the parlor and the examination was continued:

"Do you go to Sunday school?" began Mrs. Smith.

"I—yes, ma'am." Trigger's Sunday schooling had been off-and-on-ish; but he couldn't be expected to explain everything all at once.

"Well, that's a comfort!" said George Smith. "Everything in a right start."

"He looks like quite a good boy," said Mrs. Smith, "but I think we ought to make sure."

"Are you a good boy?" asked George Smith.

"I don't know."

"Every boy thinks he's good," said George Smith, adding, "for something."

"I don't think I'm good," said Trigger, "and I don't think I'm bad. I guess I'm medium both ways."

George Smith was willing to let it go at that, but Mrs. Smith didn't seem to be satisfied. "If you go to Sunday school, you ought to know the Bible stories," she said.

"Tell us a Bible story," said George Smith.

Trigger told them the story of the prodigal son. They seemed to think he did that pretty well except that he liked the prodigal son better than was right. Then he told them about Daniel in the lions' den. He lost his awkwardness as he went along. Joseph and his coat of many colors followed Daniel and other stories followed that. Then Trigger did an awful thing. He told them a story that wasn't in the Bible at all. It might have been a Bible story, but it wasn't. When he realized what he'd done, he got red in the face and wanted to run. George Smith looked queer and Mrs. Smith looked uncertain. Trigger didn't know whether they knew what he'd done or not.

Suddenly Mrs. Smith said, "Do you ever tell lies?"

Trigger was startled, but he kept his head. "Not if I can help it."

"Do you mean to say you ever do tell lies?"

"I mean I think a thing is so when I tell about it, but sometimes I find out afterward it isn't."

"What do you do then?"

"I guess I don't sometimes do anything."

"That's wicked!" said Mrs. Smith firmly.

"Yes, ma'am." It made Trigger feel better to admit as much as that. But he was afraid. He didn't want to be sent back to Calais and he thought Mrs. Smith was looking very solemn and as if she might not be willing to adopt him.

"Perhaps somebody else here wants to adopt me?" he asked.

George Smith jerked his head up at this and Mrs. Smith said quickly, "Don't you like us, little boy?"

"I guess I was afraid you didn't like me."

"Of course, we like you. Don't we, George Smith?"

"Well, well, well!" George Smith said, but he looked pleased.

"What's your name?" Mrs. Smith asked.

"Trigger."

"Yes, but your real name?"

"Just Trigger, I guess, ma'am. I don't ever remember anything else."

"But that's not a name. What name were you baptized with?"

"I—don't know."

"Weren't you ever baptized?"

"I—I—don't know."

"My mercy!" exclaimed Mrs. Smith. "You can't be confirmed unless you've been baptized and if we don't know whether you've been baptized or not . . ." She stopped, appalled.

"You can write to Calais and ask, can't you?" George Smith said. Then he turned to Trigger: "Who'd know?"

"I guess nobody down there would know much about me."

George Smith hastened to say, "We can give you a new name and begin all over again."

Mrs. Smith agreed: "Yes, if we decide to adopt you."

"Yes, ma'am."

"He might be called after me," suggested George Smith without much hope.

"Don't be ridiculous!"

"If we'd had a girl it was to be named for you."

"That's different. Besides, Myrtle is quite a pretty name."

"Got any ideas, Trigger?" George Smith asked.

"I had an Uncle Robert," Trigger said.

"That would be Bob with the boys, or Rob," suggested George Smith.

Trigger agreed, "His friends called him sometimes Bob and sometimes Rob—and some of them Rob Roy."

"Who was Rob Roy, Myrtle?"

"He was a historical person of some kind."

"He was a pirate," Trigger said, quite proudly, and Mrs. Smith, noting this, was pained and surprised.

"Do you want to be a pirate, little boy?"

Trigger didn't answer right away, so George Smith broke in, "Sakes alive, Mother! Trigger doesn't know yet just what his business in life is going to be. He doesn't have to be a pirate just because his name is Robert." He paused and then said as if trying it on himself, "Bob! Bob Smith!"

Mrs. Smith corrected him at once, "Robert!"

"Robert Smith!" Then he laughed. "But I reckon he'll be called Trigger, whatever we baptize him. Trigger's too good to get lost."

"George Smith!"

"Well, isn't it?"

"It's not a name at all; it's a part of a gun, and the worst part at that, because it causes all the mischief."

George Smith said, "Well, Robert's a good name to write in the place for it between the New and Old Testament."

Then Mrs. Smith sat up very straight, as if she were in a meeting and said, "We believe it is our duty to take in some little boy that hasn't any home of his own and bring him up. We couldn't ever treat him like as if he was born to us—flesh of our flesh and bone of our bone. That wouldn't be right to the little boy that died. But we expect to treat him as well as we know how. We expect to give him clothing and shelter and a good bringing up. But of course we couldn't ever love him the way we loved the little one that was our very own. That would be wicked." Then she addressed Trigger directly: "Wouldn't it?"

"I guess it would," Trigger said, but he didn't know why. He looked at George Smith and found George Smith looking at him and that made him feel better.

"It's time to go to bed," Mrs. Smith said.

George Smith stood up quickly. "That's settled, then!" he said quite cheerfully. He went out into the kitchen and fixed the fire.

When he came back, he found the other two sitting in an embarrassed silence.

"Is Trigger to sleep in the spare room, the guest room, or the King's bed-chamber?" he asked.

"Don't be ridiculous, George Smith!"

George Smith laughed right out loud. "C'mon, Trigger." He led Trigger out into the hall and to the foot of the stairway. He put his finger on his lips and they both listened. They could hear Mrs. Smith rocking back and forth in the dining-room. George Smith whispered: "Do I go up on your back, or do you go up on mine?"

"I don't know the way," grinned Trigger.

George Smith bent down and Trigger got on his back. "I'm the horse," George Smith said, "but you don't have to say 'Gee' or 'Haw' because your room is straight ahead at the top of the stairs." Then he neighed right out loud and made so much noise climbing that Mrs. Smith came out into the hall and called after them, "We may have to use those stairs again tomorrow!"

XI. TRIGGER AND GEORGE SMITH, PARTNERS

The next day was Sunday. When Trigger came downstairs Mrs. Smith was frying griddle cakes for breakfast and George Smith was sitting in a kitchen chair, tipped back, with his feet in the oven.

"Here he is now. Hello, Trigger!"

"Robert!" Mrs. Smith corrected him.

"Hello, Robert," said George Smith with a grin.

"Did you sleep well?" Mrs. Smith asked.

"Yes, ma'am." Trigger hadn't slept much, but when he had slept it was well enough.

"You look sleepy. Have you washed your face?"

"Yes, ma'am."

"You know what that amounts to," said George Smith. "Come with me, Trigger!"

"Robert!"

George Smith said sternly, "Trigger, you tell Robert to come with me!" He led the way to a half hogshead of water under a wooden pump on the back porch. "Stick your head into that," he said, "that'll wake you up." Trigger hesitated. "Here, I'll show you!" He bent over and put his head in the water up to the neck and then hauled it out again, spluttering and snorting like a horse. Trigger followed suit, but he couldn't snort as hard.

"What do you do in winter?" Trigger asked.

"Oh, in winter you break the ice first," said George Smith.

They grinned at each other and then went back to the kitchen and dried their faces on a roller towel hanging on the wall.

While they were eating breakfast a girl came in with a plate of doughnuts.

"Mother wanted you to try her new batch of doughnuts," she said.

"Did your mother know she sent them?" asked George Smith.

"I guess you came in to see Robert," said Mrs. Smith rather severely.

"Robert!" said the girl, very much surprised.

"How do you do," Trigger said politely.

"I do as I please," she said; then, "You've got freckles, haven't you?" That made Trigger red in the face, but she went on before he could think of a fitting reply: "I like freckles. If you don't like them you can take them off with sandpaper. I'll help." And she went away with a superior air.

"That's Kate Kerby!" Mrs. Smith said. "She's a tomboy, but nice enough for all that."

It was decided that Trigger was not to go to Sunday school till he had a new suit of clothes.

"You can sit here and read the Bible," Mrs. Smith said.

"He ought to get out," George Smith objected.

"I don't think Robert should be walking the streets with everybody in church."

"It's all right if he don't run or seem in a hurry to get any place," George Smith suggested. "Of course, he's liable to get lost and perhaps I ought to go with him. People wouldn't think things then the way they would if he went round by himself."

Mrs. Smith said it didn't matter what people thought if your conscience was clear and George Smith said his was.

Mrs. Smith said, "It's your duty to go to church."

"It's my duty to think of others, too, isn't it, even on a Sunday?" said George Smith. "And I'm thinking of Trigger."

"Robert!"

"Robert!" echoed George Smith obediently.

He said he didn't have to teach a class in Sunday school the way she did and that his voice was hoarse so he couldn't sing in the choir if he did go. Mrs. Smith said finally that they could go for a walk if they went first to the cemetery and put some flowers on the grave. She went out and cut some mignonette and sweet William for them to take and then went upstairs to put on her black surah silk. George Smith and Trigger went out the back door before Mrs. Smith could change her mind about what ought to be done.

They went up the hill to the cemetery. From there they could see the whole town.

"Where'll we go first?" George Smith said.

"I'd like to see Goosetown—by daylight," Trigger said.

They went down the hill to the main street, turned right, and kept going, passed the wagon factory and came to the tannery, and that was Goosetown.

"Nothing here but a bad smell," said George Smith. "It proceeds from the vats where they soak the hair off the hides."

"The Lodge is down there, over the bank," Trigger said.

"What lodge?"

"The gang's lodge."

"What gang?"

"Dude's gang. That's where the initiating is."

"You been initiated?"

"Yes, sir."

"Humph! Well, it's a secret, isn't it? Don't tell me any secrets. What I don't know won't hurt me. See that old woman in the window?" He pointed

Old Mrs. Hennessey's head and shoulders were framed in geraniums; she was smoking a broken clay pipe and looking at them, and her eyes and seven million wrinkles were smiling.

"That's Mickey's grandmother," Trigger said.

"You know everything, don't you? So does old Mrs. Hennessey. She lives there with her daughter. The old lady never moves away from that window. She sees everything and what she doesn't see she knows anyhow."

"Who tells her?"

"The fairies; they came with her from Ireland. They tell her the news, and when there's no news they tell her fairy stories. She keeps the news to herself mostly, but she tells the fairy stories to the children round town. Don't go near her, and if you do, don't tell anybody." George Smith waved at Mrs. Hennessey and she waved back. "The slaughter house is up the crick apiece and the swimming pool is up beyond that; but this is Sunday, so we'll go back."

Just in front of one of the biggest houses, George Smith stopped suddenly and didn't seem to know whether to go on or back. A man was coming from the house. He was big and walked importantly with a heavy heel and toe step. When he saw George Smith, he stopped.

"Why, Smith! Why are you not at Sunday school?"

"I'm showing this young man around town."

"Well, you'll be late for church if you don't hurry. The first bell rang five minutes ago." He took a big gold watch from his waistcoat pocket and looked at it. "Yes, six minutes!" Then he marched along without a single look at Trigger.

"That's Mr. Woodruff," said George Smith. "He's Burgess and the first Deacon. He owns the General Store. I work for him in a way. I'm the chief clerk."

"He doesn't look pleased," Trigger said.

"He's hard to please."

They let Mr. Woodruff get a lead, then followed as far as the wagon bridge. They crossed the bridge and went on half a mile up to Castle Garden. Trigger looked around for a castle or at least a garden, but all he saw was a round house in the middle of a huge cinder bed, and straggling cottages.

"Why do they call it Castle Garden?"

"I don't know; but I'm not to blame. It was named before I got here," George Smith answered.

They went into the round house. Several engineers and firemen and navvies were loafing around and George Smith knew them all. They asked him about Trigger. He told them Trigger was his son and had been sent to him on trial for a small advance payment, by the American Express Company. They stood Trigger up against the wall and measured him and weighed him to see if he was up to specifications. George Smith helped them, because he said he didn't want to get stuck.

Trigger was embarrassed at first and inclined to object, but after a while he fell in with the plan and said he wanted to be sure himself that he wasn't a bad bargain. That made the men laugh. They let Trigger get into an engine cab and blow the whistle and ring the bell and pull the lever that put sand on the track and throw a shovel of coal into the firebox.

They came back by way of the track and the railroad bridge. "Because you ought to know how to walk the sleepers," George Smith explained. "Everyone ought to learn how to walk sleepers before he learns anything else. Then if you get caught by a train on the bridge your feet know how to get you off before the engine runs into you and hurts itself. Only you're not ever to go on the railroad bridge."

The bridge took them to the railroad station where they met the ticket agent who was also the express agent, the freight agent, and the telegraph operator. He was a Dutchman and his name was Jake Middlekoop. He showed Trigger how to spell c-a-t on a dummy telegraph key and told him he'd let him send a message some day when he had an important one.

"He's a church member," George Smith explained afterward, "but, of course, he has to stay on his job and keep the world going and hasn't much time to go to church. But his wife goes and nobody holds it against him."

They went back through the business center, which was made up of Roach's Drug Store, the Commercial House, the *Gazette* Office, Ed Martin's Candy Store and Ice Cream Parlor, McCool's Barber Shop, and, of course, the General Store and several other places of interest.

"That's the Bank over there," said George Smith, pointing to a one-story wooden building. "Are you interested in banks? Well, anyhow, let's go over and look in the window."

They could see the safe and George Smith explained about

the combination. Trigger told him he'd learned how to work one once back in Calais.

"The Bank was robbed a while back," said George Smith, "but they only got ten dollars and the risk wasn't worth it, if you ask me."

At the barber shop they looked at the shaving mugs in the cabinet and George Smith pointed his out to Trigger. Then they looked at the two hats on display in Mary McDougal's Millinery Emporium and Dressmaking Establishment, and after that George Smith said it was time to go home.

"We can see the Jail some other time," he said.

"Have you got a jail?"

"Of course, we've got a jail. What kind of a one-horse town do you think this is, anyway?"

"I'd like to see the Jail."

"Well, you can't see everything at once. But there's the Church over there, up the hill."

"Is it a Methodist Church?"

"It's a Union Church. We're all united here. Anyone can preach in that church except Catholics and they don't want to. Baptists hold meetings there sometimes, and there's some Episcopalians in town, too. We're willing to have anyone listen to the Word of God in any way he wants to hear it. Besides, with all kinds contributing, it helps keep the building in good repair, the way a church ought to be kept."

A bell rang just then. "Church is out," George Smith said. "Hurry up. There's another service this evening and prayer meeting on Wednesdays and sometimes Fridays, but you're all right till you get a new suit of clothes."

They managed to get in by the back door just in time to make Mrs. Smith think they'd been there some time when she came in by the front.

XII. A NEW SUIT OF CLOTHES
AND A DOG

The next week a number of things happened. Kate Kerby came in early Monday morning on her way to school.

"I came to take Trigger to school," she said.

"Who's Trigger?" Mrs. Smith demanded sharply.

"Why, that fellow," said Kate, "the one with the pug nose and freckles. I'm surprised you haven't met him. Trigger, this is Mrs. Smith. Mrs. Smith, this . . ."

Mrs. Smith interrupted, "His name is Robert, and he's not going to school till next term. It's not worth while."

"When's your birthday, Trigger? I mean, Robert?" Kate asked.

"What's that to you?" Mrs. Smith said.

"I thought you might want to know. He's got to meet people and if he can't go to school, I thought you might want to give him a birthday party. All you need to make is cookies!" She went out with her head in the air.

"That girl!" Mrs. Smith said.

"She had a good idea about his meeting people. I think I'll take him over and introduce him to the teachers," George Smith said.

"What teachers?" Mrs. Smith asked quickly.

"All of them."

"Beginning with Miss Alice Brown, I suppose."

"Why not?"

"She teaches the primary and Trigger's going to enter high school. Besides, the teachers may be different next term."

George Smith said he knew what the School Committee thought about that and that Miss Alice Brown could teach in Beechwood as long as she wanted to.

"Yes, because she's pretty!"

"It's the nice way she has with the pupils."

"It's the nice way she has with the School Committee," Mrs. Smith said severely.

"That's just prejudice," George Smith said.

"Yes, it is!"

Then George Smith thought he'd hire a rig and drive Trigger over to the Minister's some evening to see if he was ready to be confirmed. Mrs. Smith objected:

"He can't be confirmed if he hasn't been baptized."

"No, I suppose not," sighed George Smith. "It wouldn't take."

"You'd better go to work."

"I was just going."

George Smith didn't try to take Trigger anywhere after that for quite a while; but he called him every morning before he went to work. He said he wanted to make sure Trigger was put together the right way so he wouldn't be wondering about it all day at the store. Then the two of them would go out on the back porch and stick their heads in the tub of cold water. Trigger improved so that he could snort almost as well as George Smith.

Trigger went back and forth between the Smiths' and the old Englishman's where he kept in touch with the gang, and did scouting in the side hills; but he didn't go into the town or meet people, because Mrs. Smith wanted him to come out first by going to church, after he had his new suit of clothes. It was known by everyone, of course, that Trigger now lived with the Smiths and several people came around and made tentative advances. Some of the girls began to meet in front of the house and swing on the gate; but Mrs. Smith put a stop to that. Some of the boys had wrestling matches near by; and couples began walking by the house evenings on their way to the cemetery. Once a large group came along on the way from school and staged a regular circus: handsprings, cartwheels, Indian wrestles, and a whole bag of tricks. Then they went to the ground and played mumble-the-peg. One of the girls got beaten and had to pull the peg with her teeth after everybody had had a turn driving it into the ground. She got her mouth full of dirt and didn't get the peg. That pleased them all, including the girl. When she tried again, she was given advice:

"You'll have to dig a hole for your nose." "That's fair." "You can't dig a hole for your mouth, but it's fair to dig a hole for your nose."

Trigger thought it was all rather childish, but he would have been glad to join the party. Mrs. Smith looked over his shoulder and saw the girl draw the peg.

"Nice thing for a girl to do!"

"Seems like fun," Trigger said.

"Eating dirt like that!"

"I wasn't thinking of the dirt."

"You stay where you are. There are three sets in this town: the good ones, the bad ones, and all the others. Those out there are the others."

George Smith came home at last with the new suit. It was blue.

"Why did you buy a blue suit?" Mrs. Smith asked. "It'll spot easily."

"He'll only wear it Sundays."

"You can spot a suit on Sunday; you ought to know that."

"Well, a Sunday spot isn't as bad as a weekday spot."

"You think you're smart. What size is it?"

"It's twelve-year-old size."

"It ought to be thirteen."

"Trigger's twelve. Robert, I mean. Besides, all boys' sizes are even. They don't have odd sizes."

"Why not?"

"Because there aren't any odd boys, I expect."

"You could get a fourteen."

"It's too big."

"He could grow up to it."

"It's mean for a boy to be always trying to catch up with his clothes."

"I ought to have bought it myself. You haven't good judgment about clothes."

"Well, I sell groceries, mostly."

Mrs. Smith told Trigger to go and try on the suit.

"Come on, Trigger, I'll help," said George Smith.

But Mrs. Smith said, "If Robert doesn't know how to dress himself, it's time he learned."

George Smith sat down in a chair, pushed it back on its hind legs and put his feet in the oven.

"I just cleaned that oven," Mrs. Smith said.

"I thought there was something wrong with it," said George Smith. He got up and went out in the woodshed; but he called back, "There's a new shirt, too, and a necktie and stockings and shoes. He'd better put them all on and see if everything's all right."

"They'll be right enough if the suit is. Time enough to get things dirty on Sunday." She looked at the shoes. "These shoes ought to have brass toes to keep them from wearing out right away."

George Smith came back. "If he has brass toes and wants to kick somebody, he can't, because it would hurt," he said.

"I catch Robert kicking anybody!"

"There's no harm. Boys are like colts that way: they kick without knowing it. The kick's in their legs and has to come out." Then he went back to the shed and began to split kindlings.

Mrs. Smith told Trigger to go upstairs and put the suit on and not to take the tags off, in case the suit didn't fit. When Trigger came back with the suit on Mrs. Smith called her husband in to look at it.

"Well, what do you think?"

"See here, Myrtle! I'm keeping still. If I say I like it, you'll

say it's because I bought it. If I say I don't like it, you'll want to know why I bought something I didn't like."

"I'd have bought a nice practical suit," Mrs. Smith said. "But it fits well enough."

"It's a little big for him."

"It's not big enough, if anything. When he grows he won't be able to get into it. Then it will have to be given away."

"Well, that ought to please whoever gets it," George Smith said.

"Why didn't you get him a hat?"

"I did get him a hat." He went out on the front porch and came back with a hat.

"How much did you pay for it?" she said.

"I forget," he said.

"That's a lie!"

"No, it isn't, either."

"Why isn't it a lie?"

"Well, it's not a lie because you know it's not the truth," said George Smith. "If I said something that wasn't so and you didn't know it wasn't so and I let you think it was so, then that would be a lie."

"You make me sick! You're ashamed to say what it cost."

"It's a good hat, isn't it?"

"It's too dressed up."

"Billy Rockwell said it's just the thing—for Sundays."

"How does he know? He never goes to church."

"He's in the clothing business."

"He's a dude."

"Well, he has to show off his goods some way."

When Trigger went to bed he didn't know whether he had a new suit and fixings or not; but in the morning he found out he was to keep everything. Mrs. Smith told him to take the tags off and remember where he put them. That was Friday.

The next day George Smith didn't get home till dark, because the store always kept open late on Saturdays, and when he came, he came in by the back door.

"What are you coming in the back door for, like a tramp?" Mrs. Smith said severely.

"I thought I'd take a look at the onions in the garden," he said. "They're coming up."

"You can't see them if they are. It's dark."

"Listen!" George Smith said suddenly, raising his hand for silence. He crossed to the front kitchen door and listened, then he said, "Shush!"

"What are you shushing about?"

"There's something out there on the porch," he said.

"Nonsense!" said Mrs. Smith, but she crossed to the door and opened it. "Goodness gracious!" she exclaimed.

There on the porch was the littlest dog in the world. He was standing on three legs and the other leg was held out as if he wanted to shake hands.

"I'll betcha he was just going to knock," George Smith said.

Mrs. Smith recovered from her astonishment and got suspicious, "Did you bring that dog home?"

"Certainly not," said George Smith indignantly: "But he looks like a dog that followed me when I left the store."

"Followed nothing!" exclaimed Mrs. Smith. "It's not much of a dog."

"Good things are done up in small parcels," George Smith said, "barring groceries. It's getting pretty dark for a little fellow like that to be out all alone. He may have lost his way. Perhaps we better keep him overnight, Myrtle." He stooped down and held out his hand. "Come here, Tip!" he said. The dog went to him with wagging tail and lapped his hand.

"How do you know his name is Tip?" Mrs. Smith said, very suspicious.

"It's the way he looks," George Smith said.

Then Mrs. Smith and Trigger both stooped down and there were the three of them squatting in a circle. Tip took a long look at Mrs. Smith and then went up to her slowly and lapped her hand. After that he went to Trigger and sat down between his knees.

"It's just an ordinary black and tan!" Mrs. Smith said.

"He's affectionate," said George Smith.

Mrs. Smith sighed and got up, "He can spend the night."

"After that we might get to like him," said George Smith.

That made Mrs. Smith very indignant, "How much did you pay for that dog, George Smith?"

"I got him for nothing," he said.

"You got cheated!" she said and burst into tears and went into the dining-room out of sight.

George Smith looked funny and then said to Trigger in a low voice, "We used to have a dog like that, but he ran away or something happened to him after—well, you see, he ran away. I thought it would be nice to get a dog to take his place. Besides, what's a boy without a dog at his heels!"

After Trigger had gone to bed that night, George Smith came to his room with Tip in his arms. He came in quietly because he thought Trigger was asleep, but when he found he wasn't, he said, "This fool dog thinks he has to have company to sleep with!" He put Tip on the bed and went out. Tip lapped Trigger and Trigger patted Tip and then they went to sleep in a huddle.

XIII. TRIGGER GOES TO CHURCH

Sunday began bright and early. By the time Trigger had put his head in the tub, eaten breakfast, done the chores, and gone upstairs to dress, the day was hot. He put his new suit on over his old underclothes, red flannels. They were thin and smooth with wear and no longer itched; besides he was used to them and he wanted something familiar next his skin. But they were hot under the serge and even before he could button up his coat he was sweating like a porpoise. He took everything off and got dressed again without any underclothes. He still felt like a stuffed owl, but his skin could breathe.

When he got downstairs he found George Smith and Mrs. Smith there. George Smith had on a black twill suit, quite shiny, a boiled shirt, turn-over stiff collar, and a black tie. Mrs. Smith vas dressed in her best-and-only black surah silk.

They left the house at ten o'clock. Mrs. Smith walked in

front, head erect, neck stiff, face set, her Bible and lesson leaves clasped in both hands in front of her stomach; she walked as if she were leading a procession and Trigger thought of the Calais Volunteer Company on parade and said "hip" to himself each time she put her left foot to the ground.

Trigger and George Smith were the procession marching in her rear; they looked at each other and grinned as if they knew it. They brushed elbows a good deal on purpose and finally, after some embarrassment, took hands brazenly.

Trigger had been to church and Sunday school, in Calais, but he had never faced anything like this. He was about to enter society. Mrs. Smith had told him so: "No matter how long you have been in town, you are not really considered, till you have shown yourself at Church. Everybody knows all about you, of course. A lot of them wouldn't approve of you, even if you hadn't given them any reason. Some of them don't approve of us either. They don't believe we're wise to adopt you. They think we are going to be sorry for it. So just you remember that everybody is looking at you and making up his mind whether to like you or not. If you don't behave yourself we'll get the blame."

To which George Smith had said to Trigger, "Look here, Trigger, don't you worry about anybody but yourself." And to Mrs. Smith, "Don't you go and make Trigger feel responsible for the Smiths."

"I want Robert to make us feel proud of him," Mrs. Smith had said.

"Well, let's try to make Trigger feel proud of us."

This conversation had taken place at breakfast. It had made Trigger uncomfortable then, and it made him more and more uncomfortable the nearer they got to church.

They went along their street, which was Fourth Street,

to Middle, down Middle to Second, turned right on Second, and in two minutes were in sight of the church, and what was worse, in sight from the church.

The church was set back from the street about twenty yards, but to Trigger this approach appeared to be four miles long. He had braced himself for a severe scrutiny within the building, but he had not anticipated the ordeal of getting in. The lower story was not a basement but was built mostly above the ground and a broad flight of steps led up to the main door. The steps were lined on both sides with men and boys, a million strong, and every eye on Trigger.

Mrs. Smith marched straight toward the church, the even beat of her steps as sure and precise as the swing of the pendulum in the parlor clock. Trigger tried for shame to unclasp his hand from George Smith's, but the more he tried the tighter he clung. His eyes were straight front, but he could see everything. And everybody could see him, and did. They looked through him and over him and to each side of him, but every eye was on him. He wanted to break and run. He got red and redder, but he stuck it out. He kept pace with Mrs. Smith: "Hip, hip! Left, left!" He almost said it out loud.

Suddenly, halfway to the door, Trigger was aware of a rhythmic beat of feet on the wooden steps: others were tuning in on the pendulum of Mrs. Smith's feet. The beats on the steps became louder, swelled to thunder. Trigger got out of step with his procession. Mrs. Smith became aware of the beat of her own feet. She looked indignantly right and left, but she marched straight on. George Smith grinned; he made desperate efforts to keep step with Trigger, but Trigger's steps were uneven and the effort was futile. He leaned over a little and said, "They all go inside when the second bell rings."

But Trigger was listening to a new sound, a hollow flat

sound like the slapping of fingers on palms. He looked quickly to one side and there in a clump of lilacs he caught a glimpse of white teeth surrounded by tobacco-stained lips. He saw hands beating out the time of Mrs. Smith's feet. Teeth and hands were instantly connected by a body and the whole became Dude. Beside him was Mickey, also assisting the march of the procession. This was the final humiliation. The gang had sent representatives to take part in his initiation into Beechwood society. Trigger went suddenly and furiously mad; he went up the steps and into the church chewing nails, with his head held high so the nails couldn't fall out of his mouth.

Mrs. Smith, ignoring Trigger, walked directly to the front of the church and sat down stiffly with the members of the choir. George Smith picked out an empty pew halfway up the aisle and he and Trigger slid into that.

"I've got to go and sing in the choir. You'll be all right here, won't you, Trigger?" Trigger nodded his head.

"They'll let you alone here till it's over and then I'll come back and stand by. That all right?" Trigger nodded again. George Smith got out his handkerchief and blew his nose; then he went forward and took his place beside Mrs. Smith, who didn't even notice him.

Trigger felt like a single sheep in a big pasture: there were women and girls all around him, but the center that he occupied was bare and he the only object in it. A whisper ran around the place like the swish of Mrs. Smith's silk skirt, only louder, and Trigger knew that he was being sized up and talked about. One girl went from group to group and wherever she went the whispering became more rapid. He took a surreptitious look. It was Kate Kerby. "Now," thought Trigger, "whatever they don't see she'll tell them." He picked up a hymn book from the seat and concentrated on that.

After a week of waiting, the second bell rang. All the men and boys came inside and with careful awkwardness stumbled to their seats. No one sat with Trigger. The Superintendent hastily took his place on the platform and opened the services by announcing a hymn. Everybody stood up, Trigger too, a lonely thing in a desolate place. He was painfully conscious of being looked at; it was easy for people standing to swing casually in his direction and the hymn books were just blinds. He wanted to pull his head down into his stiff collar; he tried to, but his jaw caught and held it above deck. He cast furtive glances here and there; one boy winked at him. He caught Kate Kerby looking at him. She smiled and nodded. Trigger knew she was trying to be friendly and reassuring, but he hated it. When the singing was over everybody prayed. Trigger got his knees down on a hassock and pulled his head below the seat top; he had never before been so grateful for a chance to pray. It was a long prayer, but not long enough. Trigger didn't even resent it when the Superintendent implored blessing on a new lamb in the flock and he almost joined in the hearty "Amen!" that followed.

When the formal exercises were over, the congregation broke up and settled down again in groups in various parts of the church. The grownups, both men and women, joined together in what Trigger knew to be the Bible class, in charge of the Superintendent. They were very stiff and formal and when they smiled at each other in greeting, it reminded Trigger of the preliminary handshake of a pair of prize fighters he had once seen in Calais. The youngsters, boys and girls, flocked up to and engulfed a smiling and pretty young woman whom Trigger took to be Miss Alice Brown, the primary teacher in the day school. Trigger thought he'd like to join her class. There was some confusion and much whispered conversation during the change of places, and Trigger was again conscious of being a center of interest. Several people went up to Mrs. Smith and shook hands, but Trigger noticed that she received congratulations, if that's what they were, with a stony and superior air. George Smith started in Trigger's direction but met with many interruptions on his way and just as he was getting near, Trigger was aware of Kate Kerby beside him.

"Come on, Trigger," she said. "I'll take you where you belong." She dragged him out of the pew and down the aisle and gave him a shove in among some boys of his own age. "Here, you!" she said to one of them. "This is Robert Trigger Smith. See if you can make him feel at home." Then, to Trigger, "You can meet the girls afterward. They're fun!" She gave the boys a disdainful look and left.

George Smith came up then and smiled at the boys and

whispered a few introductions. "This is Billy Locke. Hello, Billy! And this is Roy Kirk. And this is Sam Kreder. Trigger's new here, you fellows. See you later, Trigger." And he went off to join the Bible class.

Billy Locke dropped a lesson leaflet in Trigger's lap and then turned his head away. The other boys just stared; one of them was biting his nails and another was chewing a match —a match or a toothpick, Trigger couldn't be sure which.

Then everybody settled down to the lesson in hand. Trigger's teacher was a little man with a long pale face, short sidewhiskers and a bald head. He spent all the time explaining that he hadn't been at church the previous Sunday, hadn't got his teacher's leaflet and no one had troubled to deliver it to him, and for all these reasons he was not prepared for the day's lesson. Then he called for silence and turned around and sat down and looked as if he had been offended.

Billy Locke took out a new jackknife, opened up all the blades at different angles and passed it to Roy Kirk, who examined it critically, then passed it on to others. Roy showed Billy some picture postcards and the two boys sniggered over them. The other boys stretched out hands to get them, but Roy told them they were too young and put the cards in his pocket. In retaliation Sam and the others showed things to each other secretly, but Roy and Billy tried to look unconcerned. Nobody paid any attention to Trigger. He could see Kate Kerby and some other girls watching him from the other side of the church, but this didn't help his embarrassment any.

The lesson period was over at last; the classes broke up and everyone went back to his original place. The Superintendent returned to the platform. There was another prayer and another hymn and Sunday school was over.

Church followed almost at once. The rest of the people

filed in. Trigger didn't know where else to go so he stayed where he was. George Smith, on his way to the choir, bent over to him and whispered, "Keep a stiff upper lip. It won't last forever." The Minister came down the aisle bowing right and left and took his place in the pulpit. Silence, intensified by a swish here and a swish there, invaded and oppressed the air. The opening hymn was sung by the choir. Another hymn, announced by the Minister, was sung by the congregation. There were the usual prayers and announcements and the sermon, and another prayer, very long, and finally the doxology.

After the service, the deacons and the Minister hastily assembled at the doors and shook hands with everybody on their way out. George Smith got Trigger and tried to get him away. It was useless. All the women wanted to look him over, to shake his hand or pat his shoulder. The Minister made him a speech. In the middle of it Kate Kerby seized his hand and pulled him through the group of grownups around him to introduce him to three or four girls who chattered at him. The Minister discovered he was making a speech to someone who wasn't present, so George Smith collected Trigger hastily and took him back to hear the rest of it.

At last they were out of the church and Trigger found himself and George Smith again a procession in the wake of Mrs. Smith making toward Fourth Street and home.

Mrs. Smith relaxed as soon as the front door closed behind them. "Well," she said with satisfaction, "I think everything went off very well. Don't you, Robert?"

"Yes, ma'am," Trigger said shakily.

"Then run upstairs and change your clothes before dinner, so you won't get the new suit spotted."

Trigger found Tip asleep on the foot of his bed and he took him in his arms and hugged him.

XIV. THE MEETING

A circus was coming to Du Bois, a town much bigger than Beechwood, ten miles up the branch railroad. There was a notice of it in the *Gazette*. Dude heard about it from Matt

Dugan, the printer's devil, before the paper was printed and he came at once to Trigger with the news.

"Can we do anything about it?"

"About what?" said Trigger, who was splitting kindlings in the woodshed.

"About seeing the circus."

"I've seen a circus in Calais, two of them. One was a three-ring circus," Trigger said.

"I'd like to see a circus, especially the Indians with their war paint," Dude said. Trigger was not responsive; splitting kindlings always made him like that. Dude had come round with an idea, so he began to whittle, saying nothing. After a while Trigger said:

"We got to make some money."

"If we had money we could see the circus."

"No, you couldn't. If we have money it has to go into the cache for the old man to get to Baltimore with."

"Every cent anybody gets don't have to go into the cache."

"Yes, it does too! You agreed to that, didn't you?" Trigger said savagely. "We had a meeting about it. It's written down in the report and everybody signed it."

"I guess that's right," said Dude. "That's the trouble with writing things down; you don't get no chance to forget about them. Hang!"

Trigger was mollified, so he said, "Trouble is, we have to go to the circus to get the money to go to Baltimore."

Dude sat up straight, "How's that?"

"Well, the circus isn't coming to us, is it?"

"This is a one-horse town! No circus ever came to this town."

"Then we got to go to it."

"Why?"

"Boob!"

Dude was too much interested to remember that "boob" is a fighting word. "All right!" he said, "only you got to tell me—"

"If we get to the circus we can make some money."

"How?"

"Circuses have side shows, haven't they? Well, we could have a side show."

"What do they do at a side show?"

"They tell fortunes and have a lady with a beard and a man that eats glass and they sell things—popcorn and peanuts and—"

"Aw, what's the use! We ain't got any of them things and what would we sell?"

"We've got to sell something that nobody else is selling and we've got to sell something that somebody wants to buy."

"Yes, but—"

"Folks at a circus always want to eat. We might sell something to eat."

"Where'd we get it from?"

Trigger thought he needed advice. "I'll talk it over with George Smith," he said.

"If he tells his old woman she'll sit on it."

"He doesn't tell her everything."

"How do you know he doesn't?"

"I've heard him. When he tells her things, he tells her in spots, and he picks the spots."

"Even if we get things to sell, how we gonna get there to sell 'em?"

"I can't think of everything all at once. Call a meeting for tonight and we'll have a confab and powwow."

"Down to the Lodge?"

"Nope, up to the old man's. I promised George Smith to go up there with a batch of animal crackers that's broken and he can't sell 'em down at the store. Bad for trade." Dude got up to go. "And be sure and bring Dutch along so's we'll have somebody to object to anything you can't think of." Dude grinned and left, too excited to take offense at anything.

When George Smith came into the woodshed later, he found the pile of kindlings six inches higher than the mark. He scratched his head and sat down on the chopping block.

"What you want, Trigger?" he said.

"Me? Nothing!"

"Oh, come! I'm looking at that pile of kindlings."

"I wanted to talk something over, I guess, but that's all."

"Shoot!" said George Smith.

Trigger told him about the circus and about their wanting to sell something, and make some money and what for.

"There's several things to consider," he said. "There's what you're going to sell, how to get it and how to get it to the circus to sell it." Then he added slowly, "And there's the question of getting permission from Mrs. Smith to do all those things. Of course, you don't have to really get permission to do anything but get away from home. If you get that, you can give yourself permission to do the other things."

"I guess that's right!" Trigger said. He kept still after that, because he could see that George Smith was thinking.

"When you got to know all you don't know?" he asked Trigger.

"Meeting tonight."

"Short notice!" He considered some more. "I'm getting hold of an idea. But I'll have to see Mr. Woodruff first. Tell you what I'll do. I'll come over to the meeting after I've seen him. May be late before I get a chance, 'cause he's seeing a drummer

about a new stock of gents' suspenders and ladies' wear. You
take the crackers up."

"Are they under the front porch?"

"Yes, usual place. And I'll come soon's I can."

A commanding voice called from the kitchen, "You there,
George Smith! Come on in and bring Trigger. Supper's ready!"

"C'mon, Trigger! It's fried potatoes and sausages."

They were so preoccupied, they forgot to wash up. Mrs.
Smith sent them out to the back porch to do it. While there,
George Smith told Trigger they'd have to have a mascot for
luck. He said they could think about the mascot till he got to
the meeting.

Dude called the meeting to order at seven o'clock, but it
was later when they got down to business, because Mr. England said animal crackers didn't mean much to him, and Tip
and the gang might just as well eat them. After that Dude
stated the purpose of the meeting—to get to the circus—and
then Trigger told them to rely on George Smith and that the
first question to settle was the mascot, for luck.

Bud said the easiest thing was for Trigger to take his own
dog Tip.

"Nope," said Trigger. "Can't spend time keeping Tip from
investigating things and he hates to be tied up."

Dutch thought the fox would be a good mascot, but Mr.
England said it would be cruel to take the fox to a circus.
Somebody thought of the porcupine.

"Who's going to catch him?" asked Trigger, and they let
the porcupine drop. Mr. England said it ought to be something unusual to attract attention. Dude was impressed and
said, "Great Snakes!" and Trigger said, "That's the idea!"

"What's the idea?" said Dude.

"We'll take a snake."

"A dead snake's unlucky."

"We'll take a live one," Trigger said.

"Copperhead or rattler?" Dutch asked.

"I vote for a copperhead," said Mickey. "Copperhead looks ugly as sin and has a head like a cent and we want cents."

Dutch objected, "I'd rather take a rattler, a rattler makes a noise."

"And a rattler's just as ugly," Bud said.

"He might bite someone," Mr. England cautioned.

"Dude can take out his poison bag," Bud said.

"How about you doing it?" Dude asked.

"I don't know how."

"Huh!" said Dude, "you don't know how to do anything that takes your seat off'n a chair or a side hill."

"Well, anyhow," Dutch went on objecting. "What's the good of taking out his poison bag, just to have it grow in again."

"It won't grow in for a week," Bud said.

"Not if I take it out," said Dude. "All in favor of a rattlesnake say 'Aye.'" It was unanimous, except for Bud, who didn't take the trouble to vote.

Then George Smith arrived. He was wearing the smile that met somewhere back of his ears and tied itself in a knot. So Trigger knew the mission, whatever it was, had been successful and he settled himself to hear.

"Mind, I don't approve of this business, but I help a little because it's in a good cause," George Smith began. He paused and looked anxiously at the old man who nodded just as if he knew what the good cause was, which of course he didn't. "Mr. Woodruff had a cousin die up in Du Bois a while back and he fell heir to the things. He had most of them sold but he kept some of the furniture because it belonged in the family, and he's been waiting for a chance to get it down here without having to pay express on it." George Smith considered how to continue for some time.

"Now, Mr. Woodruff is a very positive man and likes to have his own way and he doesn't like to see a thing done unless he thinks it's right. So I said to him that along about Wednesday, which is the day of the circus, I'd like to see the supply room at the store rearranged to be more convenient and he said that would be a good plan and he'd been thinking about that very thing, but that I couldn't spare a clerk to do it. Then he got an idea and said Pat Mullen could do it. I said it was too bad to give the delivery wagon a day off like that and that the horse didn't need a rest the middle of the week. Well, one thing led to another until at last he asked me to have Trigger and another boy—or maybe two—take the rig up to Du Bois and get his furniture and bring it back."

A cheer interrupted him at this point, and that gave him a sense of responsibility. "But, mind you, it's a long trip. Mr. Woodruff says it's got to be done in a day, too. He says you can start early and he won't mind if you're a bit late getting back. What I say is, you had better start a bit earlier than he says and get back a bit later, and then you could have the day to spend in the good cause."

Dude jumped up and led three cheers and a tiger for George Smith. Mickey got up on a chair to be higher than anybody else and said, "This gang's got one honorary member already."

Everybody turned and looked at Mr. England, and the old man bowed and smiled. Then Mickey shoved his fist high in the air and shouted, "I move we make us another!" His fist came down with one finger sticking out of it at George Smith. Everybody shouted, "George Smith!"

"Elected unanimous," declared Dude.

XV. CAPTURING A MASCOT

"You going with us to catch that snake?" Dude asked Trigger.

"Sure I am. I've never seen a snake caught and I want to see how it's done."

They were up at the shack. Dude got a piece of copper wire about four feet long, from the old man's supply of odds and ends. He made one end of it into a loop with a slipknot, and they set out.

On the way up to the ledges, Mickey cut two willow sticks, each about five or six feet long. They fastened the loose end of the wire to one end of one of the sticks. The other stick they trimmed so it left a small two-tined fork at one end.

"We got all we want now," Dude said. "Except the snakes."

They reached the ledges in half an hour. The sun was out strong and beating right down on the face of the cliff.

"If there's a rattler anywhere around he's out on these ledges," Dude said.

They worked a cautious way around the ledges and up above them, where they could look down. There, sure enough, were a couple of snakes stretched out. Trigger thought they looked like the same two he had seen before.

"Might get them both," Mickey said.

"We've only got one snare," Dude objected.

"One's enough," Trigger said. He sat down on the edge of the cliff to watch, because catching a poison snake wasn't in his line.

Dude inched his way down the cliff and out on the shelf of rock where the snakes lay. The snakes never moved, they were asleep. He got up close enough to one of them to put the forked stick over the snake's neck just back of its jaws, and as soon as did that, he pressed down hard on the stick to hold the snake's head in place. The snake came to rather slowly, but as soon as he found he was pinned to the rock, he began to draw himself up and try to strike, but Dude held him and he couldn't make it. The other snake coiled up, but as soon as he found out nobody was bothering him, he un-coiled and lit out under cover.

"Hurry up, Mickey, with that lasso," Dude said. "This baby is tough as your grandmother."

Mickey had slid down behind Dude and was right at hand. He slipped the noose over the snake's head and pulled it up back of its jaws. Then he ducked back and held the stick so it pulled the wire taut like a fish line with a fish on the hook. Dude let go his hold with the forked stick.

"Here you are, Trigger," he said. "He's a pretty fair

specimen and he ought to make a good mascot. Shall I take
out his poison sac?" He got out his knife and waited, while
Trigger considered. "If I take it out he can't kill anybody, but
if I leave it in he'll have a lot more pep."

"You could take it out later."

Dude took the pole from Mickey and raised the end of it
so the snake's head was off the ground. The snake raised itself all over when Dude raised its neck. It stuck right out
horizontally, writhing and wriggling to beat four of a kind.

"He's pretty strong in the neck," Trigger said.

"That's right," said Dude. "Any snake that's worth his salt
can hold himself right out straight like that and make himself think he's crawling along the ground. 'Course, he gets
tired after a while and sags down, but he comes up and goes
on again soon as he gets rested."

That's just what the snake did, all the way down the mountain—up and wriggle, down and rest, and then do it again. By
the time they got down to the woodshed, the snake was fagged,
and Dude said they ought to let him rest up before they
showed him off.

They lowered him into an empty barrel where he'd be safe
until they needed him to take to the circus.

XVI. RATTLESNAKES AND A CIRCUS

It had been a long journey and the aged horse struggled up the last hill with the boys walking before and behind him and some of them helping him with shoves on his flanks. The downward slope was easier. The wagon pressing the shafts helped him along and down into the town.

The sun was well up and the circus men already had the great tent spread to raise. The lifting of the poles into the air took the weariness out of the gang's legs.

"Two poles!" said Trigger. "It's only a two-ring circus."

"No matter," said Dude, "it's a good-enough circus for me."

"Well, anyhow, the people that come to see it all eat and that's what we're after."

A fence enclosed a field that bordered the town and into the field drove the gang, now back in the wagon, gesticulating and whooping and Mickey doing a clog till a lurch of the wheels sent him overboard. This enthusiasm was out of themselves, and not for exhibition, but nevertheless they attracted some attention.

"Look who's here!" shouted a man who was stretching and pegging the side of the big tent. His fellow workers looked up and laughed, but continued with their work. "Who you looking for, sonny?" he asked Dude, who was in the driver's seat.

"Nobody!"

"He ain't here," was the good-natured reply.

Trigger slid to the ground. "We want a place to set up for business."

"Business? What business?"

"We got a rest'rant. We want to set it up right along where the people come by to the circus."

"Say, you boys got a concession to work with this shebang?"

"What's a concession?"

"Have you paid the big boss to set up a rest'rant?"

"Mean to say we have to pay somebody something for the chance to sell our own food?" asked Trigger.

"Sure! Didn't you know that?"

"How much?"

"Mebbe fifty bucks, mebbe more. You'll have to ask the boss." And with a nod he settled to work, grunting with each stroke as he sledged the big pegs into the ground.

Just then a clown came along, only half made up, munching a hot-dog sandwich. He had on bloomers and pointed shoes that curled up at the toes and giddy stockings, but above the waist, nothing. He saw the boys, stopped in mock surprise and counted them: "One, two, three, four, five, six, and SEVEN!" —more and more amazed with each succeeding number—"The seven wonders of the world!" He threw back his head and admired them openly.

"That's a clown," Trigger explained, "up to the waist."

"And what can a clown up to the waist do for the seven lords of creation?" He dropped to his knees and supplicated: "See, I beg to do them service."

Trigger took up with the offer at once: "We want to find a good place to set up our side show."

"Oh!" said the clown, jumping to his feet. "And what have you to show that is more wonderful than yourselves?"

"We're selling sandwiches."

"Alas! Eat, eat, eat! I was looking for a miracle, but nobody does anything but eat!" He discovered his own sandwich and proceeded to eat. Giving the last of it a shove into his mouth he suddenly popped the end of the sausage out again and wiggled it with his lips.

The gang howled. "Come with me, bones of my bones!" he said.

He led the procession to the side of the tent. "Here's a nice lonely spot!" he said, admiring the bare ground. "Here you'll be all by yourselves and none to bother you."

"He's a nut," Dude said, and Mickey made a noise like the cracking of a nut.

"We want a place where there's people passing. We got cheese sandwiches to sell," said Trigger.

The clown studied him: "A philosopher hath said, 'If ye cook a good meal the world will make a path through the forest to find it.' "

Trigger grinned. "We're not so sure of our good meal, Mr. Clown. Please help us find a good spot where we can do some business."

"Follow me!" said the clown, picking up a stick and twirling it like a drum major's baton. He led them around the tent to the business department of the circus. They were just in time to see the start of the parade, which had been forming in the seclusion of canvas walls. The gorgeous band, mounted on a gorgeous chariot, struck up with the first step and led the procession from its place of concealment out into the street.

"Gee!" exclaimed Dude. And the rest of the gang gaped in wonder.

"Behold!" said the clown.

Mounted men, mounted women, all in gay colored tights, passed before them. Monstrosities on painted wagons, animals in barred cages, elephants with kings on their backs, Indians in war paint—the whole marvelous wonderland.

"I seen the circus for nothing!" Dude said in an awed tone.

"That's not the circus, it's a promise," said Trigger. "It's a parade. They parade through the town and when folks see the parade they want to see the circus."

"It's nothing," said the clown, "because this is my day off and without me—" He spread his arms out. "Come!"

They found their way through the welter of workers, the clown leading, the gawking gang at his heels, and the horse led by the halter following the gang. Presently they came face to face with a short squat red-faced man in shirtsleeves, who stopped them.

"Friends of mine, O Master of the Household," introduced the clown.

"Huh!" said the man, his eyes first on the gang and then on the horse. "What you want?"

"A place in the sun, O Master. They have wares to sell."

"What?" The man glared.

Trigger spoke up bravely, "Sandwiches."

"Can't be done. I've already sold the sandwich concession."

"But these are cheese sandwiches, O My Master," elaborated the clown.

"Fried cheese," added Trigger.

"Fried cheese!" exclaimed the man, holding his nose.

The clown looked aggrieved, "You didn't tell me the cheese was fried."

"It's got to be fried," explained Trigger. "It's an old—that is, it's not a new cheese."

"Get out!" ordered the man and turned his back on them.

The clown bowed his head, then he was inspired. "Come! Follow me!" He led the way to the entrance gate and just beyond it. "Here is the spot. Here the populace passes. It is outside the sacred limits, but it is alongside of the road to heaven. Set your shop up here. Here the people will smell your fried cheese. They may even buy it." He smiled quizzically. "Bless you, my children!" He slipped two complimentary tickets into Trigger's hand, made a deep bow and departed, before Trigger could thank him.

Dude seized the tickets. "Gee!" he said.

Trigger snatched the tickets back. "You can draw lots for the tickets after we set up shop, if there's time for it," he said.

They had come prepared. They unloaded the wagon and set to work and in half an hour an open-faced booth was erected close to the ticket tent. It was done the easier and quicker, thanks to several big pieces of canvas which Mr. Woodruff had provided as a protection for his furniture and which served as top and back for the booth. They set the board counter with empty wooden plates which George Smith had provided along with the cheese, "Because when it's frying, it oozes and you need something to catch the drip," he had said. Several boxes and a broad board provided a workbench at the rear of the booth. The ancient half-cheese, bags of soda crackers, a two-burner oilstove, and two skillets completed the equipment.

"How about breakfast?" asked Mickey.

They had forgotten about eating in the excitement but with Mickey's suggestion they all became suddenly hungry. All lunches had been eaten in the early dawn and there was nothing left but the cheese and crackers.

"Well, we might spare enough to make one apiece," Trigger said. "It would be good practice, anyhow. Bud, you're the cook, you drew the low card."

If Bud was cook, it was in name only, for everyone took part in the cooking. They forgot to put butter or bacon in the skillet, and presently a ferocious odor of burning cheese assailed their nostrils.

"Butter!" shrieked Trigger. "We forgot the butter."

They began again, first melting butter in the pan and this time with more success, but the odor of frying cheese was strong and persistent. It spread like a smoke cloud and penetrated the ticket tent, where the sleepy attendant, not yet at this early hour occupied, came suddenly to life and shouted, "Fire!" A crowd of youngsters, eager for excitement, especially fire excitement, took up the call. Circus people rushed up. The boss was called. Scenting the trouble, he stepped up to the booth.

"I told you to get out, didn't I?" he said savagely to Trigger.

"Yes," said Trigger.

"Well?"

"Well?"

"You think you own the whole town and county?" asked Dude.

The man started to leap the counter, but was brought up short by a dose of hot frying cheese which Bud flipped at his face. He retreated, ridiculed by the assembly. "I'll get the cop," he said.

The cop was a constable, in a one-button waistcoat, a battered straw hat and a match in his mouth. He was also a philosopher.

"Don't see's I kin do anything about it," he drawled after a slow and careful consideration and a hearing of both parties. "You got a right to say what goes on in the field, but this here side show's outside the field."

"Don't they have to get a license to peddle goods in this man's town?" demanded the boss.

"Mebbe," sighed the constable, "mebbe they do according to statute. Only trouble is, everybody in town peddles something sometimes and none of 'em has a license and I don't see as I can pick on one party just because you don't like the smell he makes."

"It's a public nuisance!"

"Wall, Boss, I'll stick around and see if the folks agrees with you." He looked over his spectacles at Bud. "Is the taste as good as the smell, sonny?" he asked.

Bud took the hint and made him a fat sample. "I allus sorta liked fried cheese myself," he said and, munching his sandwich, turned and departed, leaving the circus boss furious but dumb. There was nothing he could do but go back to his job, followed by the jeers, catcalls, and other noises of his enemies.

The first performance was at eleven, but it was not more than nine when the first arrivals straggled up to the ticket tent. They had come in from the surrounding countryside and were bent on getting their money's worth. Inside were many minor attractions, some free, like the caged animals, others calculated to attract extra nickels and dimes. These firstcomers paid no attention to Trigger's sandwich shop. They had food aplenty with them and the odors of frying cheese neither attracted nor repelled. Trigger put Mickey in front of the booth as Barker. His line was, "Fresh cheese sandwiches, piping hot." It made no impression and brought no customers.

The returning parade brought in its wake the usual procession of the youth of the town; the boys actively taking part, the girls arm in arm at aloof distances, an admiring audience. Following them presently came the town itself in larger and larger groups. The line of ticket buyers formed. Straight at first, it gradually assumed a bent direction, and the bend was away from the odor of frying cheese. They even made remarks. The women put handkerchiefs to their noses. Mickey shouted himself hoarse and was cursed and laughed at, but he brought no buyers to the booth. The constable wandered up.

"They don't like it much, do they?" he said to Trigger, one arm on the counter.

"No," admitted Trigger. "They don't!"

"I might eat another," said the constable. "Jest to set the example!"

Bud made him another, and he ate it with glum deliberation. After that he ate a third.

"Quit hollering, Mickey, and come on in here," said Trigger. "We got to attract their attention, but we're doing it the wrong way. Where's the snake?"

Trigger had forgotten the mascot. Now he remembered it. It was in a box covered with chicken wire. Dutch got the box from the wagon and put it on the counter, open side to the front.

"Listen!" commanded Trigger. "Can you hear him rattling? I can't."

"Yeah!" said Dutch. "He's rattling, but he's sort of weak."

"It discourages a rattler some when you take his poison bag," Dude explained.

"Well, tickle him or something," said Trigger. "He's got to make more noise than that, or nobody'll ever hear him."

"Let's all of us rattle," said Dude with a grin.

Trigger took him seriously. "I forgot about that." He was businesslike at once. "Here, you fellows, come here, everyone but Bud, get down under the counter and help the snake make a noise."

They all carried rattlesnake rattles among their keepsakes, some of them several. And each boy had at least one rattle strung on a twisted silk thread. When the thread was alternately stretched and released the rattle vibrated and made just the same noise it made when it was on the snake's tail. The five boys out of sight below the counter vibrated their cords together and the rattler on the counter seemed to be making five times as much noise as he knew how to make.

The bent line had straightened itself with the dying out of the cheese odor and the withdrawal of Mickey from his post. It now passed within ten feet of the face of the booth. Two women were just abreast of the rattler on the counter when the boys began to rattle underneath. They heard the vicious sound instantly. One of them shrieked, picked up her skirts, and fled. The other fainted outright and fell into the arms of the man behind her. The constable, who had been surveying the scene with appreciation, heehawed spasmodically, and ducked behind the booth and made off, before his professional services would be called for. The line to the ticket booth broke apart and spread out suddenly, everyone giving a quick look to the ground at his feet. Then a man spotted the snake in the box.

"Ho!" said the man. "Look, them boys has a rattler in that box."

The man had a youngster with him and the youngster was interested in the snake, so the two stepped up to examine it, followed by a crowd. The snake writhed and rattled and threw out his forked tongue. The youngster was delighted, he wanted his father to buy the snake. One woman squealed in alarm. Another woman, seeing the man hesitate, became indignant.

"A rattlesnake for a plaything! The very idea!" She looked at the man who was still considering. "If that child's mother was here!"

The man defended himself. "I reckon Jimmy doesn't care so much about the snake; it's the rattle he wants." The child nodded a vigorous, eager assent to this. "What'll you take for the rattles?" he asked Trigger.

"What good's a rattler without any rattles?" Trigger stalled, but he was thinking fast.

"What'll you take for the snake?" the man asked.

"Don't know as I want to sell that snake," deliberated Trigger. "It's a sort of a pet snake. His name is Wigglebottom. See." Trigger tilted the box and the snake began to writhe rapidly to keep from sliding forward. "That's why we call him that. He's safe too. His poison bag has been taken out."

"I don't believe any snake is safe," the woman said firmly.

"Want me to let him bite me to show you?" asked Trigger.

"NO!" the woman shrieked and fled, followed by several other women who had crowded up.

The man warmed up. "Snake's no good to me. I'd kill him soon's I got him. It's the rattle I want."

"Just rattles?" Trigger asked, as he reached down and seized Dutch's rattles.

"Any rattle's good enough. Hey, Jimmy?" Jimmy agreed.

Trigger lifted Dutch's rattles above the counter. "Here's a good set of rattles." He put his thumbs in the silk loops and stretched and relaxed the thread, the rattles rattling vigorously. Jimmy shouted in delight and the man was sold.

"Give you a dime for them," he said.

"A dime!" Trigger was disgusted.

"Fifteen cents," said the man. Trigger shook his head. "Twenty cents?"

"A quarter," Trigger said.

"Done!" The man handed over two dimes and a nickel and Trigger gave the rattles to the youngster. The man took them at once. "Here, Jimmy! I'll show you how to use 'em." The two broke back through the crowd that had gathered.

Trigger looked the crowd over for children and saw several all eager. He picked out a boy who was held firmly between his mother and father, but just as he was about to begin his sales talk, a man spoke up.

"Say, son! Can you tell how old a snake is by the rattles?"

"Sure!" said Trigger. "He get's a new rattle every year."

"How long does he live?" Trigger sized the man up as a drummer and a drummer who felt pretty smart.

"It varies considerable," said Trigger.

"At a guess?"

"Fifteen years or so."

"Huh!" said the drummer. "Take that snake you got in the cage now. He's a good-sized snake, but he's only got seven rattles."

"May be big for his age," Trigger said.

"Don't believe any snake lives to be fifteen years old,"

declared the man. "Tell you what I'll do. I'll give you a dollar for a rattle from a snake that's fifteen years old." The drummer led the laugh that followed.

Trigger felt a jab on his shin and, glancing down, saw Dude seize Mickey's string of rattles and deftly slip them over his own string. Trigger began to see light. He said, "Is that a bargain?"

"Sure it's a bargain." The man pulled out a dollar bill and slapped it on the counter. Trigger reached for it. "No, you don't. You show me the fifteen rattles first."

"Let that gentleman hold the dollar then," said Trigger, indicating a man beside the drummer.

The drummer looked doubtful, but he handed the dollar over. "Now then," he said.

Trigger's hand slid under the counter and came up with a string of rattles. He gave them to the stake holder who counted them.

"Fifteen!" He handed the dollar to Trigger and the rattles to the drummer. Several men and all the boys, knowing the trick, laughed. The drummer's jaw dropped. He looked uneasily around, then he counted the rattles.

"Stung!" he said. "Don't just figure it out, but I'm stung somehow." He backed away and disappeared toward the ticket booth.

After that things were easy. Trigger cleaned the gang of rattles and sold all of them, for a quarter each. Boys on the outskirts began to offer unstrung rattles for sale, but no one wanted to buy their rattles—they had no living wriggling snake on exhibit to make them more attractive. One boy, a prospective purchaser, said to his father, "Who wants a dead rattle? Get me one that rattles." Trigger bought all the outlying rattles for a nickel apiece, passed them under the counter

to Dude, Mickey, and the others, who attached strings to
them, and sold them again for a quarter a rattle. It was a
flourishing business till the supply gave out. By that time it
was eleven o'clock, the circus was on and all genuine buyers
with money to spend were inside the big tent.

Trigger wiped the sweat from his face. "This isn't any sandwich shop we've got, it's a rattlesnake den." He counted his
money. "Ten dollars and a quarter. Trouble is, we're out of
stock."

The gang was up from under the counter now. Dude cast
a speculative glance at the surrounding hills and Trigger caught
it.

"What you thinking, Dude?"

"Nothin'."

"Aw, come on!"

"Well," Dude said reluctantly, "I was just thinking there's
a whole pile of ledges up there and it's dollars to doughnuts
they's a lot o' rattlers sunning themselves on the ledges. But
it's a tough climb on a hot day."

Trigger whistled, just once, then he got down to business.

"Boys," he said earnestly, "we got to get money. We got
to get the old man to Baltimore. This circus doesn't give another show till three o'clock. We've got to get a new supply
of rattles by an hour before that. Dude, you're captain of this
outfit. Lead the way! Take the gang up yonder, and don't
you dare come back till you've peeled the rattles off of every
darn snake in this part of the country!"

Dude looked suspicious. He pointed a finger at the two
complimentary tickets that were sticking out of Trigger's shirt
pocket.

"And while we're sweating up there on the mountain, you
go in and see the circus."

Trigger gave Dude a look of contempt, he took the tickets from his pocket and held them up:

"Boys," said he, "are we here on business or pleasure?"

"Business!" yelled the gang.

Trigger tore the tickets in two, and threw the pieces on the ground.

"I'll collect that furniture while you get the rattles. Then we'll dig out as soon as the next show starts. We don't dare stay for the night performance. If we do, we won't get home till daylight and the old nag will be dead and no good to deliver goods. George Smith'll get Hail Columbia. He might even lose his job. So we got to make hay—I mean, we got to sell rattles while the sun shines."

They didn't want to go but they went, each one with a pocket full of crackers and a hunk of unfried cheese.

By two o'clock they were back with a big bunch of rattles and one live snake which Dude had collected out of pure enthusiasm. They put the second rattler in with the first. "It's an added attraction," Trigger said. In addition, Trigger had a sign over the booth. While collecting the furniture he had observed and appropriated a new pine board and chalked on it: "The Rattlesnake Den." He had laid in a spool of silk thread, too, but he had paid money for that.

Business began right away. The circus was something everybody knew about, but the live rattler, the threaded rattles and the fried cheese were news. Reports had spread quickly and brought many parents who had no idea of coming. But a homemade product taking an active part in a real circus was too much for them. Not everybody bought a rattle. Some came to jeer, others came merely to look on. But enough people bought to keep Trigger busy. He met all requirements in rattles. He sold rattles for their width as well as their length. He sold them for color, dark or light. He sold them as from male and female snakes. He amazed everyone, including himself, by the variety and scope and general interest of rattles. And as he hawked and bartered, the two snakes in the box and five boys under the counter rattled and continued to rattle. By the time the second show opened, Trigger was hoarse. He had three rattles left.

"What'll we do with them?"

Then came the triumph of the day. Out from the gate strode the big boss, a sheepish grin on his red face.

"I got three kids back home," he said. "They've never seen a rattlesnake. How about it, boys?"

"You're very pleasant when you want something," Dude said.

But Trigger said, "Sakes alive, Boss! I'd like to oblige you, honest I would. All the rattles we've got left is three rattles that we didn't dare sell. We had plenty of chance, but they belong to my little baby brother and if I sold 'em he'd cry his eyes out."

"I'll give you fifty cents apiece for 'em. How's that? Hurry up, I've got to get back to my job."

"Nope," said Trigger sadly. "I'd like to, but that baby brother of mine——"

"Seventy-five?" Trigger shook his head. "A dollar apiece! That's as high as I'll go. Take it or leave it!"

"If it weren't for my baby brother——"

"Oh, can that baby brother," said Dude.

"All right!" said Trigger. The deal was made and the man left quickly. "That makes twenty-five dollars and seventy-five cents."

XVII. THE BIRTHDAY PARTY

The gang did not tell how much money they made at the circus but it got out, and what they raised it for got out too, as Trigger discovered at the party Kate Kerby gave in his honor.

"You're late," she said, opening the front door even before he had knocked. "And at your own party, too!"

"The clock was wrong in the kitchen, I guess. Mrs. Smith said I ought to get here exactly five minutes before supper."

"It's not a supper, it's a party, I tell you. Everybody's here but you." She opened a door and thrust him unceremoniously into the parlor.

Trigger found himself in the middle of a group of boys and girls spread around the room.

"This is Robert Trigger Smith," Kate introduced from the door. "He's the guest of honor. It's his party. Mrs. Smith couldn't give the party because it's a birthday party and she didn't think it would be right to give a birthday party unless Trigger knew his birthday and he doesn't. He was born in the woods down East among the Indians and they didn't have any calendar."

Everybody laughed and Kate said savagely, "Don't you laugh at him. He couldn't help being born without a calendar!" Then she laughed too.

"Trigger, you'll have to meet this crowd gradual, it'll take too long to do it all at once. That's Rose Kerby over there. She's my baby sister and wants to count your freckles. That's Elva Whiting alongside of her. That's Billy Locke, you met him at Sunday school. And that's—oh, all the rest."

Trigger was as red as a beet. Much undertone comment went round the circle. Trigger could make out fragments. So could Kate Kerby.

Kate stamped her foot. "You're a lot of pigs!" she exclaimed. Her fury was suddenly lost in a listening attitude. She raised her hand for silence, "Hush!"

Mrs. Kerby's soprano voice floated in from the kitchen. Kate explained to Trigger: "Mother sings in the choir and she's always practicing. She sings when she works and the high note comes when she gets through what she's doing! Listen!" Sure enough, the voice went way up in the air, quavered a bit and broke off. "There!" exclaimed Kate, "Thank goodness she did it—almost. Sometimes she cracks."

"Katie," came a singsong call, "Katie"—the accent on the second syllable.

"Yes, Mother-ee," she mocked the voice.

"Supper's ready," sang Mrs. Kerby.

"It's just beans, and brown bread for filling," Kate apologized, adding with more assurance, "with ice cream and cake."

She led the way into the dining-room. An extension table stretched the length of the room and on each end of it was a large platter of beans and a big loaf of brown bread. Trigger, wanting to look at anything except the faces still smiling at him, looked at the beans. He looked away again immediately, because he remembered what Mrs. Smith had said about Mrs. Kerby's beans and was embarrassed:

"They'd be all right if she left them in the oven long enough to get brown, but she don't. As it is, they look like boiled beans. She doesn't come from down East like you and me, and people here don't know any better. You must remember to be polite and not take any special notice of the beans. The brown bread will be good enough. The ice cream will be good, because Ed Martin made it. He keeps the candy store and makes ice cream for all occasions except the church suppers. It's too expensive for that. He has a son, Eddy Jr., and you'll most likely meet him at the party, and if you do and don't know what else to say, you can say you like the ice cream." George Smith, overhearing this admonition, had remarked, "If you eat her beans, she won't mind how you look at them. These women are all alike!" "Indeed!" Mrs. Smith's comment had been. So George Smith added, "About food, I mean."

Kate seated Trigger at her right and kept him in place till all the other places, after much confusion, were occupied.

Trigger ate three plates of beans, because Mrs. Kerby appeared as he had achieved his first plate and again after the second, and was pleased to observe the empty plate and replenish it. Kate had urged, "If you don't eat them every licking last one, Mother'll think they're not up to par."

Trigger knew he'd never want beans, white or brown, again.

He was too full to eat his ice cream, and Kate ate it for him. "Because Eddy'll notice it if your saucer isn't empty and tell Ed Martin—that's his father—and Ed's feelings'll be hurt."

After supper they played Blind Man's Buff, London Bridge, Ring Around the Rosy, and other games. Then the older ones objected to being childish and wanted to do something worthy of their years and experience. It was agreed to play charades.

Kate Kerby and Elva Whiting chose sides and each wanted Trigger on her side. Elva won the toss.

Kate lost her temper and said, "Let's make it all the girls against all the boys."

"Good business!" agreed Billy Locke.

"All you men get out in the dining-room," directed Kate, "and don't you dare to listen at the keyhole! When I rap three times on the floor, you can come in and see if you can guess what we've got."

Trigger became the center of the group as soon as the boys were together in the dining-room. None of them knew much about Trigger, but they were all curious about him and perhaps a little antagonistic. Billy Locke as spokesman began at once to put him on the defensive:

"You belong to the Goosetown gang?"

"That's my business."

"You're ashamed of it."

"I am not."

"You wouldn't want them to come to this party, I betcha."

"They wouldn't wanta come."

"They wouldn't get asked."

"They wouldn't come anyhow."

But Billy was curious in spite of his slighting manner. The Goosetown gang was a mystery in his set and therefore interesting. He wouldn't have admitted it for the world, but he couldn't help showing it.

"You're a member, aren't you?"

"Yes," Trigger was quick enough to answer since it was a matter of standing by his friends.

"A regular member?"

"Yes."

"How do you know you're a regular member?"

"Done all the things to make me a member."

"What have you done?"

"Took the oath, and—"

"What's the oath?"

"It's a secret."

"Oh! What else?"

"Chewed the bark of the slippery elm tree."

"There's not any slippery elm tree around here."

"Yes, there is."

"Where?"

"It's a secret."

"I guess so!" This with derision.

"Believe it or not!"

"What else?"

"Learned the grip."

"What's the grip?"

"It's the way you shake hands."

"How do you shake hands?"

"That's a secret, too!"

"Only girls have secrets," said Billy with scorn. He glared at Trigger. "I know one of your secrets."

"What?"

"You're trying to raise money for the old man that lives up the gully."

Trigger was amazed. "How'd you know that?"

"I know it all right. All us boys know it." Trigger and Billy glared at each other.

Eddy Martin walked up close and said, "It's just us boys know about it. We won't tell anybody if—" He stopped short and gave Billy a nudge with his elbow.

"Quit poking me!" snapped Billy, "I know what I'm up to!" Then he turned to Trigger and said ingratiatingly, "Why don't you take us fellows in?" Trigger stared. "We might be able to help—you know, raise some money."

Trigger gasped. "You mean—take you into the gang?"

"We're as good as you are," Eddy Jr. said.

"Shut up!" commanded Billy. "Well, what d'you say?"

Just then there came three thumps on the floor. There was a strained silence and everyone looked at Trigger. Trigger grinned. "I'll speak about it at the next meeting," he said.

The door to the dining-room flew open and some girl said sharply, "Any time tonight!"

The party broke up quietly. When Trigger got back to the house, he found Mrs. Smith sitting up for him.

"Well," she said, "were the beans white like I said?"

"Yes'm."

"I hope you ate enough to be polite."

"I ate three helpings."

"Goodness me!"

Trigger wanted to say good night to George Smith, but when he went upstairs, he heard George Smith snoring. He got out his bedroom window to the porch roof and down to the shed. He found Tip and took him to bed with him.

XVIII. A COMMITTEE OF ONE

Trigger was downstairs and had the kitchen fire built, while George Smith and Mrs. Smith were still abed and snoring. He puttered around doing anything to kill time, except wash his face. That he saved as always to do with George Smith when they ducked their heads in the hogshead. At last he became impatient. He rattled the stove covers and kicked the coal hod. Then he went to the foot of the stairs and listened. The snoring was still going on. He lost his temper, went back into the dining-room, and upset the spoon-holder. The spoons scattered and clattered on table and floor. Trigger grinned and listened. A sudden snort overhead told him that someone had awakened. He hoped it was George Smith, but it wasn't.

Mrs. Smith came hastily downstairs, her feet going ker-thump in George Smith's big slippers. She stopped in the dining-room doorway amazed and indignant. She had for-gotten to pin on her switch. She looked wild.

"For goodness' sake, what happened!"

"I upset the spoons."

"Goodness gracious! I forgot to put them away in the bureau drawer. I got to wondering how I could tell Martha Kerby how to brown her beans, and I just forgot everything. It's a mercy there wasn't a burglar around to steal them!" Then she remembered her duty and said sharply, "You pick those spoons up and wash them!"

"Yes'm!" said Trigger who was already on his way to the kitchen sink with the polluted spoons.

"What you listening at?"

"I thought I heard something."

"It's George Smith getting his feet into his boots. I waked him. Time he was up. He was snoring like a freight train get-ting under way! I'll go get dressed. See that those spoons are washed and back where they belong before I come down again."

She departed. Trigger went into the kitchen, gave the spoons a lick and a promise, and put them back in the holder. George Smith came down wearing a broad grin. "What you getting us up so early for, Trigger?"

"I want to ask you about something."

"Why didn't you ask Mrs. Smith?"

"She went right upstairs."

Trigger and George Smith looked at each other.

"Myrtle can't help the way she is anymore'n I can help having funny feelings and you can help freckles," George Smith said.

Trigger knew that, but the way she was he couldn't talk to her. "She takes hold of everything by the wrong end," Trigger had told Dude. "She finds out what she wants to do just so she can stop herself from doing it. The only fun she gets is not having any. It's a wonder she don't walk backwards, and sleep standing up." He had added out of loyalty, " 'Course I like her all right and she's good to me, but we just don't gee."

But Trigger and George Smith did gee. Trigger could talk to George Smith and did.

"Let's take a plunge first," George Smith said. They went out to the hogshead and blew and snorted like colts in a pasture. "That's better! No use trying to listen with my eyes glued shut!"

They withdrew to the woodshed, just to be on the safe side. George Smith sat on the chopping block and Trigger on the floor with his back to the pile of kindling.

"Now, then?" George Smith prompted.

"That party I went to," Trigger began. "Billy Locke was there, so was Roy Kirk, and Eddy Martin."

"Is that all?"

"No, but I'm just talking about them."

"What about them?"

"They want to join our—that is, they want to join the Goosetown gang."

"It's all right with me. I'm not a member." Trigger looked up, hurt. "I mean I'm just an honorary member."

"But what do you think?"

George Smith was silent. "Sort of oil and vinegar, isn't it?" he said at last.

"They don't mix, you mean?"

"Well, what do you think?"

"Trouble is, Billy Locke has found out somehow about our raising money. He says they can help."

"That's bribery!"

"Yes, but if they can? We got to raise a lot more money."

George Smith considered this. "Well, now I tell you," he began. "It's like this. Clothes don't always make the man, though they do mostly. It's not just a social question, especially when you're young enough not to know any better. Take you, now. You're sort of betwixt and between. Got a foot in both puddles. Of course, Myrtle don't know about the other puddle, but there it is and you're in it and you seem to be able to navigate around as well as the other tadpoles. What I mean, those other fellows, Billy Locke and Roy and Eddy Jr., they may be as good as you and Dude are when you get to the bottom of them. Seems like they have an idea. That's something." He slapped his knee. "That's an idea, too!"

"What's an idea?" demanded Trigger.

"Why don't you find out what their idea is first?"

"If we knew that, we might be able to work it without them," Trigger thought.

"You wouldn't do that, would you?"

"They might think we would. We might too, if it was a good idea. I wouldn't want to risk knowing what it was, unless those fellows were promised something for it."

"All right. Promise them something."

"What?"

"Well, promise to put them on probation."

"What's probation?"

"That means it's up to them to make themselves worthy to become members of the Goosetown gang. They have to make themselves so important, that you can't do without them. You promise to give them a chance to do that. Then they'll go to work on this idea they say they have. And they'll dig up all the ideas they can to try to make good."

"Suppose they can't see it?"

"They can't help seeing it. Everybody knows he has to make good to get into anything, unless he's born to it. When I was made a Mason, didn't I have to do everything I was told to do before they'd have me? Of course I did!"

"But who's going to say when what they've done is enough to say they've made good?"

"You and the rest of the gang."

"But we might keep them at it forever. When you started to be a Mason you just had to do a certain number of things, didn't you?" George Smith nodded in agreement. "But if we say to those fellows to go ahead and not tell them how much they have to do, they might never get done."

"All right. Set a limit."

Trigger took this under consideration. George Smith prompted: "It's a question of money, isn't it?"

"That's part of it," Trigger admitted.

"Well, then, how much more have you got to raise?"

"Seventy-four dollars and twenty-five cents," said Trigger promptly.

"Then make them raise half of it. That's the way Andrew Carnegie used to give libraries to people. Tell them they can be members of the Goosetown gang, as soon as they've raised thirty-seven dollars and twelve cents."

"Twelve?" questioned Trigger.

"You can look generous and agree to raise the extra cent yourself."

Trigger's forehead lost its wrinkles of perplexity. "I'll think it over," he said. Trigger always said he's think it over when he was pretty well satisfied already.

"Breakfast!" called Mrs. Smith from the kitchen door.

George Smith and Trigger stood up and shook hands solemnly, then, with Tip at their heels, went into the house following the fragrant odor of liver and fried potatoes. Tip got some liver under the table, unknown to Mrs. Smith.

Trigger waylaid Dude on his way to school, and told him to call a meeting. He had some difficulty, because he didn't want Dude to know ahead of time what the meeting was about. He knew Dude would be prejudiced against Billy and the others and would work up a rebellion among the gang that it might be hard to subdue. Trigger was always willing to face trouble but he wanted it to come at the right time.

"Where'll we meet?" asked Dude.

"You're the president, aren't you?" Trigger never fought over unimportant details.

"The old Englishman's?" said Dude tentatively.

"That would be a good place only we want to talk about something to do with him."

"The slippery elm tree, then!"

"That's the place!" agreed Trigger. "Right after school."

The meeting that followed began in sullen silence. Dude was disgruntled and he had imparted his mood to the others.

"Trigger's got something on his mind," was Dude's sour introduction, as soon as he had called the meeting to order.

Trigger was tactful. "This gang's sore because vacation's coming and all the loose change anybody's got has to go into the treasury for the old Englishman's new eyes. There won't be anything for anybody to have a good time on till we raise the rest of that hundred dollars. So I've been trying to figure some way to get that money quick."

This looked like something to the gang, and interest picked up at once.

"How you going to do it?" was Dude's challenge.

"I got an idea. Why don't we get some more people to help?"

"Huh!" derided Dude. "Help this gang raise money?"

"That's the point, Dude!"

"What's the point?"

"This gang is raising that money and we want to stand to that. We don't want to share the honor of curing the old man's eyes with anybody outside the gang, do we?"

"You bet we don't!" exclaimed Mickey, and there was unanimous agreeing.

"But," continued Trigger craftily, "there's seventy-four dollars and twenty-five cents left that we got to raise. That's a lot of money."

"I'll say!" said Mickey.

"What I say is, let's elect some more members!"

Amazement and silence was the response to this. Trigger went on: "This gang isn't the right size, anyhow. It's not big enough for a baseball nine."

"It's as big as Castle Garden is!" retorted Dude.

"But we want it bigger, don't we? There's only enough for one outfielder, if you don't count me, and you don't know whether I'm any good or not. We ought to have a full nine and a substitute besides me. I could be bat boy or manager. Then we'd look like something." He let this sink in for a moment, then continued, "Besides, if we only had a full nine we might get engagements and get our fare paid to places."

"Huh!" Dude was disgusted. "We'd have to walk and put the fare money into the old man's eyes!"

"No, we wouldn't," answered Trigger, "because we'd raise the eye money first. And after that we'd have to buy uniforms. We couldn't take on engagements without uniforms."

"Uniforms!" exclaimed Dude. He began to scratch himself. The idea of a uniform made him itch.

"We might charge admission to the game with Castle Garden for the mitt and mask," ventured Dutch.

"Huh!" objected Dude. "That would keep folks away, and we want plenty people present when we wallop those navvies."

"Besides there isn't any fence around the ball field to keep folks out," sighed Mickey.

Trigger feared the object of the meeting was being lost sight of, so he repeated with emphasis: "Anyhow this gang wants to be a real gang and that means a full nine and a substitute and a manager."

"Who you going to get?" demanded Dude.

Trigger felt that he had made his first point.

"I've been thinking," he said.

"Huh!" from Dude.

"We want to get men that know how to get money."

"And who'd that be?" asked Dude.

"I've been looking round. I went to a party the other night. You fellows know Billy Locke and Roy Kirk and Eddy Jr. Martin? Well, those fellows look pretty good to me."

"Those dudes!" from Dude.

"That's just their clothes," retorted Trigger. "You can't spit on a man just because he wears shoes. 'Sides, they could take their shoes off when they came to a meeting or anything."

"I can just see that bunch doing that!" Dude laughed.

Trigger laughed too, and then everybody laughed.

"And they've got some money."

"They never treated me to anything," said Mickey.

"But they would if they belonged to this gang. Members of a gang always share what they've got."

Everyone thought this over, then Dude shook his head. "Even if we wanted them, and I'm not saying we do, they wouldn't want us."

"How do you know they wouldn't?" demanded Trigger.

"Aw, I know!" retorted Dude.

"You don't think enough of your own gang!" scorned Trigger. "I've been around and I tell you this gang is known and looked up to and respected. Those fellows have a gang of their own, but what is it? They don't have any fun and they haven't even got any secrets, not one. I know that."

"I wouldn't want to ask them and have them turn up their noses," said Dutch.

"Nor me either," added Bud.

"Bud's waked up!" Trigger said and got another laugh. "Anyhow you don't have to ask them. I'll ask them—if you fellows make me a committee."

"Well, I don't know!" Dude temporized. But Trigger could see that Dude was tempted.

"Look here," he went on, "I won't even ask them. I won't give them a chance to turn us down."

"What'll you do then?" Mickey asked.

"I'll make them ask us."

"What?" Dude was astonished.

"We'll tell them they have to do something to be worthy of this gang, and if they do it, we'll let them belong and initiate them. What they'll have to do is raise money for the old man's eyes."

"All of it?"

"Half of it," amended Trigger. "We don't want anyone to get the idea we're not able to do our share."

"Sounds like a tall order," said Mickey.

"You can't do it," said Dude.

"You just make me a committee and see!"

Dude thought this was a good way to let Trigger undermine his growing importance in the gang, so he grinned and said, "Motion is in order, gents."

"I move Trigger's a committee to do what he says he can do," offered Dutch.

Mickey seconded the motion.

"All in favor say 'Whoop.'" Everyone whooped. "Carried unanimous! Now do we adjourn and go home to supper?"

XIX. MEMBERS FOR
THE GOOSETOWN GANG

Trigger met Billy, Roy, and Eddy Jr. by appointment in the shed back of Woodruff's General Store, the place of his historic fist fight with Dude. It was unlocked because empty of hides and so accessible. Trigger had a strong sentimental regard for the place, for old time's sake. Besides he liked the smell of leather which clung to it. He had Tip with him, having smuggled him out of the house under a superfluous coat, partly as companion, partly as subject for initial conversation.

"Not much of a dog," Eddy Jr. said, as soon as Tip had been presented to the three boys.

"He's all dog," returned Trigger, "and he knows more than most folks."

Trigger made a cushion of his coat and Tip went to sleep on it.

"Have you had a meeting?" asked Billy.

"Uh-huh."

"What about it?"

"What was your idea about how to raise money?"

"Huh!" snorted Eddy Jr.

"We want to know first if we can get into the gang," Billy answered.

"The gang isn't anxious about any new members," Trigger said carelessly. "But they don't want to be stuck up."

"How much is the initiation?" asked Eddy.

"What?"

"My Dad says to find out how much I have to pay to get initiated?"

"Oh," said Trigger. "That's five dollars."

"Five dollars apiece?" gasped Roy.

"Sure, but you don't pay that till the time comes."

"I've got a lot more than five dollars right now," bragged Billy. "My father's conductor on the Valley Branch, and he gives me a quarter a week for getting in wood."

"Well, I guess I can get five dollars off Mother," said Roy, recovering from the shock.

" 'Course you can," said Eddy Jr., "and my Dad'll give it to me. He makes a lot off of ice cream in the summer."

"Do your folks know you want to join the Goosetown gang?" asked Trigger, somewhat surprised.

"Mine does," answered Eddy. "At least my Dad does. Mother's dead a long time. He says I got to mix with all kinds and I might as well begin early. But he said not to brag about it round town, because some folks wouldn't understand."

"Mother doesn't care what I do," said Roy, "as long as I don't bother her with it."

"What about you, Billy?"

"Aw, I don't tell anybody anything, 'less it's good for them to know it."

Silence followed. At last Trigger got his speech in order. "It's like this, you fellows. This gang's a club and you can't get into a club unless you got something the club hasn't got and wants. This gang's only got seven men in its nine and it wants to get the other two and a substitute. Can you play ball?"

The three boys knew that the Goosetown gang could play ball and though not modest by nature, they hesitated.

"I guess I'd be all right in the outfield," Billy said at last.

"Me, too!" echoed Roy. "But I don't run any too fast. My folks say I've grown too big too fast, but I'll outgrow it."

Trigger concluded: "All you'd have to do is get the fouls, because Skinny Muldoon can cover any fly between third and first. Can you bat?"

"Oh, I can bat all right," admitted Billy.

"Me, too!" agreed Roy.

Trigger looked at Eddy Jr. who hadn't said anything. "I could be manager, and look after the money. My Dad's a business man," Eddy Jr. ventured.

"Don't kid yourself, child," Trigger spoke severely. "There's only one manager and treasury and I'm it. I get the money and hold on to it. You can be substitute, I guess."

The three boys looked relieved, this seemed easier than expected. Trigger, observing the obvious relief, felt that he had not been difficult enough. " 'Course we'll have to try you out," he said.

"Oh!" said Billy, dubiously. "How?"

"Well, I'll tell you. We got to raise seventy-four dollars and twenty-five cents more money to send the old man to Baltimore to get his eyes fixed. The 'nitiation will be fifteen dollars all told. That leaves fifty-nine dollars and twenty-five cents. You can raise half and the gang'll raise half."

"That's twenty-nine dollars and sixty-two and a half cents," figured Eddy Jr., the business man.

"Let it go at sixty-two!" Trigger waved a careless hand. "The gang'll raise the extra cent."

Roy and Eddy Jr. looked troubled, but Billy spoke up, "I know how to do that. Didn't I tell you we had an idea?"

Roy and Eddy nodded, but with a questioning look at Billy, who evidently had not confided his idea to them.

Billy made a speech: "My father's a conductor, as I said. His job takes him a long ways off and everywhere he goes he hears things that folks living round here don't hear till afterward, unless he tells them. Well, the other day he was up at Du Bois. He laid off there overnight and went to see a minstrel show. He thought it was pretty good and said so to the ticket man. He said, 'Why don't you come to Beechwood and give a show?' The ticket man told him they were planning to come right through here on their way to Renova, but they'd stop off for a night if we could guarantee to sell a hundred tickets at fifty cents and twenty-five reserved seats at sixty cents and get them a hall for nothing and put them up overnight."

"Uh-huh?" Trigger was noncommittal.

"Gee, that's business!" said the astonished Eddy.

"Who's going to do all that?" Roy asked.

Billy swelled up: "We are, you and me and Eddy." This made Roy and Eddy look proud, but doubtful. Trigger just sat detached and waited for more. It came. "It's easy as rolling off a log. Look! Dad already spoke to Will Mitchell and he said we could use the auditorium over to his place if we'd clean it up ourselves and furnish the coal-oil for the lamps. There's only fourteen or fifteen men and we could spread them around for the night. Folks would be glad to entertain actors just to hear them talk."

"I guess that's right," Roy conceded.

"Sure!" agreed Eddy. "My Dad would put up three or four and give them ice cream after the performance."

"All right," commented Trigger, from his aloof position, "but where is the twenty-nine sixty-two coming from?"

"Oh," Billy said, "of course we wouldn't be doing all that for nothing; selling those tickets brings in sixty-five dollars and we get one third of the gate receipts. That's better than twenty dollars, isn't it?"

"Twenty-one sixty-six and two thirds," supplied Eddy.

"Well?" asked the cool-looking Trigger.

"Well, I guess me and Roy and Eddy could make up the difference."

The three looked at Trigger with some pride and waited expectantly for a word of praise. Trigger looked them over thoughtfully, then put two fingers in his mouth and gave a shrill whistle, adding, "All right, Dude!"

Instantly Dude's face, wearing a broad grin, appeared above the floor at the open doorway. He climbed up and in, followed by most of the gang. The candidates were startled and Eddy Jr. retreated a few steps.

Billy gasped, "You all been listening?"

"Naw," said Dude, "what would we be listening for? We all been having a snooze down there under the floor where it's nice and cool."

"Meet the gang, you fellows!" commanded Trigger. Everybody shook hands. Then Dude said, "This isn't any regular meeting, but you all might as well come to order."

He sat on the floor back to the wall and kicked his heel on the floor for order. The others squatted or sprawled, and an embarrassed silence followed. At last Dude turned to Trigger.

"Trigger, it's your turn to report. You're the committee, aren't you?"

Trigger repeated what everyone already knew, adding, "There ought to be some announcements and posters hung up around."

"I could get Matt Dugan—he's printer's devil over at the *Gazette* office—to see if he could get Joe Jackson to let him print some circulars," Dude suggested. "You fellows want any other help from the gang?"

"You could help sell tickets," Billy offered as a favor.

"We got plenty to do," countered Dude; "it's just if you need help."

"We don't, only there isn't much time, that's all. We could do it, if there's time. Maybe there isn't. It would have to be two weeks from last night. I guess Dad'll take care of most of the arrangements."

"Is this all made a motion, or isn't it?" Dude directed his voice and eyes at the gang.

"I move it is!" said Mickey.

"Second it!" said Dutch.

"Carried!" said Dude. He turned to the three prospects. "Now, you fellows, there's some things you got to know. You got to get out and practice. That's one thing. Sometime pretty soon, we got to play Castle Garden for the mitt and mask. Another thing is, if any of you wants to be president, he has to lick Trigger first and if he licks Trigger, he has to lick me. If he can lick the two of us, then he can stand for election." Dude spat in the direction of Eddy, who rolled quickly out of range. "Any other business?"

Billy came back boldly, "When's the initiation?"

"When you fellows make good," Dude said.

"We've told you our idea already and you've agreed to it. Goes without saying, we can sell the tickets and raise that money, specially if you all help. If we can't, we can get it some other way. And we've already said we'd play ball. Seems to me we ought to get something for all that," Billy said firmly.

"What you want?" challenged Dude.

"You've got secrets, haven't you? I guess we've earned the right to one or two of them."

"Huh!" exclaimed Dude.

"Billy's right, Dude," Trigger said. "We might tell them the grip. Especially as we'll have to have some way of knowing each other from now on."

"Huh!"

"I motion it," said Mickey.

"Second!" said Dutch.

"Oh, all right," said Dude. "Carried unanimous! But we can't tell them right here in public."

"The lookout," suggested Trigger.

"Carried!" said Dude. "Let's go!"

"Wait a minute!" Trigger objected. "If they know half the secrets, they ought to pay up half the initiation fee."

"That's agreed!" Billy spoke for all three.

"You can pay it to George Smith direct, whenever you can. George Smith puts all the funds in the safe."

On the way to the lookout they passed Kate Kerby, and a couple of other girls. Kate looked them over with a knowing eye. "Well, will you look who's here!"

"We ought to have come by the crick," said Dude under his breath.

Billy said, "You ashamed to be seen in our company?"

Dude stared at him, then grinned widely. "Come on!" he said.

At the lookout, Dude showed them the grip, explaining how the right hand did it and the left hand covered it. Then he lined the gang up and made the new members pass down the line shaking hands with each one. After that, Dude, in an open-hearted way, showed them the slippery elm tree and told them it was a deadly secret and how later on they might be allowed to chew the bark and swallow the spit. After that, they would all be taken some night to the Lodge, and initiated and introduced to Pumpernickel.

The meeting broke up with everyone very pleasant and the old gang and the new part of it pursued separate ways back to town, each group congratulating itself on results to date.

When Trigger reached home, he found Kate Kerby swinging on the gate.

"If Mrs. Smith sees you doing that—!" he began.

Kate Kerby waved this aside and got right down to business. "The Goosetown gang been taking in some new members?" she asked.

"What's it to you?"

"Nothing! Only I thought if they were taking on Eddy Jr. Martin, they might as well take on a real girl."

"Who?"

"Me!" Kate went off, slamming the gate, her head in the air, leaving Trigger gaping after her.

Trigger told Dude that same night.

"One girl might be useful," urged Trigger. "You know, to clean up the gulch and the Lodge and get meals sometimes. Not a regular member, of course, but auxiliary. Like a sewing circle in a church."

"Gosh a-mighty!" said Dude.

XX. SAMBO SLEEPS AT THE CLUBHOUSE

Minstrel shows didn't matter much to Beechwood. As a rule, that is. The town had them pretty often and nobody ever got excited about them.

This minstrel show was different. It was for charity, and that gave people a sense of duty about it. It was more fun, too, than most of the charity things they worked for. Most of them were suppers or raffles or fairs, and when they had a charity show, it was pretty sure to be a cantata, with all the children in the Sunday school howling out of tune and the big-boom and high-screech voices dragged in from the Bible class. It was new and pleasant to have a sense of duty coupled with something that had some fun in it. The Ladies' Aid took it up, and whenever there was a gathering anywhere, somebody spoke for it. Even Mr. Woodruff spoke for it at Wednesday evening prayer meeting. He said he'd bought three reserved seats and contributed a dollar for nothing. Nobody came right out in public and said what the charity was. Either they didn't want to hurt the old Englishman's feelings, in case what they said got around to him, or they thought fixing an old man's eyes didn't sound as much like charity as foreign missions did.

The *Gazette* printed a story about it on the front page, and the gang was mentioned by name in the write-up, thanks to Kate Kerby. Joe Jackson, the editor and proprietor, didn't want to mention them. He said the Goosetown gang would queer everything, but Kate Kerby said it wasn't fair not to mention them. She did not tell Joe that she was trying for the gang herself.

Besides getting the write-up in the *Gazette*, Kate Kerby organized the sale of tickets. She distributed the tickets among people and clubs and centers and told them how many they had to sell to fill their quota. Then she turned to and sold twice as many tickets herself as anybody else sold. The gang didn't help much. Billy, Roy, and Eddy did a lot of bragging about what they were going to do, but they didn't do it. None of them sold even as many tickets as Trigger. Dude and Mickey and the rest of the gang sold almost none.

Kate Kerby got Trigger in a corner the night of the performance, when they were all drawing the shades and lighting the lamps in the auditorium just before the doors were opened, and claimed her reward.

"What do you want?" he asked.

"I want to be elected."

"You can't. It can't be done all of a sudden. You have to

do different things in different places and it takes time. Besides, you're a girl."

"I don't care if I am a girl. I've earned something. I don't have to be elected a regular member. Anyhow, I don't care about being at meetings with your dirty gang, but if there's anything interesting going on I want to be in it. And I've earned the right."

Trigger called Dude and the others into the corner, and explained how things stood.

"Give a girl an eel and she takes the whole fish basket," Dude said, disgruntled.

Kate Kerby burst out at this: "You wash your face, Dude Quinlan, before I'll even look at you in public. But I've earned something and I'm going to have it, just to show you girls count. I can do everything you can do and do it better, only I don't want to. I don't want to give the whole town the heebie-jeebies."

"She could be an Eastern Star, couldn't she?" Billy offered, partly to show off his knowledge.

"I don't want to be an Eastern Star, or anything else any other woman is," Kate Kerby said, furious. This cooled everybody off while she thought what she did want to be. "I tell you. You can elect me a Western Star. Nobody has ever been a Western Star."

Trigger made the motion and Billy seconded it. Dude was so mad he couldn't think of anything but putting the question and saying "Unanimous!" before anybody had a chance to vote.

He was still more disgruntled, when the doors were thrown open, to see Kate Kerby walk up and take a front seat with Herbie Lord and the girls. She had bought one of her own tickets with her own money.

"Look at her!" he growled. All the rest of the gang had to stand up in the back, because they were pledged not to spend money on themselves and couldn't buy seats.

Kate crowded through the audience as soon as the show was over and the curtain had stopped going up and down. "That swell end-man is real," she whispered to Trigger and Dude, "the rest are just blacked up."

"What of it?" demanded the wrathful Dude.

Kate glared at him. "Bah!" she said, "I'm just telling you something." She joined Elva and Rose and the three went off together. Dude looked after her disdainfully. "She thinks she's smart. I could have seen that too, if I'd been as close as she was."

After the audience had gone, the boys saw the real Negro himself coming from the dressing room, carrying his banjo. He walked along alone and lonely-looking.

"Hey!" Dude addressed him.

" 'Lo, Bo!" returned the Negro.

"Where you bound?" asked Dude.

"No engagements," grinned the Negro, lighting a cigarette.

"Say, I betcha—" began Dude; then he whispered to Trigger, "All the other actors were invited out."

Trigger whispered back, "Let's take him up to the Lodge."

"Want to put up at our clubhouse?" invited Dude.

The Negro looked at the ragged, dirty Dude. "Well, I dunno," he hesitated.

"We'd sure like to entertain the best actor in the show," said Trigger enthusiastically.

"Where-all's this here clubhouse?" grinned the Negro.

"Uptown a piece."

"Let's look her over," agreed the end-man.

They put out the last lamp, and started off together in embarrassed silence.

"You-all's gentlemen," the Negro said by way of ice-breaking. "My name's Sam, Sambo for short, Sam Watkins."

"Mine's Dude and this is Trigger here with me. We belong to the Goosetown gang."

"You shore enough do!" Sambo was pleased if astonished.

"Well now, I understands you gentlemen put over this here show tonight. I feels proud to be your guest."

Dude let this remark pass, not knowing what it meant, but Sambo's friendly manner and gayety had put an end to all embarrassment, and it seemed no time before they were at the Lodge.

Dude went in and lighted the lantern. Sambo followed and looked around. "Well, well! This is a regular, real clubhouse, sure enough!"

Dude pointed to the only chair, "Have a sit-down, Mr. Watkins."

Sambo took the chair, still holding his banjo. Trigger and Dude sat on the floor near by and leaned back against the wall.

"This is my real style! Fact is, gentlemen, Ah's glad not to have to live the social life when the chance offers." Sambo managed to look comfortable in spite of the battered chair.

Suddenly someone rapped five times on the door, three raps and then two more. "Come in!" called Dude.

The door was flung open so hard it banged against the wall of the Lodge, and there was Mickey with his squirtgun held tight in his hands, his eyes big, and ready for battle. He glared around.

"Gad!" he said, wilting, "I saw a crack of light and I thought the place had been broke into."

"This is Mickey. He's a member," said Trigger. "Mickey, this is Mr. Watkins from the show—Mr. Samuel Watkins."

"All boils down to Sambo, if you're friends o' mine."

Trigger got a sudden idea, "You're not planning to stay round here a while, are you, Mr. Watkins?"

"Can't say Ah was," Sambo drawled.

"Do you have to go every place yourself?" Trigger asked wistfully. "Wouldn't all the rest be enough once in a while?"

Sambo laughed: "Now, gentlemen, Ah ask you? What would that show be without me?"

"That's right!" Dude and Mickey exclaimed together.

Sambo laughed aloud, pleased with the compliment. Then he asked, "What-all's on your mind, Trigger?"

Trigger told him about the old Englishman, and that they still had to raise twenty-nine or thirty dollars. Sambo was interested. He began to look as if he were trying to think out some way to help. He picked up the banjo and began to hum an old Negro spiritual. The boys listened, entranced.

Suddenly Sambo gave a sharp twang to the strings, stopped humming, and said, "That show's laying off over the weekend. Ah'll stay and help you gentlemen."

The boys set up a cheer. Sambo put his banjo aside, and the boys quieted down.

"We'll keep this show a secret and surprise the town," said Trigger.

"Now you're talking," laughed Sambo. "Ah'll hide out here, but Ah tells you, this floor don't look too good to me."

Mickey jumped up. "There's a canvas cot in our woodshed, Mr. Watkins, Sambo, and a blanket."

Sambo smiled, "That's just the ticket!"

Mickey was gone in one flash and back in another. When everything was ready, Sambo said, "This 'minds me of old times, when Ah took the barns by storm. Come around in the mornin', gentlemen, and tell me what you-all plans."

XXI. CAPITALIZING SAMBO

"We got an actor," Trigger told George Smith the next morning, as soon as they got through snorting and blowing, with Tip looking on and listening.

"What actor?" asked George Smith, leaning sidewise to shake the water out of his right ear.

"The only real actor in the show."

"Where is he?"

"In the Lodge. We invited him. He says he'll help with the old man's eyes."

"How?"

"We're gonna give some kind of a show and surprise the town, when we can think of what kind to give."

"Breakfast!" called Mrs. Smith from the kitchen door.

George Smith put his finger on his lips and told Tip to keep still if he'd heard anything, and the three started in.

When George Smith and Trigger got to the table, they both looked as if they had a rabbit hid under their shirts. Mrs. Smith took one look at them and saw the rabbit.

"You two!" she snorted. "You've been up to something, but I haven't got time to attend to it now."

"Liver and bacon!" Trigger exclaimed, with enthusiasm.

Mrs. Smith just looked at him, but George Smith spoke before she could say anything. "I hear Boney Remick butchered Locke's cow yesterday up at the slaughter house."

"This is fresh western beef!" Mrs. Smith declared.

"Yes, that's what Boney always says," was George Smith's comment.

After breakfast Trigger was sent downtown with George Smith to get ten pounds of sugar for strawberry preserves. When they got to the Kerbys' gate, Trigger stopped.

"I got to see Kate Kerby, she—"

"Don't tell me!" George Smith whispered.

"Oh, all right!"

"She's as bad as you are. I shouldn't wonder if you'd both grow up to be Democrats. Only you be careful not to stay too long. Those strawberries are half hulled already, and if Myrtle gets the rest done before you get back, there'll be questions asked." He started on, then turned back. "I'll do up the

sugar and if there's anybody coming this way, I'll have them
drop it at the Kerbys'. You'd better ask there before you waste
time coming down to the store." And he went along.

Trigger looked after him the way you look after a person
you like pretty well, and then began to swing on the Kerbys'
gate to attract attention. The gate squeaked.

Kate Kerby came out right away and told him to get off
the gate.

"I want to ask you something," Trigger said. "Let's go
somewhere where we can't be heard. When you get to talking, everybody can hear you."

They went across the street and sat on the Mitchells' front
steps. The Mitchells were away visiting relatives.

Trigger got right down to business. "We got that actor
down at the Lodge. He's willing to earn money for the old
man's eyes, but somebody's got to have an idea about how
to do it."

After several suggestions had been offered, argued over, and
discarded, Kate said, "He might be a Medicine Man."

"Indian Witch Doctor?" Trigger asked.

"What's that?" Kate asked. "I mean patent medicine man."

"What's a patent medicine man?"

"That's the kind we have around here."

"You said once you didn't have any Indians around here!"

"We haven't. It's the medicine that's patent, not the man.
But they always claim it's Indian medicine they're selling. The
fellow that sells it wears a string of feathers to prove it, but he
doesn't claim to be an Indian himself. We could get Tubby
Roach to mix up the medicine."

"Well, anyhow, that sounds like a good idea," Trigger
said, getting to his feet. Kate Kerby got up too. When she
got to her own gate, she turned back and said, "I know where

to get the feathers and I'll get him some other things to wear so he won't spoil his good clothes." After that she went on into the house with her nose in the air.

Just at that moment Tubby Williams came along with a bag on his arm. He was the fattest boy in town, and the dullest.

"Is that sugar?" asked Trigger.

"Yeah, it's sugar. It's for Mrs. Kerby."

"It's for Mrs. Smith," Trigger said and took the bag away from Tubby.

Tubby protested, "But George Smith said maybe Mrs. Kerby would give me a nickel for bringing it up."

"Maybe she will," Trigger answered, heading for home.

"My goodness, Robert!" Mrs. Smith exclaimed as Trigger appeared in the kitchen. "You back already and me not through hulling these berries!"

"I'm pretty quick, Mrs. Smith."

Mrs. Smith stopped hulling long enough to look at him. "Sometimes you are," she said.

Trigger was quick enough to leave. He went out the back door with Tip and sauntered up through the garden to the grape arbor at the rear. Here he found Dude and Mickey. They often waited there if they wanted to see him. Dude didn't like to go nearer, because he didn't like Mrs. Smith because Mrs. Smith didn't like him.

"Where you been?" Dude demanded.

"I've been busy," Trigger said.

"Mickey got Sambo some breakfast. He begged it off his grandmother; but we got to get busy with the show." Dude was excited.

"Sambo's got to be in Renova Monday night," Mickey added.

"Come on!" Trigger said.

He told them the plan on the way to the lodge.

"But what about the actor?" asked Mickey.

"Oh, he'll like it," Trigger said, with more assurance than he felt.

" 'Mornin', gentlemen," smiled Sambo. "How's tricks?"

"We got an idea," Trigger began. "Can you act a medicine-man part?"

"Man, that would be just pie to me! Once down in Oklahoma the Indians down there was putting on a show for some tourists and their one and only Medicine Man was so drunk he couldn't even grunt. They hired me on to take his part and when I got through, they offered me the job permanent. All Ah needs is some copper-colored grease paint and a few feathers and I can walk, talk, and grunt like an Indian!"

"Gee, but folks would buy that medicine!" exclaimed Mickey.

"Medicine!" repeated Sambo, sort of drawing in his horns. "What medicine?"

"The medicine you're selling to them," Mickey offered.

"Patent medicine," Dude amplified.

"Patent medicine?" Sambo repeated, grasping the idea.

"It has to be patent," Trigger said, "to prove it's the genuine real article."

Sambo was reduced to silence, but after a while he recovered enough to ask, "You-all want Ah should sell some patent medicine?"

"That's the idea!" Dude said.

"How about it?" asked Trigger.

Sambo could see they were all hanging on his words and he hated to throw cold water. "But Ah just can't see Samuel Watkins Bones standing out on a stump selling something, even if it's good enough to drink." He looked around hopeful of understanding.

"Don't you-all see you-all's making me out just a salesman?"

Trigger had held himself in reserve, but now he cut loose: "Salesman!" he snorted. "What makes you think you're a salesman?"

"What you think then, you Trigger?" asked Sambo.

"You're not a salesman. You're just pretending to be a salesman. And what's pretending? It's acting, isn't it?" Trigger was shouting.

"Shore now, Trigger, don't you go and get all het up over this here business!" Sambo soothed the irate Trigger.

"Well, it makes me sort of mad to have you think we're insulting you like that, and ourselves, too!" Trigger lowered his tone.

"There, there!" Sambo coaxed. "Nobody's feeling insulted."

"You're acting being a salesman, and you're acting being an Indian! And you got to act mighty well! Hasn't he, Dude?"

"I'll say!" Dude agreed, but not very strongly because he was occupied with wondering whether Trigger was mad or pretending to be.

"Hasn't he, Mickey?" Trigger demanded of Mickey.

Mickey was quick enough: "You bet he has!"

"The question isn't, are you a salesman, but are you an actor, and are you actor enough to play two parts at the same time!" Trigger relaxed after this and just challenged Sambo.

Sambo said presently, "Yeah, Ah see you see this here question different." He threw back his head and laughed aloud.

"I see it the way it is!" Trigger was emphatic.

Sambo laughed again and then considered. "It's not that Ah can't act an Indian, specially just a imitation Indian. And

Ah can act being a salesman too. But a actor has to say something, he has to have lines. What's my lines? Ah needs words for my mouth, man!"

"Well, it's Indian medicine," Trigger thought aloud. "So it ought to be Indian words."

"Sinnamahoning's an Indian word," Dude said.

"So's Susquehanna," added Mickey. "This here crick's a branch of the Susquehanna River."

"I heard tell there's a tribe called Ojibways," Sambo contributed.

"And there's 'The Last of the Mohicans,' " Trigger supplied.

"Come on now," Sambo began to get excited, "we've got four words already. Four more good mouthfuls like them and the part's set!"

Trigger added them out of his Calais past. Then he suggested, "You could be the Witch Doctor, Medicine Man, and Personal Representative of Chief Red Feather. I know him and he knows me. I could get him to agree, if he was here or I was there."

"Chief Red Feather!" Sambo rolled it round on his tongue. "Yeah, that's good. Gentlemen, consider that medicine sold!"

Dude led a cheer for Sambo Watkins.

Then there was a knock on the door. Dude opened it a crack. "Girls!" he snarled and tried to shut it. But Kate Kerby was too quick him. She pushed him head over heels to the floor, then she turned to Sambo: "Here's your costume, Mister!" She threw a bundle in and disappeared, slamming the door.

"Jimminy!" exclaimed Sambo.

Dude spoke from the floor: "She's not a real member of this gang. She's just a Western Star!"

"Western Star!" gasped Sambo. "Shootin' star if you ask me!"

XXII. PATENT MEDICINE MAN

Trigger couldn't do much himself, but he knew what everybody else could do, and he could see that they did it. Billy borrowed his father's camp tent without saying anything about it. Eddy Jr. got permission from Ed Sr. to set the tent up on the vacant lot next to the candy store and ice cream parlor. Kate Kerby got Joe Jackson's permission to let his devil print posters, and Dude got his personal friend the devil to do it.

Everyone sat in on what was said on the posters—the old gang, the new gang, and the Western Star. The meeting was up at the Lodge, because Sambo wanted to know what was

said about him. Kate Kerby sat on the threshold of the open
door, and when Dude looked at her she held her nose to show
what she thought of the place. That made Dude furious, so
whenever she said something, he said something else. It wasn't
easy to agree about the poster, anyhow, because all of them had
too many ideas and all the ideas took too many words. All
except Trigger. Trigger said, "We don't want to print a whole
newspaper. Who'd read it?" When they got it ready at last,
and everybody had about agreed to it, Trigger and Dude took
it to the *Gazette* office. The devil set it up in big wooden type
and printed it on the back of some old circus posters he found
in the storeroom. It looked something like this:

SAMUEL WATKINS BONES
World-Famous End-Man
Personal Representative
OF
Indian Chief Red Feather
FOR SALE
Wild Root Remedy
The Chief's Own Sure Cure
FOR
Coughs, Colds, & Stomach Complaint
50 cents a bottle

They printed twenty-eight copies. Trigger distributed them
to the gang and Kate Kerby made out a list of where each
member was to get his posters on view.

"That's enough for all the stores and the two lampposts
and the hotel and railroad station," Trigger said.

Dude and Mickey got Tubby Roach to make the medicine.
They had some trouble reaching an agreement, because Trigger had told them they had to make twenty-five cents on every

bottle, and the posters said that each bottle had to be sold for
fifty cents. Tubby claimed that didn't leave much profit for
him if the mixture was going to be a sure cure for anything.
However, an agreement was reached in the end—only the
bottles were pretty small. Tubby didn't have any appropriate
labels but he pasted big plain ones on the bottles, and Kate
Kerby decorated each by hand in red ink, because, she said,
"Indians means scalps and scalps means blood and red ink
stands for blood."

Trigger consulted George Smith late that afternoon.

"Well, I don't know," he said. "I have a sort of feeling there's
going to be trouble but I can't seem to put my finger on what
it is. Probably it's just because it's unusual and folks always
get het up when a thing's unusual and make trouble about it.
But it reads all right. You say what you've got to sell and how
much it costs to buy it."

The gang set the tent up before dark without attracting
much notice, because everybody was acquainted with tents.

Sambo was smuggled into the tent the next morning before
daylight by Dude and Mickey and most of the old gang. Trigger stayed in bed, like a manager.

Some posters were put up on the lampposts and hotel and
station before anyone was around, and the rest of them were
posted on the inside of the store-front windows as soon as
the stores were open. As soon as the gang had the posters up,
they came back to the tent and hung about without remembering to go home for breakfast.

Kate Kerby got around very early. She had done her best
to look like a squaw. Her hair wasn't black, but she had brushed
it down straight all the way round her head so that it looked
like a lambrequin and she held her head high and stiff so that
the hair wouldn't get out of place. Over her shoulders she had

draped a red and yellow horse blanket with the stripes running around instead of up and down, to make her look fat. And she had a big red pasteboard star pinned in a conspicuous place on the horse blanket. She had a folding campstool, too, which she set up at one side of the tent flap and sat down on. For a wonder she didn't say anything, she just sat there like a squaw in front of the Indian side show at the circus, to attract attention.

Dude had borrowed a snare drum and a trombone from the town band, so they could have an orchestra. Mickey was pretty good with the drum, and Dude could make a noise with the trombone. They got out the instruments when everything else was set.

Trigger showed up last. He was dressed up for Sunday and said he was the Barker and that everybody was to keep still while he barked, including the band.

Quite a few men passed by on their way to work, but they hadn't time to stop.

Ed Martin was the first regular customer. He came early to open the candy store and ice cream parlor.

"Got a stomach-ache and want a bottle of this medicine." he said to Trigger, keeping his face pretty straight. The medicine was in with Sambo, but Trigger had a sample bottle in his pocket. He handed it to Ed. "You can have it for nothing," he said, "on account of donating the lot."

"No, you don't!" Ed countered. "I'm going to pay for it, but I want to get my medicine from the doctor himself."

Trigger grinned and put the bottle back in his pocket. "All right," he said. He opened the flap of the tent. There was Sambo.

Sambo looked real and terrible. Instead of his own clothes, he had on blue overalls and jumper, but these didn't count for much because of what he had over them. There were buckskin leggings and moccasins pretty well fringed and beaded, which covered him up to the knees, and a beaded buckskin jacket much too small partly concealed the jumper from shoulders to waist. He wore a crown of feathers with a couple of feather streamers trailing behind, and a blood-red sash tied tight around his waist with a bow and long ends. A hunting knife was tucked in one side of it, and a hatchet with a red handle in the other. Trigger had contributed his own genuine bow and a quiver of arrows, a present from Chief Red Feather himself, and these Sambo wore over his shoulder.

Dude and Mickey struck up a few notes by way of introduction.

Sambo stepped forward, a bottle in each hand. Ed started back and exclaimed, "Jimminy crickets!" Sambo didn't pay any attention to him, but just repeated his lines in a big voice: "Sinnamahoning, Susquehanna, Ojibway-Mohican, Schoodic, Meddibemps-Aroostook, Katahdin, Mohawk-Cherokee, Milwaukee, Winnepesaukee!"

"Golly!" muttered Ed. Then he recovered himself. "Well, anyhow, I'll take one bottle." With an eye on Sambo, he held out a half-dollar vaguely and Trigger took it. Ed accepted the bottle from Sambo at arm's length. Sambo instantly disappeared and the suddenness of it startled Ed backward. He backed right into the arms of Sam McCool. Sam took the bottle from Ed and looked at it.

"What's it for?" he asked.

"It's for what ails you," Ed answered.

"Thanks!" said Sam. He drew the cork and took a long drink, almost emptying the bottle. "That's better than Koonan's Hair Petrol. How much?"

"Fifty cents," Trigger answered.

"I'll have a bottle," said Sam, stepping forward.

"You've had your bottle," objected Ed. "Buy one for me!"

"I'll have two bottles," announced Sam.

"One dollar!" said Trigger.

Sam handed him the dollar, and Trigger pulled open the flap of the tent.

Sambo appeared, "Sinnamahoning, Susquehanna, Ojibway-Mohican, Schoodic, Meddibemps-Aroostook, Katahdin, Mohawk-Cherokee, Milwaukee, Winnepesaukee!"

Sam McCool looked at Ed and Ed looked at Sam McCool, and Ed said, "It's all right with me!"

"Me too," said the barber, "here's your bottle." He took the two bottles from Sambo and gave one to Ed.

Then he and Ed both turned around to go. By this time

quite an audience had gathered and they had to fight their way through.

Trigger pushed Sambo back, closed the flap and began to bark: "Samuel Watkins Bones," he began and went all the way through the poster.

"Heck!" said one of the men. "What is it?" said another. "Medicine!" said Trigger, "fifty cents a bottle!"

"I'll have a bottle," said the first man. "I'll have two bottles," the second man called out.

Trigger collected the money. Then he went to the tent, poked his head in and told Sambo he wanted three more bottles. Sambo was indignant, "Look here, you Trigger, who-all's acting this part?"

"I was just saving time," apologized Trigger. He stepped back, pulled the flap and let Sambo show.

The band played for the last time.

After that Sambo didn't have any chance at all to retire from view. The cause was good, Tubby Roach had made the medicine good, and buyers were plenty and business was fast and furious. In an hour, they had a line and everyone joking and laughing and very good-natured.

Then things began to go wrong. George Smith came hustling up from the back door of the General Store, so that he wouldn't be noticed much. He grabbed Trigger by the elbow and took him back of the tent. "Better all cut and run for it, Trigger," he said.

"What's the matter?" Trigger asked.

"Mr. Woodruff is out on the sidewalk reading the poster. Herbie Lord told him about it. He went blind mad when he read it the first time and had to put on his gold-rimmed specs to see to read it again. He'd be right here now only he's so mad he can't think what to say that's Christian language and bad enough at the same time."

Trigger was crestfallen. "What's he mad about?"

"I don't think he knows yet. It may be because nobody consulted him, and his importance is hurt. Or it may be a moral scruple. I can't tell yet and he can't. When he finds out, he'll break loose. If it's his importance, he'll go into the store and bawl out the clerks for letting the placard get in the window. If it's moral, he'll be here. Watch him!" They could see Mr. Woodruff from where they stood. Suddenly he whipped off his spectacles, thrust them into their pasteboard case, and thrust the case into his vest pocket. He made a military left face and started up the street toward the tent.

"It's a moral issue," sighed George Smith.

The Burgess came along heavily, even heel and toe steps.

"What'll we do?" gasped Trigger.

"It's too late to move out," George Smith said.

"We're not doing wrong, are we?"

"That isn't the point."

"Gosh!" Trigger was furious.

"Now, don't get excited, Trigger. Just treat him gentle and turn the other cheek. It may turn his wrath." George Smith gave Trigger a smile and ducked back to the store.

Trigger went to the front of the tent, turned his back toward the approaching madman, and kept on with his barking, only more gently. Suddenly he was seized by the shoulder and swung around.

"What are you doing?" Mr. Woodruff demanded.

"Barking." Trigger was gentle, a little surprised.

"What!" barked the Burgess himself. He glared around, and most everyone stopped smiling. Some that worked for him looked worried and one or two sneaked off.

Trigger explained, very innocently, "We've got a show here and I'm telling folks about it."

"I forbid it. I absolutely forbid it!"

Trigger was astonished all over his face and his voice was too. "We didn't any of us know you wouldn't like it."

Mr. Woodruff stared at Trigger, "You're George Smith's new boy, aren't you?"

"Yes, sir!"

"Does he know you're doing this?"

Trigger dodged, "I don't think he'd mind, sir."

Mr. Woodruff began to get angry again, "He will mind when I speak to him about it."

Kate Kerby snickered.

"Young woman!" bellowed the Burgess.

Kate Kerby looked at him and was pretty snappish, "I'm not deaf!"

This made things worse than ever, especially when some of the gang snickered right out loud, and Dude nearly choked on his quid of tobacco. The Burgess drew himself up big and puffed his fat cheeks out and addressed the multitude: "This town is a clean town! I'm Burgess here and I mean to see that this town remains clean. This thing stops right here and now. I'm getting the constable to see to it. If he finds anyone here after fifteen minutes, that person or persons will be arrested." He took out his big hunting-case gold watch and looked at it and snapped it shut and back into his pocket. When he looked up again, almost everybody had gone, except the gang.

Mr. Woodruff turned on Trigger. "How much money have you collected?" he demanded.

"Eight or nine dollars." Trigger began to count it.

Kate Kerby spoke up sharply, "Don't offer him any, Trigger. It wouldn't be enough to keep him quiet."

The Burgess glared at her. Then he told Trigger, "See that that money is returned to the rightful owners."

Trigger was doubtful: "I don't know's I can remember, sir!"

"Then see that the money is used for charity."

"Oh, yes, sir, I will!" Trigger said quickly.

The Burgess about-faced and strutted back to the store.

As he went in the front door, George Smith came out the back door. He came waltzing along and just as he got to the tent, the Burgess came through the back door following him.

Dude said, "Hist!" and George Smith took a quick look over his shoulder and saw Mr. Woodruff coming. He dropped down on his knee and untied and tied up his shoe strings, and talked fast, under his breath: "Hide everything in the store-house when the coast is clear. The tote team is just in from Sawyer's lumber camp. It's going to load up right away with supplies and start back at four in the morning. Tomorrow's Saturday and the next day's Sunday. There's sixty men out there and they haven't much to do and lumberjacks are pretty generous-minded. You can plan it all out this evening. Only don't tell me anything about it." He got up and seemed surprised to see Trigger. "Why, little Trigger!" he spoke right out loud. "What are you doing here?" Then he started off quite fast up the street.

"George Smith!" The Burgess was near.

George Smith turned round. "Oh, Mr. Woodruff! I just came out to look for you," he said.

"Me?"

"Yes, sir. There's a customer just come in that says we sold him some bad eggs!"

The Burgess scowled. "He'll have to prove that!"

"Well," George Smith said, "it ought to be easy to prove it if an egg's rotten."

That ended the show for that day but the next morning at four o'clock Henry Hicks, who was driving the tote team, took Sambo and four of the gang out to the lumber camp. Out there Sambo put on such a good show that they made seventeen dollars and twenty cents and as Sambo wouldn't take a cent and said his work was his contribution to the old man's eyes that made up the whole hundred dollars. After supper Billy Fustleback drove the tired but happy crew back to town, singing. Sambo led the singing.

XXIII. THE OLD ENGLISHMAN DEPARTS

The next morning when George Smith came downstairs, he found Trigger waiting for him by the hogshed on the back porch.

"Back already?" he said. "Quick work! You look like the cat washing up after the canary. Better stick your head in the tub and wash off the feathers before Myrtle comes down and sees them."

As soon as the snorting and blowing was over, they went into the woodshed where Trigger told George Smith everything, and gave him the money.

George Smith blew his nose and got over a lump in his throat and then said, "And now what?"

"You've got to tell him."

"Me? Tell who what?"

"You've got to tell the old Englishman about the money and what it's for."

"Me? The gang ought to do that. You ought to tie the hundred dollars up in a fancy candy box and make a speech."

"Look here, George Smith," Trigger said, decidedly earnest, "none of us can tell him."

"There's Kate Kerby; she could do it."

"Yes, she could," agreed Trigger; "but she won't get the chance. She's only a Western Star, anyhow."

"But what do you want me to say?"

"It's no matter what you say, so you get the money to him and let him know what it's for. But you got to do it right away."

"Without any breakfast?"

"Well, it ought to be soon enough right after breakfast."

"What's the hurry?"

"Because his eyes're getting worse every day and he ought to catch the early train in the morning and there's a lot he'll have to do."

"What's he got to do?"

"Well, he's got to pack up and put things to rights. And the fox and porcupine have to be told, don't they? I mean the fox has to be taken up in the woods and let go."

"It's going to be a busy day for a Sunday," George Smith said.

"Breakfast's ready," Mrs. Smith called from the kitchen door, and when she saw Trigger she said, "Humph! you look like butter wouldn't melt in your mouth. George Smith said you went away to do a good deed, but it's a good thing I promised not to ask about it."

After breakfast, George Smith said he was going to take Trigger out for a walk and look around. Mrs. Smith looked suspicious, but she said nothing, just began to wash the dishes.

George Smith and Trigger started off across the field and went over through the edge of the woods to the old Englishman's. When they got pretty close, Trigger sat down back of a clump of alders. He picked up a dead pine limb and began to whittle. George Smith went on into the shack, as Trigger could see by peeking through the alders. Trigger kept getting up and down, whittling a while and stopping and peeking through the bushes. Before long he was having chills and fever, his hands trembled so he couldn't whittle and he put them in his pocket to keep them out of sight.

George Smith came out at last and they went back through the edge of the woods and across the field. They climbed over the back fence and when they got down on the other side George Smith went over to the cucumber patch and Trigger followed. They both bent over to look at the cucumbers. George Smith said, "Everything's all right, and he's to go off on the early train. He says he'll let the fox go right after dinner if anybody wants to be present to help."

They went into the house and got dressed and went to Sunday school, walking behind Mrs. Smith in her surah silk.

Between the time Sunday school let out and church took in, Trigger went out and hid a note under a stone that he and Dude used for Sundays. Then he went back to church and looked as if he was listening to the sermon.

Dude came along after a while, got the note and notified the old gang about the fox. Trigger told Billy after church and told him to tell Roy and Eddy Jr. Nobody told Kate Kerby anything; Trigger just acted as if he didn't see her when she came up to him after church.

George Smith took Mrs. Smith for a walk up to the cemetery after dinner, so Trigger could have a chance to get away without answering questions.

When Trigger got over to the old Englishman's, he found Billy, Roy, and Eddy sitting right out in plain sight not very far away. The old gang was hid around back of the trees and bushes all over the ravine. As soon as Dude saw Trigger, he said, "Hist!" Trigger went up behind the tree where Dude was.

"What'd he say?" Dude asked.

"I don't know," Trigger answered.

"Didn't he say anything?"

"I guess he did, but I didn't hear him."

"Didn't you tell him?"

"George Smith told him."

"Scare-cat!"

"Scare-cat, your own self!"

"How we going to get the fox up in the woods without his getting away?"

"How do I know? I never took a fox to the woods before."

"Go and find out from the old man."

"You go!"

Just then the old Englishman came out the door and sat down on the steps. Dude grabbed Trigger by the wrist and pointed him out, just as if Trigger and all the rest of the gang didn't see him anyhow.

Then Trigger and Dude sauntered down toward the shack. The old man was sitting still as a stone, except that he was smoking an empty pipe. Close up, his eyes looked like there was a slow tear or two trying to run down and when Dude got the idea the old man had been crying, he turned on Trigger and gave him an awful wallop. Trigger gave Dude another and in a minute they were in a mix-up; but they couldn't seem to get very mad about it. The rest of the gang came out of their holes and began to sick them on, but the fight didn't amount to anything.

When everything got still, the old man spoke: "I've got a crate in here ready for Freddy. If you want to get him."

Dude and Trigger went in past the old man and brought out the crate. It was big and shaped like a peach crate, with the partition taken out and one end made to open on leather hinges. The old man knocked the ashes out of his pipe, only there weren't any ashes in it, and got up and went around to the back of the shack with everybody following. There was Freddy running back and forth and stopping, and back and forth again.

The old man told them what to do. They shoved Freddy up into his covered pen at one end of the run, and closed the door to the pen on the run side. There was Freddy all closed in. Then they lifted up the loose end of the crate, and put the

opening up against the pen where there was a door that slid
up and down in a groove. They raised this door so that Freddy
could go into the crate from the pen. Freddy wasn't for going
—not at first. They coaxed and threatened and everybody had
a different idea, but Freddy wouldn't go. The old man just
stood and smiled and smiled, but he never said a word. Then
Dude pried some slats off and got into the run and opened the
door on that side and looked in at Freddy. As soon as Freddy
saw Dude he ran into the crate and Trigger pulled the crate
away from the pen and shut the end of it before Freddy had
sense enough to run out. Now they were ready.

Everyone turned and looked at the old man. He started
off up the ravine and they all followed. He stuck to the path
and went along just as sure-footed as if he could see it, but
slowly on account of the gang coming behind with Freddy.
They took turns, two at a time carrying the crate, and when
they'd got up to the place where the path died out, everybody
had had a turn. They stopped there, because there wasn't any
way for the old man to go farther without somebody leading
him. They put Freddy down and waited.

Pretty soon the old man said, "I always thought we'd let
Freddy go on his birthday, and that's a Friday. Well, this is
a Sunday, but Sunday's the best day in the week for some
things. I guess Freddy'd agree that Sunday is a good day for
him." He stopped there and thought about what he wanted
to say: "It's as if Freddy here had been blind a long while,
because he's been shut up and couldn't get around and see
what's going on in the world. Now he's going to be given
back the use of his eyes. I guess he knows he owes it all to
this gang. He'd like to say so, but he doesn't know just what
to say, and anyhow he knows the gang would feel more comfortable if he didn't say it. So we'll just let him go, and the

way he goes, just as this gang wants him to go, is his way of saying, 'Thank you!' "

The gang shifted around a while and then Trigger and Dude together got the crate door open after fussing over it a good deal and stood back.

Freddy didn't move for a minute or two. At last he stuck his nose out and looked around, puzzled. Then he did a quick sneak for about twenty feet and stopped. He looked back over his shoulder on both sides and then trotted off pretty slowly for him. He came back once after he'd disappeared and took a last look and then went off for good.

They all turned and went down the ravine. When they got to the shack, the old man stood near the door and every one of the old gang came up and shook hands. Billy and Roy and Eddy Jr. didn't seem to feel as if they belonged, so they didn't come very close. The old man sat down on the steps, took out his pipe and began to have another dry smoke. The gang slipped away in embarrassed silence.

Next morning George Smith went over to the old Englishman's. He gave the old man his ticket and a wallet. He told him there were bills in the wallet and that every bill was a dollar, so nobody could cheat him when he used them. He gave him a lot of silver, too, and said he could tell what it was by the feel of it. Then he helped the old man lock up. Mr. England gave George Smith the key and told him the gang could use the shack for meetings and whenever they wanted to. At train time he and George Smith went off down to the station, and George Smith carried the valise.

The gang were hid up the bank above the station, and after the train pulled out and the old man with it, they all went up to Castle Garden and had a good fight with the gang up there and walloped them plenty.

XXIV. THE BALL GAME

As soon as the fight was over, they all settled down to business to decide when to play off the game for the mitt and mask.

"It's about time!" Nils Nielson sneered. He was captain of the Castle Garden team.

"We couldn't play before," Dude said.

"No," Nils answered, pretty sarcastic, "you had to practice up some!"

"That's a lie!"

Trigger stepped in to prevent a fight. "We've been busy raising money ever since school let out."

"You could have played before school let out if you hadn't been afraid to."

Trigger had to stop Dude from fighting again, before Trigger had a chance to say, "Don't be foolish!"

"You calling me a fool?" Nils snarled, shoving his face up into Trigger's.

"Aw, dry up and listen. What sense was there in giving Herbie Lord another chance to stop the game?"

Nils quieted down, but he was pretty sulky: "He's still around town, isn't he?"

"Yes, he is," Trigger admitted. "He's got a singing class for part of vacation."

"Girls!" Dude was disgusted.

Trigger went on: "Anyhow, he can't do anything now that school's let out." He stepped back and looked at Dude.

"Let's make it tomorrow," Dude said.

"All right," agreed Nils.

"What about Skinny and Socks and Jim?" Trigger asked.

"They have to quit work for the game," Dude answered.

Trigger suggested, "Why not Wednesday? That's a holiday for everyone, all afternoon. Then everybody could come to the game, and we'd let them come for nothing. That way, we could show our appreciation for what they all did to help about the old man's eyes."

Goosetown thought this was a good idea, and Castle Garden didn't care. So they set the game for Wednesday.

The Western Star met the gang on the way back to town. As soon as she found out about the game, she hustled up to the *Gazette* office and got Joe Jackson to say he'd print a local about it. She stood at the case beside him while he set up the stick of type, and told him what to say. It was an invitation for everybody in town to come to the championship game between Goosetown and Castle Garden.

The invitation stated that Miss Alice Brown would be present and would present the mitt and mask to the winning team.

"Have you asked her?" Trigger demanded.

"No, but I'm going to right now," Kate Kerby said.

And Miss Alice Brown said, "I'll be pleased and proud to do it."

The game was called for two o'clock. It was a good clear day and hot as blazes.

There was a big wicker armchair for Miss Alice Brown right back from the line between first base and home plate, just where she could see who struck out and who was safe after a hit. It was full of cushions and Miss Brown was delighted with them before she sat in them, but after a while they got pretty hot and she was helped to unload them one after another till she got down to the cane. The gang had got some chicken wire from somebody's henyard and nailed it on slats for a screen in front of the chair so she couldn't get hit by a liner.

George Smith came along as soon as the store closed with a big yellow and red umbrella which he said was a lawn-party umbrella there hadn't been any call for, so he borrowed it without saying anything to Mr. Woodruff, who wasn't expected at the game. He had a crowbar too. He made a hole with it and set the umbrella into the hole and opened it up so the sun would be kept from the chair.

Then Ed Martin appeared pushing a wheelbarrow with a big freezer of vanilla ice cream in it, three cardboard boxes of lady fingers, two boxes of candy bonbons, and a lot of chewing gum. He said it was for Miss Brown to distribute around to anybody she wanted to. She was pleased, but she said she thought it would be nicer if it was just set down handy where everyone could help himself. Ed set it up on a board, but it was too near the chair and nobody took anything. Gradually most all the town—men, women and children— arrived singly and in groups, laughing and good-natured in spite of the heat.

It was two-thirty when Dude and Nils Nielson went up the bat hand over hand, and at the end of it Dude was stuck with just the nob. He said he could get enough of a hold on the nob to throw it over his head, but he couldn't. He dropped it right away. That meant Castle Garden could say whether they wanted to bat first or field first and Nils said they'd bat first.

Dude got out in the box and threw the first ball before anybody discovered there wasn't any umpire. Then the two teams couldn't agree who would make a square umpire. Dude wouldn't trust anybody from Castle Garden and Nils wouldn't trust anybody from anywhere else. Then the crowd began to tell them to play ball and that made them sweat. Nils saw George Smith over talking to Miss Alice Brown and he said he guessed they could trust George Smith. He was square every other way and he guessed he couldn't help being square as an umpire in a ball field. George Smith didn't want to umpire, but the boys said he was the only umpire both sides could agree on so he said he would. Then the game got under way.

Dude's pitching started out wild as a hawk. He could pitch when you let him alone or when he was fighting mad, but hearing himself cheered by the great crowd of fellow sympathizers undermined his stability. He gave three men a base on balls right away and then he gave two more and forced in the men on second and third. That was two runs Dude had made for his opponents, and that made him furious.

He got the umpire to declare an accident while he went

to the benches and made Eddy Jr. rub his muscles over with Glover's mange cure. After that Dude went back into the box, and Eddy lay down behind the backstop because the smell of the mange cure made him sick.

Dude had his out-shoot pretty well under control and he got nearly every ball close enough to the plate for Mickey to stop it with the new mitt. Dude said he put two right over the plate, only the batters misjudged the ball and jumped forward on the plate and got hit. George Smith practically admitted those two balls were strikes if the batters had let them alone, but he said he couldn't hold a batter responsible for not having judgment and so he sent them to first and that forced in two more runs for Castle Garden.

Dude said if Castle Garden didn't know how to judge a curve and keep out of the way of it, he'd have to give them a few straight balls and see if they could dodge them.

Nils said they'd try to dodge them, but he'd rather Dude would throw them a couple near enough to reach with the bat, just to keep his team's courage up and give them something to hope for.

"This game is baseball," Dude told him.

"Yeah, I guess that's right," Nils shouted. "We got plenty of bases and balls, but what we want is a chance to bat."

"Play ball!" called George Smith from out back of the pitcher's box; and that reminded everybody about the game.

Goosetown got three outs on Castle Garden by about three-thirty p.m., but not till Castle Garden had cut thirteen notches in their side of the new pine board they were scoring with.

"Thirteen's unlucky!" Dude said to Nils.

And Nils said to Dude, "Yeah, but whose luck?"

Dude was right, because Goosetown got seventeen runs that first inning before Castle Garden could stop them.

Then it was after four-thirty. George Smith said it was a good thing there was a full moon, because they'd have to play the last three innings after sunset. So they settled it to have a six-inning game. But it was five-thirty at the end of the second inning, and they decided to make it a five-inning game. After the third inning, Goosetown had forty-six runs and Castle Garden twenty-nine and it was six-thirty. Then George Smith said he'd have to go home to supper pretty soon or he'd be in hot water and they all agreed to call it a day after only one more inning.

Nobody was much interested in that last inning. It was pretty certain that Goosetown was the superior team, and the Castle Garden part of the crowd dribbled away home. The Goosetown supporters began to entertain themselves to keep interested enough to stay. Some of them had a scrub game of their own over at one side, but they only had a hollow rubber ball and a broom stick to play with.

Kate Kerby got herself blindfolded and made up like a gypsy and told fortunes; but Billy Locke told her that she had the blindfold fixed so she could peek, and that spoiled that. She took off her get-up and made a face at Billy and said she hated him and he said he didn't care. So she went home.

Miss Alice Brown was tired, but she had to stay to present the mitt and mask to the winning team. Toward the last nobody said anything to anybody. They just sat or stood around. When Goosetown got the third out on Castle Garden, the cheer that followed wasn't very loud. The score stood 46 to 37, in favor of Goosetown.

Mickey took the mitt and mask right over to Miss Alice Brown. She smiled but she had hard work to do it. Then she stood up to make the presentation speech, but Mickey saw the ice cream freezer. He was thirsty so he dug into it and both teams followed suit. Miss Brown couldn't do a thing but smile and wait till the freezer was empty.

Just about then Kate Kerby came tearing back. She grabbed the mitt and mask right out of Miss Brown's hands and hid them under the pile of cushions.

"Why, Kate!" exclaimed Miss Alice Brown.

Kate tried to get breath enough to talk, but all she could manage was: "He's coming!"

"Who's coming?" asked Miss Brown.

Kate just pointed, and they looked around and there was Mr. Woodruff getting out of his buggy.

"He's found out all about it," Kate said.

"Gosh!" exclaimed George Smith, and he jerked the red and yellow umbrella out of the hole and hid it under the cushions with the mitt and mask.

Mr. Woodruff wasn't thinking about any umbrella. He just heeled-and-toed it right over to Miss Alice Brown and planted himself in front of her and puffed out his cheeks and looked like a thunder cloud.

"Why, Mr. Woodruff!" she said to him, as if she were surprised and pleased, and sweet enough to melt a stone. But old Woodruff wasn't melted.

"Where is it?" he demanded.

George Smith looked pretty guilty, but Miss Brown just looked more surprised.

"Where is what?" she asked, pulling a cushion over an end of the umbrella where it stuck out.

"Don't try to hoodwink me!" he shouted.

"Mr. Woodruff!" she said, and she looked as if she'd get cross herself in a minute.

He glared all around and then he looked around for something he didn't see. "You're concealing it!" he shouted.

"I have nothing to conceal, Mr. Woodruff!"

"Then where is the thing those boys have been gambling for?" he demanded.

That let the cat out of the bag for everybody. They knew he was talking about the mitt and mask, but it hadn't occurred to anybody that there was any gambling about it. When he said that they knew they were in for trouble as anything he could call gambling was like a red rag to a bull for him.

"Gambling!" he shouted.

Everyone shook in his boots, except George Smith and Miss Alice Brown. George Smith was so relieved that it wasn't the umbrella he didn't care about anything else. Miss Brown looked amused. She reached down among the pillows and pulled out the mitt and mask, being careful not to uncover the umbrella, and showed them to him.

"Those are the desecrated articles!" he bellowed.

That made Dude mad. "They're not desecrated!" he answered back. "They're good enough for the Phillies. They're first class and they cost ten dollars!"

Mr. Woodruff glared at Dude. "I have nothing to say to you, young man; you know not what you do. I am speaking to your elders who should know better."

"Mr. Woodruff," Miss Brown said in a voice that was awfully sweet, "will you kindly explain yourself?"

"If that is necessary, I will," he said. "I understand that these misguided children are competing for a—a—a stake! These articles are the stake. A stake means gambling. This town has an ordinance against gambling. I am the Burgess of this town. Do I make myself clear, madam?"

"Miss, if you please!" she said.

"Do I?" he shouted.

"Quite!" she said. "And I'm sorry to say, quite ridiculous."

Mr. Woodruff stared at her, surprised that she dared oppose him like that. Then he grabbed the mitt and mask. "I'll confiscate them!" he said.

He made a right about face like a wooden soldier, but he found Dude in his way.

"How'd you know all about this?" Dude demanded.

Mr. Woodruff pushed Dude aside at first, then he thought better of it and said: "I have my information from the best of authority, the principal of the high school."

"The black-hearted—" Dude began one of his long oaths.

"Silence!" bellowed Mr. Woodruff. Then he stalked to his buggy and got in and drove off.

"Well," George Smith said, "you can't blame a man much for being the way he is, and he's like that."

XXV. A PLAN FOR THE FUTURE

Dude was mad at Mr. Woodruff, but he was a great deal madder at Herbie Lord. "That mitt and mask belongs to us," he said to Mickey. "Here it is vacation and the mitt and mask's locked up in the safe and Herbie Lord's to blame!"

"We ought to do something about it," Mickey said.

"Are you telling me something?" Dude demanded.

"Let's ask Trigger what to do," Mickey suggested.

"I know what to do without asking Trigger or anybody," Dude fired at him. "You lend me your big squirtgun and I'll get a quart of red ink and put it in the gun and when Herbie leaves town I'll squirt it all over him. Then I'll trip him up and we'll have the gang hid around and they can come out and everybody jump on him and kick him in the ribs."

"Yeah!" Mickey was doubtful. "Only if he has a singing class he won't be leaving town."

"He'll leave afterward. I can wait."

"He's coming back again next term," Mickey said. "You wouldn't dare do much to him, because he'd take it out of us after school took in next fall."

Realizing this Dude wasn't so sure about his plan to squirt red ink all over Herbie and tramp on him, so he called a meeting up at the old man's shack. Dude always called a meeting when he wanted to find out what Trigger thought about anything. Dude told the gang about his plan and why it didn't look so good if Herbie was coming back. And Mickey told the gang what he'd already told Dude, which was just repeating what Dude had said.

Trigger agreed with Dude and Mickey: "You can't mess him up if he's going to have a chance to get even with us next term."

"But every one of this gang agrees we ought to do something to him, don't they?" Dude demanded.

They shouted their agreement.

"What?" asked Dude, as if he knew but wasn't telling.

"Let him alone till a chance offers," Trigger said.

"What kind of a chance?"

"A good chance."

"What's a good chance?"

"Well," Trigger thought it out as he talked, "what we want is to see Herbie messed up some, so he won't look pretty or feel pretty, either. We don't care who does it and we don't care how it's done. If some big fellow picked a fight with him, it might work out right."

"Aw, nobody likes Herbie enough to want to fight him."

"Maybe somebody hates him enough," Mickey said.

"Maybe," said Trigger. "Anyhow, he's got to hang around to give those singing lessons."

The schoolhouse had to be shut up for the summer, so the girls got the deacons to allow the singing lessons to be held in the social room of the church. The social room was half-way underground below the auditorium and the windows were right on the ground. You could lie on the grass outside and see everything that went on inside.

After the singing lessons started, quite a lot went on. Trigger said it was enough to satisfy their revenge to see the way the girls made a fool of Herbie. But Dude said that like as not Herbie thought he was making fools of the girls and it wasn't much satisfaction to see a fellow made a fool of if he didn't know it. Trigger agreed to this and so did the rest of the gang, so they just lay out there on the grass on singing nights, watching and waiting for something to happen that could be made use of. After a while something did happen, though it didn't look very important at the time.

There was a young fellow just come to town who painted stripes and curlicues and did all the fancy work on the bodies of the wagons that were built at the wagon factory. His name was Fred Pitcher. He was only about eighteen, but he was big and strong as an ox and he had quite a name for being a fighter. Some said he was training to be a prize fighter and that was why he never lost a chance for a scrap.

Fred Pitcher had a girl and the girl went to the singing class. Her name was Laura Remick. She didn't join the class till nearly the end, but when she did she made just as much of a fool of herself over the principal as all the rest of the girls did. Herbie treated all the others pretty evenly, and distributed his at-

tentions about the same all around; but when Laura came in,
his judgment slipped a little and he began to pay special attention to her. There wasn't very much difference, but some. The
boys didn't notice it at first, but they did notice that the other
girls cold-shouldered Laura a good deal and after a while they
figured the thing out and then they could see it clear as day.

When Trigger found out that Laura was Fred Pitcher's
girl, he said that ought to mean something to somebody. The
gang watched and waited and hoped, but nothing came of it.
Then on the very last night of the singing class, the thing they
had hoped for came to pass. Herbie took Laura home, and was
quite a long while saying good night to her at the front door.
It was too late for the gang to do anything about this now, as
Herbie was leaving the next day. They had to satisfy themselves with the consoling thought that Herbie was coming back
again in a few weeks.

Fred Pitcher found consolation in this thought, too, when
he and the whole town read the following item which mysteriously found its way into the *Beechwood Gazette* later:

"Work up at the singing school in the basement of the
Union Church has temporarily stopped while Mr. Lord is
on his vacation. But it has proved very popular and been
proceeding up to now, one might say, with considerable
results. The students have been learning to sing under the
helpful coaching of Mr. Lord (principal up at the high
school), and they all hope to learn to sing enough to get
private engagements or anyhow get into the church choir.
All the pupils go to high school except one young lady, and
it is probably because she doesn't go to school that she gets
more attention from Principal Lord than he has to give to
others. It is said she doesn't go to school because she is getting ready to be married to an eminent artist in this town."

XXVI. VACATION

With the old Englishman in Baltimore, Herbie gone, the big
game played and won, and the mitt and mask locked up in old
Woodruff's safe, the gang found themselves face to face with
vacation and time hanging heavy on their hands.

Then one day George Smith had something to tell Trigger.
He had a letter from the hospital in Baltimore. The operation
on the old Englishman's eyes had been performed and was successful. He was all right but the doctors wanted him to stay
there long enough to insure a perfect cure.

"I wish we could tell him how glad we are," Trigger said.

"Go ahead," George Smith advised, "send him a telegram."

The gang got together right away and wrote one. Then they rushed it down to the telegraph office and helped Jake Mittlekoop send it. After that they went into conference to decide how to get the money to pay for the telegram.

Pretty soon Trigger thought of Mrs. Smith's cookie basket. Mrs. Smith had just baked a big batch of her best sugar cookies to take to a church supper. They filled the cookie basket chock-a-block and it was a half-bushel basket. She always hung it on a piece of baling wire from the ceiling of the pantry so the mice couldn't get to it, and you couldn't take a cookie out of it without making it swing around. If she came into the pantry any time inside of an hour she could see it go and knew what was up. Trigger knew that everybody knew about Mrs. Smith's sugar cookies, and would give something to get a handful. He figured that a good cause was as good as a church supper and better, but he didn't like to hurt Mrs. Smith's feelings. He got George Smith into the wood shed. After Trigger had talked a lot, George Smith said, "Well, I don't know what you're talking about, but I'm planning to take a walk with Myrtle and make a call on the Lockes right after the supper dishes are done up."

Trigger told Dude and Billy Locke and Kate Kerby to get as many as they could out back of the wood shed and, as soon as George Smith and Mrs. Smith went out, to line them up at the south pantry window with their nickels ready. The pantry was just off the end of the kitchen wing and there was a window in each end of it. Everybody was to climb in the south window, hold his left hand behind his back and take as many cookies as he could with his right hand out of the swinging cookie basket, then climb out the north window. If he dropped a cookie he had to put all he had back in the basket. Most of them got only about four cookies, because the first two got more than they could hold and dropped one and had to pay another nickel for a second try, and the rest took that as a warning, especially those who only had one nickel. Kate Kerby collected the nickels at the south window. Trigger was in by the cookie basket to see that the rules were lived up to. It wasn't so easy to get a grip on those cookies with the basket sashaying around. They cleaned out the cookies in half an hour except for two apiece that Trigger had hid for Kate and Dude and Billy and himself. They made two dollars and forty cents.

Trigger had decided that Mrs. Smith would just have to think her cookies got stolen, but he didn't reckon on Eddy Jr. Eddy was saving his cookies to eat later, and Mickey took one away from him on their way home. Eddy was a crybaby and began to bawl. Just as he got his holler way up to the high point, George Smith and Mrs. Smith came along. Mickey told Eddy to run, and he ran himself, but Eddy just stood and howled. Mrs. Smith stooped down to sympathize with him. It was still light enough for her to see his cookie, and of course she knew her own cookies. She grabbed Eddy and wanted to know where he got it. Eddy stopped crying right away and went dumb. She couldn't get a word out of him. She marched him home, and as soon as she looked in at the cookie basket, she stood Eddy up in the corner of the kitchen and sat down in front of him and gave him the third degree.

After a while Eddy broke down and told her everything. When she found out that Trigger was to blame, she sent Eddy home and then George Smith had a bad time. Trigger heard everything because he had seen them coming and ducked, and when Mrs. Smith began to talk turkey to Eddy, Trigger had sneaked back and knelt down on the porch under the kitchen window and listened. He thought he'd better not show up right away so he went up to the shack and whittled shavings till nine o'clock. Then he came back and went up on the porch roof and in through his own window to bed.

Next morning Trigger found out that George Smith had taken the blame, so he and George Smith had an argument right at the breakfast table about who was to blame. Mrs. Smith said she was broken-hearted and hurt to the core to think she had menfolks like Trigger and George Smith. She said what they'd done was a wicked deception and they said it was, too. She said they had to give the two dollars and forty cents to the supper committee and anyhow she'd have to bake a new batch of cookies.

Trigger had to tell her about the telegram. George Smith helped him tell the story. After a while Mrs. Smith's sympathy was awakened and she said he could pay for the telegram out of the cookie money, though she didn't believe it was right to do it.

XXVII. BOUQUETS FOR HERBIE

Herbie Lord came back to Beechwood on the last train he could take to be in time for the fall term. Two delegations were on hand to meet him: the girls, most of them fluttering and flaunting themselves right out on the open platform; and the Goosetown gang hidden around behind stacks of boxes and barrels.

The summer service Pullman was still on and Herbie had treated himself to that, though it was only a two-hour ride up from Lock Haven. He got off the train behind the porter, who lugged out a lot of new satchels and bags. The porter was just swank and swagger to the gang. Besides the porter, Herbie sported a colored shirt, a red necktie, yellow spats, and a flowing soft felt hat. Herbie took off the hat and made a sweeping bow and smiled as soon as he saw the girls. There was too much noise for him to make a speech. After that the girls gave the school cheer pretty high and shrill, which ended with, "Beechwood, Beechwood, rah! rah! rah!" and on the tail end of this Mickey bellowed out a big "Goosetown!" before Trigger could stop him. Nobody on the platform paid any attention, beyond being startled for a moment, but there was a sudden yell from down behind the creekbank back of the station, where Castle Garden had taken up a secret position. They had planned to see and not be seen, but the "Goosetown" was too much for them and they came back with three tigers and a whole flock of "Castle Gardens!" Goosetown had come armed with a collection of reception missiles, but with Castle Garden down behind the bank they decided to let up on Herbie and hold fire for the other enemy.

"Besides," said Trigger to Dude, "we haven't any call to mess up all those pretty dresses. They can't help being foolish."

When the girls began to present bouquets and boxes of fudge to Herbie, both Trigger and Dude lost patience.

"Go get me a big bunch of goldenrod," Trigger told Mickey. Mickey went and got it, some fresh and some not. Trigger weeded out most of the fresh and threw it away and then waited. The girls had worked out quite a nice way to present the things and then relieve Herbie of them so as not to embarrass him by having to hang on to an armful. The first girl offered her bouquet and Herbie smiled sweetly and took it, not suspecting how many of them were coming. Anna Kerby had been appointed to stand beside him as flower girl, and just as soon as Herbie honored the present by taking it, Anna took it away from him and held it. After three or four times he got the idea and then she didn't have to reach, he just passed the things to her. When all the presents had been presented, there was a long time of just being embarrassed when nobody had anything to say and less to do. They fiddled and faddled. The train had pulled out and everything was quiet. So Trigger slid from behind his drygoods box and stepped forward with his bouquet of faded goldenrod and a mighty innocent expression.

"Some of us boys wanted to do something, too," he said, presenting the bunch. Herbie was so surprised he never looked at the goldenrod, he just took it because he wasn't up to not taking it and he didn't know what to say or what to do. Before he got around to anything, Anna Kerby snatched the bouquet out of his hands and threw it down and jumped on it. "You're a nasty mean thing, Trigger," she said, "and I'll go right and tell on you."

"You don't dare!" Trigger said.

"I don't dare! Why don't I dare?"

"Because you're not mean like me."

That spiked her guns and all she could do was reach out and slap him. Herbie just stood there in a daze with a half-sick smirk on his face.

They all got under way after that, and escorted their idol up to the Colemans', where he was to board that winter.

The gang got their ammunition together and began a stealthy approach toward the creekbank where Castle Garden lay concealed. But before they got well under way, they were brought up short by Fred Pitcher, who came around the end of the station on the hot-foot, pretty nearly out of breath. For obvious reasons of his own, he had intended to be on hand and meet the train, too; but somehow the time had slipped by him.

He stopped short, took a wide look around and gasped, "Where is he?"

Dude knew there was an opportunity here somewhere, but he didn't know just where it was, so he looked at Trigger. Trigger stepped up to Fred and said innocently, "Were you looking for somebody?"

Fred's jaw tightened up and he said to Trigger, "You said it. I'm looking for that blankety-blank principal up at the high school. I just been told he came in on that train."

"Oh," said Trigger, "you mean Herbie Lord. He did, but he's halfway to the Colemans' by now."

That was all that Fred wanted to know, but before he had taken two jumps after Herbie, Trigger stopped him.

"You'll get stung," he said.

"What's that?" Fred Pitcher stopped and stared.

"He's got a whole beehive with him," Trigger explained.

Fred Pitcher stared at Trigger and a broad grin spread slowly over his face. "Reception committee?" he asked.

"Girls!" said Dude.

Fred Pitcher scratched his head. "Was—" Fred began.

"No," said Trigger quickly, "she wasn't."

Fred relaxed, took out a cigarette and lighted it. Then he grinned again. "I guess you kids know everything," he said.

"Well," began Trigger modestly. Then all of a sudden he got his big idea.

"School opens tomorrow. Why don't you come around?"

"School? Me?" Fred exclaimed.

"A lot of things can happen in school," Trigger concluded.

Fred Pitcher looked Trigger and the gang over with much appreciation. A humorous expression spread slowly over his face. He took a long pull at his cigarette and blew the smoke into the air.

"I'll be there!" he said.

He gave everybody a pleased smile and sauntered off.

The gang were excruciated with joy. They shook their own hands and did somersaults right on the platform. Then they turned on Trigger and almost ate him up. Trigger got embarrassed with this show of appreciation and diverted it with the magic word, "Castle Garden!"

The gang whooped and made in a body for the creekbank, and expressed their happiness on the rival gang all the way up to the roundhouse.

XXVIII. REVENGE

When school opened next morning it was the beginning of a day long to be remembered in Beechwood.

The first surprise was the number of new pupils that appeared in addition to all the old ones. Nobody knew there were so many in the town. There weren't either, for many of them came from outlying places and ought to have been going to district schools.

Rumors about what might happen were going around. Everyone was pretty sure that they had something to do with Herbie. Most everybody thought he'd find a garter snake in his desk or gum on his chair or some silly thing like that. The girls had gone to school early and looked things over for tricks, to protect Herbie's dignity, but they hadn't been able to find anything.

The first thing on the program was the enrollment. Everybody's name was put down on a list alphabetically, so the teachers could call the roll every morning and find out who wasn't there and then later check up to see who was out because he had a right to be and who was hooking jack. The ones that were caught playing hooky got switched. Herbie did all the switching, no matter whose school they belonged to. The other teachers sent the delinquents in to him and he switched them. That is, Miss Sarah Biddle did. She was always having somebody switched for something. Miss Alice Brown never had anybody switched. She said it wasn't right to switch youngsters. She just talked to hers if they were bad and hugged them sometimes and made them feel ashamed; but she never had much trouble anyhow.

It looked that first morning as if Miss Sarah Biddle would want everybody in her room switched. She'd made out her roll call ahead of time so as to be forehanded. She thought she could do it because she knew who was coming in from the primary school and who was going out to the high school. But so many were there that she hadn't expected that her list was all wrong. She had to do it all over again and she was as sour as a dill pickle.

Miss Brown had a good many new ones too, but she never did a thing about her roll call that first day. Somebody said later that she knew something was up and that she decided to wait till things shrunk to normal. It was probably true, because she could tell that some of her new pupils were old enough to be in the grammar school or even in the high school.

Herbie didn't bother about his roll-call list. He just went into his private office and left the door open and had the girls make the list. Anna Kerby was one of them, and whatever Anna was in she bossed because bossing things ran in her family. When she saw a lot of older boys that had been out at work for two or three years, she began to ask them questions. But they all knew that all they had to say was that they were under twenty and had never graduated and were entitled to schooling. She couldn't get a thing out of them.

Finally, Herbie came out of his office. He had on a violet shirt and a green tie and walked as if he owned the earth and most of the planets with a few stray stars thrown in for good measure. You could hear the girls sigh as he passed along in front of them, like a lot of leaves fluttering. He spent some time putting things in his desk and getting ready to settle down generally. After a while he raised his head suddenly, and looked around quite surprised, as if he'd only that moment thought there might be somebody else present. Then he smiled, and stood up to make a speech.

Before he made it, he sent for Miss Sarah Biddle and Miss Alice Brown to come in and hear it. They came and sat down where he pointed, right in front of him at his feet. Miss Sarah Biddle took the speech hard, but Miss Brown had a twinkle about her somewhere. The speech was rather long, but it boiled down to about this: he was glad to be back, he was obliged for their cordial welcome and it looked to him as if the school were growing.

It didn't mean the same thing to Trigger and the gang and most of the other boys that it meant to the girls. The girls thought it meant, "Here is your humble servant back to serve, and he's glad there are more of you to serve than last year."

Trigger said he looked like a tame pheasant showing off in a daisy field and that the speech meant he was glad to be back where he was admired so much last year and he was tickled to death to see his popular appeal had rounded up a lot more of them to admire him this year.

The girls made a lot of noise applauding because they wanted to show Herbie how much they liked him and the speech and the way he made it. The boys made a lot more noise applauding because it was a good chance.

After the speech everybody stood up to sing. Miss Sarah Biddle and Miss Brown went across the hall to lead the singing in their rooms. All three schools sang *America* more or less together. When the singing was over, Herbie had one of the girls shut the door between the high school and the hall and after that each school was on its own.

Herbie told Anna Kerby to call the roll and everybody had to say "Present."

During the roll call, Herbie had been looking at Dude, and after Anna sat down, he took a sheet of paper, stepped up to Dude, made him stand up, and said severely, "Spit it out." Dude did and it was gum. Herbie was surprised, because he had switched Dude quite often for chewing tobacco, but he was fooled this time. He couldn't very well switch him for gum, but he made him go and stand in a corner. Then he said, "Face the blackboard, Master Quinlan!" It made Dude furious to be called "Master" and Herbie knew it, but Dude didn't dare do anything except turn around with a jerk.

Fred Pitcher, who had been waiting for any kind of a chance, boiled over and sang out without getting up or even putting up his hand, "That ain't fair!"

Herbie considered Fred in a way he said was "more in sorrow than in anger," then he turned to Anna, "Who is the young man, Miss Kerby?"

Anna stood up and said very demurely, "His name is Fred Pitcher."

Herbie turned back to Fred. "Fred Pitcher? When you desire to speak, Master Pitcher, it is first necessary either to rise or to raise your hand." He was speaking smoothly, but now he struck his desk with the ruler that was in his hand and said sharply, "Stand up!"

Fred Pitcher grinned and got up slowly. Dude swung around so he wouldn't miss anything, but Herbie saw him, "Master Quinlan, face the blackboard." So Dude had to swing back again.

Herbie turned his attention to Fred Pitcher and spoke to him in a puzzled sort of way and all the time as if taking the girls into his confidence, "You say I have been unfair. If you have no objection, may I ask why?" He shot out the "Why."

"It ain't fair to treat a kid like that," Fred said.

"You are insolent, Master Pitcher!"

"Mebbe. I don't know what it is."

"And impertinent!"

"Oh, come now!"

"Step forward, please!"

"Sure!" said Fred, slouching up to the desk.

"I failed to anticipate trouble on the first day of school and I have provided no switches. I regret using a ruler, but it's all I have. Hold out your hand."

"What's the idea?" Fred said, putting his hands behind him.

"The idea is that you have been insolent and insubordinate. I intend to punish you."

"You mean you are planning to lick me?" Fred Pitcher tried his best not to look pleased.

"You may call it that."

"Then give me a ruler, too."

"What?"

"You ain't meaning to lick me without giving me an equal chance, are you?"

"I intend to punish you."

"And I just stand here and take it?"

"Hold out your hand!"

"Not on your tintype!"

Then things happened. Herbie began it. He tried to glare Fred down, but all he got out of him was a grin. That maddened Herbie and he leaned across the desk and gave Fred a rap on the cheek with the ruler. He got in only one blow. Fred went over the desk with a whoop, caught Herbie by the throat and backed him up against the wall. The girls shrieked and then grabbed each other and kept still, looking to see what would happen. Nothing happened. Herbie just stood there propped up against the blackboard, his hands clutching the chalk gutter that ran along underneath it. His eyes bulged out and his mouth fell open. He was frightened stiff in a minute.

When the girls saw their hero look like that, they sneaked out in huddles without stopping to get their hats or anything. The boys gathered around in a sort of half ring.

Fred dropped his hold on Herbie and looked him over. "Don't you know how to fight?" he asked, bewildered.

"N-no!" gasped Herbie.

"Then I'll teach you!" Fred said. He slapped one side of Herbie's face with one hand and then the other side with the other hand. Herbie got scared as a rabbit, and turned tail and tried to run into a corner. The boys formed a tight ring and prevented him. He just squawked and fell on the floor. Fred took him by the scruff of the neck, hauled him to his feet and shoved him into his chair like a bundle of empty mealsacks.

Fred stood looking at him. "Gee!" he said, "to think a thing like that could tickle my girl any!" Herbie looked up at that as if he was beginning to see light.

Dude weaved up and shook a fist under his nose: "And you would tattle to old Woodruff, would you?"

Trigger just stood around and looked as if things had gone off pretty well anyhow.

All at once everybody was embarrassed. They all got their caps and left, but they had to fight their way through the crowd from the other schools that were jammed in the doorway.

Herbie called a meeting of the School Committee that night, but they told him they had to have a principal that knew how to keep discipline, so he left town on the first train next morning.

There wasn't any delegation to see him off.

XXIX. MR. WOODRUFF TAKES
A HAND

But that wasn't the end of it for Trigger and the rest of the
gang. Mr. Woodruff went on the rampage again, and ordered
the School Committee to come to his office in the General
Store to discuss holding an investigation. He had George Smith
with him to act as secretary and to furnish ideas.

"It's a disgrace to the town," Mr. Woodruff said.

"Any town ought to feel disgraced that has a principal that
gets to look the way Herbie Lord did this morning," said
George Smith.

"How did he look?" one of the School Committee wanted to know.

"Bad!" George Smith said. "Like a dog coming home after trying to be friends with the mother of kittens." Everybody laughed.

Mr. Woodruff banged his desk: "I called this School Com- mittee here to tell you that you must do something about last night's disgraceful affair."

Nobody could suggest anything. After a while George Smith asked if they didn't know what to do, wasn't it better to reach a decision and decide not to do anything. That made the Burgess madder than ever. He said the town was disgraced and had to do something about it. George Smith said he ex- pected the town would feel the disgrace if Mr. Woodruff said they had to, but he was sure they'd be willing to forget it if he'd let them. Mr. Woodruff said he wouldn't. His duty forced him to demand action. He glared around: "Something must be done!" he repeated, banging the desk harder than ever.

"But what?" asked George Smith.

It was long past bedtime and in spite of much talk, George Smith's question was still unanswered when the meeting ended.

A day or two passed and still the Burgess had been unable to get suggestions from anybody. The conviction was forced upon him that if there was to be any investigation he would have to hold it himself.

For a long while he couldn't figure out what to do, be- cause finding out about things without telling anybody what he wanted, was a new line for him. He had a suspicion that the gang knew more than they were telling.

Dude was amazed and nonplused when Mr. Woodruff

stopped him on the street in front of the ice cream parlor, shook hands with him, and said, "It's hot. Let's go into Mr. Martin's and have a dish of ice cream." Old Woodruff took out his big bandanna and wiped his perspiring brow.

Dude had just got a new chew off Pat Mullen and didn't want to lose it, but he was so flabbergasted he spit out the quid, and followed Mr. Woodruff into the ice cream parlor, and began on a dish of chocolate ice cream.

"I hear you had a fight up at the high school," Mr. Woodruff said, as soon as Dude had a mouthful.

"Just a massacre," Dude said. "Takes two to make a fight."

"What did Fred Pitcher have against the principal?"

"Ask me another," Dude answered.

"I have made up my mind to consult you boys about the facts of the matter," continued the Burgess.

Dude grinned. "I'm not one of the boys, Mr. Woodruff."

Mr. Woodruff considered and twisted a little in his chair. "I want certain information," he said finally. "It is contrary to my principles, but the circumstances are unusual and I am prepared to pay for it." He took a long billfold from his pocket and extracted one crisp dollar bill. He held it toward Dude.

Dude swallowed twice and shook his head. "It's too much for nothing, Mr. Woodruff." He shoved back his chair and got up to go.

"Just a minute, young man," said old Woodruff, holding up a fat hand. "I have, locked in my safe, certain articles which would, I believe, be of value to you. Am I right?"

The precious mask and mitt floated before Dude's eyes in a red haze. He couldn't trust himself to speak, but he nodded.

Old Woodruff wiped his brow again. "I want you to understand," he said, "that I am acting for the School Committee.

This is not a personal matter, it is a public duty. Those articles
were confiscated as a punishment for misdemeanor. I am sure
that the School Committee would be disposed to authorize
me to return the articles if you and your friends will give me
any information you may have about that fight."

Dude's jaw dropped. "Gee whittikers!" he said at last.
"Bribery!"

"Sir!" Old man Woodruff rose to his feet in righteous wrath.

Dude left him flat and began right away to round up the
gang, like a dog collecting a pack for a pig chase. He went
up to Goosetown and got Mickey and Bud and Dutch, then
all four headed back downtown after Billy Locke and Roy,
and Eddy Jr. Kate Kerby was swinging on the gate as they
all passed her house. Dude didn't look at her but he said out
loud to himself as he went by her, "Confab and powwow,
pretty important." And she said to nobody in particular, "All
right, I'll get Trigger and the key," slammed the gate and
started off for the Smiths'. She and Trigger got to the shack
about as soon as Dude and the others. Trigger unlocked the
door and they all went in.

"What's up?" Kate Kerby wanted to know.

"Plenty!" Dude fired at her. "Old Woodruff has turned
detective and he's going around asking questions."

"Oh, pshaw!" Kate said, "what can he do?"

"I don't know, but most everyone knows Fred Pitcher was
jealous of Herbie and hated him on account of it, and that
somebody put Fred up to going to school."

"He doesn't know who," Mickey said, looking at Trigger.

"I didn't do it, not exactly," Trigger said.

"No," Mickey grinned, "but we got to give you credit,
you got the idea."

"I don't know about that!" Dude objected. "The idea sort

of grew up out of the gang, and anyhow everybody has to stand by everybody else."

Trigger began to feel uneasy. He knew George Smith was all right, but he was thinking about Mrs. Smith. "Nobody's done anything to go to jail for," he said.

"Heck!" exclaimed Dude. "Jail's nothing, jail's just a soft snap. What I'm thinking about is the disgrace it would be to have something put over on this here gang. I don't care if everybody knows we run Herbie out of town, but I want us to tell it our own selves when we get around to it, and not have it choked out of us by any old investigating committee the way you make a dog give up a bone."

Everybody agreed to this.

"We can take an oath to keep our mouths shut," Mickey suggested.

"That's what!" Dude said. "We can do it first right here, and we can do it again after dark up at the Lodge on the skull and shinbone."

"Oh!" Kate Kerby squealed and shivered, "I'd love that!"

Dude looked at her doubtful, "A woman ought to be honorable and keep an oath the first time she swears it."

"Then I won't swear this time," Kate declared.

"Oh, let her do it both times," Mickey said.

"Mind you, then!" Dude frowned, "you can only do it twice this once. This gang isn't going to have its auxiliaries swearing all over the place all the time."

"All right," Kate agreed.

"Then all of you raise your right hands and swear not to tell old Woodruff anything about anything. And cross your heart with the other hand while you do it." They all swore and crossed their hearts.

"That's done," Dude said with a sigh of relief. "Now it's

in order to move to adjourn till eight o'clock, when it's dark
up at the Lodge and then everybody swears again on Pumpernickel."

"Pumpernickel?" exclaimed Kate.

Dude looked at her in disgust. "That's the skull and shinbone," he told her.

"Oh," said Kate, pleased and proud to be let in on it.

They adjourned and scattered, so nobody would see them
together.

Trigger went home pretty thoughtful, and when he had
a chance to get George Smith into the woodshed, he told him
all about everything and George Smith shook his head, and
looked very sober, too.

XXX. THE CULPRIT

The Burgess sleuthed around for a week, with the School Committee afraid he'd find out something and he himself afraid he wouldn't. Then he told the committee he'd learned all he wanted to know, but he wouldn't tell them what it was. He said, "Public interest has been aroused and must be satisfied. We will hold a public investigation."

Mr. Woodruff was nearer right than he thought when he said public interest had been aroused. He had more help than he'd bargained for in building up an audience. Joe Jackson printed a piece about the coming investigation in the *Gazette*. Then he tipped off his newspaper friends in near-by towns that a good time was going to be had by all, and he even sent word to some editors in Williamsport and Harrisburg that they'd better send some men up to cover the occasion.

The investigation was held in the high school at eight o'clock at night and the lamps had to be lighted. It was a full house. The outsiders were there for the fun of the thing, the home folks because they wanted to be, and the witnesses were there because the Burgess made them come—all but the gang which was conspicuous by its absence. Mr. Woodruff was right back of the Principal's desk and the School Committee right back of him on the platform. They looked pretty sheepish. The Burgess made Daddy Coleman, the constable, come and stand right beside him so that order would be maintained.

The Burgess rose: "Ladies and gentlemen, I have been called upon by the School Committee of this town to conduct an investigation into the causes of a recent unfortunate affair."

He stopped there and shuffled his papers, pretending he had stopped talking because he had to arrange things. Then he took a long breath and began again:

"There were two participants in this affair. One, the principal of the high school, I have been unable to locate." He got a laugh there, but it quieted down. "The other is, I believe, present." He looked over at Fred Pitcher and said, "Will Mr. Fred Pitcher please come forward?"

Fred got up and down front somehow, and stood looking at Mr. Woodruff as if he wished the Burgess was Herbie and nobody was around.

The Burgess made Fred admit he had a fight with Herbie, which everybody knew anyhow; and then he proved that Fred hadn't come to school for anything but just to have that fight. He couldn't make Fred tell why, so he let him sit down again. Then he held up a clipping and waved it around. He said it was a clipping from the *Beechwood Gazette*. It was the same one that had appeared some time before.

Mr. Woodruff put on his glasses and read, giving particular emphasis to the last part:

"All the pupils go to high school except one young lady, and it is probably because she doesn't that she gets more attention from Principal Lord than he had to give to the others. It is said she doesn't go to school because she is getting ready to be married to an eminent artist of this town."

The Burgess went on: "The editor and proprietor of the *Beechwood Gazette* is Mr. Joseph Jackson." He looked down and then up and then called out, "Mr. Jackson!"

Joe Jackson got up with a broad grin on his face. He wasn't letting the boys from Williamsport and Harrisburg think he was the kind of newspaperman that takes anything to heart much, so he said, "Well, Mr. Burgess? Shoot!"

Mr. Woodruff made Joe admit that the item appeared in the *Gazette* without his knowledge or consent and that it was put in by the printer's devil who sometimes did that sort of thing to please his friends.

This got a laugh from almost everybody and the newspaper fellows set up a little singsong: "Hear! Hear!"

The Burgess asked: "What first brought this item of news to your attention, Mr. Jackson?"

Joe took a look around at Fred Pitcher and grinned at the way Fred was scowling. "Fred Pitcher came in to see me about it. He thought he was the artist referred to."

"Why should he be offended to be called an artist?"

"Well," said Joe, "you'll have to figure that out for yourself." He sat down. Harrisburg and Williamsport gave him a hand, and Joe got up again and gave them a bow.

The Burgess announced that obviously Mr. Pitcher's jealousy in connection with Mr. Lord's singing class was the cause of the fight.

After that he called for Matt Dugan, the printer's devil. Matt stuck to his seat and Daddy Coleman was sent to get him to his feet. Finally he admitted that he'd slipped the item in to please the Goosetown gang. Daddy let go and Matt slouched down in his seat.

Then Mr. Woodruff made a statement on his own account. He said the Goosetown gang had a grudge against Mr. Lord for causing them to lose the mitt and mask. He explained all about it. A lot of remarks ran around the room and they weren't just whispers. The Burgess gathered the idea that the crowd sided with the gang. That made him angry. He marched up to Daddy and gave him an order. What they said couldn't be heard on account of the buzz and chatter, but it was clear enough they were not agreeing about something. Pretty soon Daddy gave in. He hitched his suspenders up till his trousers were six inches off the ground, sort of buttoned up his mouth, ambled over to the door and went out.

The crowd, getting the idea that something was up, stopped talking and listened.

Suddenly, outside the schoolroom windows, somebody said, "Go!" in a loud voice. In about two seconds everybody knew there was a free-for-all and rough-and-tumble going on and they wanted to see it. They got up and craned their necks at the windows, but they couldn't see anything because it was dark as a pocket. The noise didn't last long. The crowd just listened expectantly. Pretty soon a loud trampling and scuffling was heard out in the hall. The Burgess stepped over, stuck his head out the door and said, "Come in!"

It looked as if nobody was anxious to come in. The Burgess

went out and came back leading Daddy Coleman who looked as though he was ashamed to be alive and didn't care whether school kept or not.

Mr. Woodruff looked around at the door expecting some more to come in, but nobody did so he went back to the door and made a big gesture. The whole gang, except the Western Star, was shoved into the school room and lined up against the blackboard.

The Burgess introduced them: "Ladies and gentlemen! Allow me—the Goosetown Gang!"

It brought the house down. The crowd roared and clapped and stamped. The gang looked befuddled and didn't know whether they were getting a razz or a welcome.

Mr. Woodruff teetered down the line and looked them over one after another. Suddenly he missed Kate Kerby and stopped short. "Where's the girl?" he asked.

It was a group of strangers that had brought the gang in —two boys to a man. One fellow had only one boy and that

was Trigger. The fellow was holding onto Trigger with one
hand, and the other hand was busy with a bloody nose. The
Burgess turned to him: "Where's the girl?" he said sharply.

The man looked at Trigger, and Trigger looked at the man.
"She got away," he said.

"Idiot!" bellowed the Burgess.

"She'd have got away from you, too, if somebody'd cracked
you on the nose." The man gave Trigger a dirty look and
went back to mopping his nose.

The crowd laughed.

"We got everybody else. Isn't there enough of them?"

Gradually the crowd saw what the Burgess had been up to,
and it was clear what they thought of it. Mr. Woodruff explained: "I regret as much as you do, ladies and gentlemen,
that I have had to take certain coercive measures, but duty
is duty. Wrongdoing must be detected and justice admin-
istered. It was necessary that the Goosetown gang should be
present at this investigation. I invited them to be present. They

declined. It became necessary to use force and—strategy."
He was pleased with the "strategy" part of it. He looked the
gang over and said it again—"Strategy!"

"Pursuant to my duty, ladies and gentlemen, I caused to
be present here tonight a group of men whom you may regard as properly constituted deputies. These men, under my
direction, and I regret to say, without the very active co-
operation of the local constable, secreted themselves in the
environs of the schoolhouse. At the proper signal they acted.
The result is before you, because, ladies and gentlemen, I was
availing myself of the well-known maxim, to wit: 'The criminal
always returns to the scene of the crime!' The criminal, ladies
and gentlemen, is, collectively speaking, the Goosetown
Gang!"

This sounded pretty good to some of the crowd, not so good
to others, but when Dude looked over at the Burgess and said,
"It's a dirty trick!" the roof came right off.

The Burgess waited for quiet, then he said sourly: "That,
ladies and gentlemen, is Dude Quinlan. Why 'Dude,' I don't
know, unless it refers to his clothes!"

They laughed at that and there was no getting around it,
Dude did look pretty funny. He didn't have on any more than
usual and that was ragged enough, and what there was had
got quite a bit raggeder in the scuffle outside the schoolhouse.

Mr. Woodruff continued. "I see, ladies and gentlemen, that
you are dissatisfied. You perceive, as I did, that a gang acting
as a whole could not conceive and execute this ingenious plan
of revenge. No, not the gang as a whole, but some single
individual is responsible." He turned to Dude: "Dude Quinlan,
step forward!"

Dude didn't step, he stuck. One policeman couldn't move
him. It took two. They shoved him forward a little and held

him and everybody had a good look at him. Dude just stood there and faced them and chewed. After a while he looked at Mr. Woodruff and chewed faster, and anyone could see how he felt about the Burgess.

The Burgess addressed the School Committee: "Gentlemen of the Committee! You have before you the culprit. What are you going to do about it?"

The School Committee didn't want to do anything and that was clear enough.

"Can you," said the Burgess, "allow this boy to go unpunished? He is the type that becomes a confirmed criminal. He possesses the instinct for trouble and the ingenuity to make trouble. Severe handling at this time may change the direction of his nature from bad to good. I call upon you, gentlemen of the Committee, to instruct me to hail this delinquent before the court and have him remanded for his own benefit and yours to the reform school."

The crowd was rather stunned by this idea. It didn't look like the right end to a pretty good show, but they didn't know what to do about it. The School Committee fiddled and faddled. Dude stopped chewing right away and looked glum. He knew something about the reform school. Trigger took a look at Dude, broke away from the man with the bloody nose, and went up to the Burgess.

"Dude didn't do it," he said, "I did it."

The Burgess was astonished and the crowd held its breath. "Did what?" he said, just as if he didn't remember what it was all about. "What did you do?"

"I got the idea and wrote the piece in the paper and got Dude to get it printed. If you don't believe it, ask the gang. They won't tell, but they can't deny it. I'm not going to see Dude go to jail for what's my fault."

It didn't take any wit at all to see that Trigger was telling the truth—and the crowd went wild! Trigger was a hero right off, with everybody but old Woodruff.

The Burgess jumped up and down and shouted and the crowd quieted down. He said, "This is getting out of order. Here is a boy who is a self-confessed criminal. He is a member of the high school and as such I command the School Committee to exert their authority."

The Burgess was furious. The School Committee just sat there. When the Burgess told them Trigger had to be expelled from school, they let it go at that and expelled him on the spot.

George Smith got Trigger and they went home together and all anybody said on the way was what George Smith said when he said, "Well, folks is funny!"

XXXI. IN THE DOLDRUMS

Next morning George Smith and Trigger both got up an hour ahead of time just as if they'd planned it, but they hadn't. They ducked in the hogshead, but the snorting and blowing was pretty weak. After that they went to the wood shed and George Smith sat on the chopping block and took a piece of white pine and began to whittle. Trigger sat on the floor and whittled, too.

"Well, I don't know," George Smith said after about a quarter of an hour.

"I expect Mrs. Smith will find out all about everything," Trigger said.

"I guess a lot of the neighbors will come around and offer sympathy," George Smith agreed.

"What'd I better do?"

After a long while George Smith said, "Well, I tell you what, Trigger. If Myrtle just gets mad, all you have to do is hang around where she can relieve her mind whenever she feels like it and then things will work out all right. But what I'm worrying about is that she'll take it to heart and get a sense of duty or something. If that happens, I'd keep out of sight mostly, if I were in your boots."

Then they went on whittling. When they heard Mrs. Smith getting breakfast, they got up and threw away the pine sticks, and George Smith said, "Trigger, you know I feel all right about everything."

Trigger said, " 'Course I do, George Smith."

Kate Kerby came in while they were eating breakfast. "Hello, everybody!" she said. Then she looked at Trigger. "Hello, Trigger! How's your knuckles?"

"What's wrong with his knuckles?" Mrs. Smith said, quick as a flash.

"He smacked a fellow's nose with 'em," Kate said. She went up to Trigger and stood looking at them. All of a sudden she began to cry and that made her mad! She brushed the tears out of her eyes and said, "Cat!" at Mrs. Smith and ran out of the house.

"Hussy!" Mrs. Smith said. She got suspicious. "What happened last night?" she demanded. "I ought to have gone to that investigation myself. I don't suppose I'll ever know what happened, now!"

"I guess you'll hear everything sooner or later," George Smith said. He left after that and Trigger and Tip went, too.

Mrs. Locke met them at the gate. She looked at Trigger and never said a word but went on into the house.

"Well," George Smith said, looking after her, "there goes the first bell now. We'd better hurry or we'll be late for church." He went along to the store. Trigger left him at the corner and went up to the old Englishman's. Tip stopped a while to decide, but at last picked up his feet and followed Trigger.

Mrs. Smith was surprised to have a caller at that time, but she offered Mrs. Locke a rocking chair in the living room. Mrs. Locke wouldn't sit in it. She went right on into the parlor and took a straight-back chair with a seat covered with black horsehair, so Mrs. Smith knew something was up and sat down and folded her hands and waited.

"Well, I hope you're satisfied now, Myrtle Smith!" Mrs. Locke said and Mrs. Smith just sat and dropped her mouth open. "Everybody said you'd be making a mistake, adopting that boy. If the Good Lord didn't see fit to give you another child, it's nothing but wickedness to go against His wishes. Well, it's your business and you're paying for it and folks said you would, and I leave it to your own conscience. But I will say this: I don't want my William to associate any more with that boy, because evil companions corrupt good manners and William's manners are getting worse. I'm forbidding that boy to come into my house or into my yard in future and William is not to come here again, not as long as that boy remains here, and I'll thank you for doing your part to see that my rules are carried out and you can do no less with any self-respect or any consideration for the feelings of others. For goodness' sake, what's the matter with you? Don't you know what I'm talking about? Haven't you heard anything at all about what happened in the high school last night?"

Mrs. Smith was just about able to say, "I guess I heard Robert had hit somebody's nose but—!" Only Mrs. Smith wasn't able to see why a crack on the nose should cause all this disturbance unless— "It wasn't William's nose, was it?"

"What are you talking about? I suppose you knew there was an investigation held last night at the schoolhouse?" Mrs. Smith had heard that. "Well, the School Committee took action as a result." She held back to give the rest a running start. "They expelled your boy, Robert—if that's what you call him. Everybody else calls him Trigger and I must say it fits better."

"Expelled!" gasped Mrs. Smith.

"Yes, expelled!" Mrs. Locke drove it home. "The Ladies' Sewing Circle are meeting at two o'clock to make a resolution of sympathy for you in your time of trouble!"

Mrs. Locke told Mrs. Smith everything about the investigation and didn't need to be coaxed much to do it. When she got up to leave Mrs. Smith just sat still and all she noticed was that Mrs. Locke had on her black kid gloves.

If the women felt like that, the men around town felt differently. George Smith began to find this out as soon as he got to the store. Sam McCool was on the steps when George Smith unlocked the door.

"That's a great kid you've got," Sam said. "A lot of fellows have talked to me and they all say he's a great kid the way he acted."

Then Mr. Woodruff came, heel and toe, kplack-a-kplack, like a fat wooden soldier, with his head back. He didn't take any notice of Sam, but he gave George Smith a look to come on in. George Smith gave Sam a wink and followed. Sam went on up the street to open the barber shop.

Mr. Woodruff unlocked the safe, took out the ledger, opened it, and put it on his desk. He sat down in front of it and then he was ready for business. He called George Smith up on the platform and said:

"I hear some men around town are getting up a petition to have the School Committee rescind their vote and allow that boy you adopted to go back to school. I don't want you to think anything is going to come of it. That petition is not worth the paper it's written on without my name on it, because everyone on that committee is dependent on me. My name will not be on it. It hurts me more than it does you to have to be firm in this matter, but I couldn't absolve myself if I failed to do my duty. I hope you understand."

George Smith said he guessed he understood pretty well and went back to begin sweeping up. He had swept up the night before, but he forgot and did it all over again till Mr. Woodruff began to sneeze and told him to stop. That's the way he was all day, doing things twice over or not doing them at all. At noon he carried some crackers and cheese and chipped beef up to Trigger. He knew Trigger wouldn't want to go home alone to lunch.

Trigger spent the day whittling shavings and Tip spent it with him. Part of the time Tip went out back and smelled around Freddy Fox's empty run and a couple of times he went over and gave a little attention to Billyus Porcupine's dead tree, but Billyus didn't come around. Most of the time Tip just lay and looked at Trigger.

After school Dude and Mickey scouted the Smith house, but couldn't see anything of Trigger. They went downtown to see George Smith. They tossed up a nickel to decide who'd go into the General Store, because neither of them cared much about meeting "Old Woodruff." It was Bud's nickel they tossed. Bud had given it to Mickey to get some all-day suckers as a present from the old gang for Trigger. Dude lost and had to go into the store. While he was gone Mickey went to Ed Martin's to get the candy.

When Dude and Mickey got up to the shack they found Trigger and Tip, looking pretty lonely.

"Hello, Trigger!"

"Hello, Dude!"

" 'Lo, Trig!"

" 'Lo, Mike!"

Mickey gave Trigger the candy. Trigger shared it and gave some to Mickey for Bud and Dutch.

After that they just hung around, everybody busy doing nothing. They whittled so much they filled the barrel that the old man kept for shavings handy to the stove. When they had cut up every pine stick in sight and shut up their jack-knives and got up to go, Trigger said:

"How's the new principal?"

"He's all right," Dude said without much enthusiasm.

"He's the kind it's no fun to bother," Mickey said. "Sort of goes round smiling and doesn't see anything."

"Just walks around in his sleep," Dude said. "Bet you he's thinking all the time about Miss Alice Brown."

"That's all right, isn't it," Mickey demanded, as if he were ready to fight about it.

"Who said it wasn't, you bullet-headed mummy," answered Dude, as if he were ready to fight, too.

They threatened up to each other but there wasn't any kick to it, and the fight blew up, so they just went along home.

Mickey spent the evening listening without hearing anything while his grandmother told fairy tales. Dude couldn't think of anything he wanted to do, so he got his lessons for the next day.

George Smith came up to the shack on his way home to supper. Trigger had spent a bad day trying to keep away from himself and he was tired. He thought George Smith looked like the big buffalo robe his Pop used to have, and you could roll up in it and go to sleep and forget to keep count.

"Come on home to supper," George Smith said, just as if nothing had happened.

Trigger wasn't anxious to see Mrs. Smith and he just kept working at a loose knot in the floor, trying to get it out with the toe of his shoe.

"I tell you, Trigger, we'll go over and you can wait outside while I go in and see how things are."

Trigger kept on with the knot. He wanted George Smith to stay with him, but he knew he couldn't.

Tip was hungry and stood around with first one leg up and then another, all ready to start. He couldn't understand the delay, so he barked and that gave George Smith another idea.

"I tell you what, you can leave Tip here for a nest egg, and then it'll be an excuse to come back after him if you don't want to stay."

"All right," Trigger said. He gave Tip the rest of the chipped beef, but Tip was looking for a hot supper and wouldn't eat it. "Then don't!" Trigger told him. He and George Smith went out and shut the door, leaving Tip inside mad as hops and telling the world.

When they got to the house, George Smith went in alone. Mrs. Smith said right away, "That boy hasn't been here all day, but about every other boy in town has."

"Well, he didn't want to hang around underfoot," George Smith told her. "He's outside now."

"I won't scold him before he's had his supper, if that's what you mean," she said.

"Oh, well!" George Smith said, "after supper he can go out again."

"No!" Mrs. Smith said pretty firmly.

"Yes!" George Smith said just as firm, and that surprised Mrs. Smith so much she almost forgot Trigger. They stood there like a couple of roosters for a moment, and then Mrs. Smith sighed and said:

"Well, let him go. Then we can talk among ourselves. I feel kind of responsible, anyhow; and you would if you had any decency and sense of sin about you."

George Smith brought Trigger in, but nobody ate much. After supper, Trigger went back to Tip and took him some food.

When the dishes were done and put away and everything cleaned up, Mrs. Smith sat down in the rocking chair and began to rock, but George Smith didn't wait for her to look up.

"Now, then, Myrtle!" he said, as if he expected her to speak up, and she did.

"Don't you speak to me in that tone of voice!"

"Well, I've got a cold coming on."

"And don't try to be funny!"

"I don't try, it comes natural."

"Do you mean to stand there, George Smith, and tell me you approve of evil doings!"

"I think you ought to see there's some difference between evil doings and prankishness."

"Prankishness! I suppose it's prankishness to inveigle money out of people and instigate prize fights and be the head and front of everything bad and underhanded that's been going on."

"You've been hearing quite a lot all of a sudden!"

"Yes, I have! And been blamed for it, too!"

"Blamed? Who's blaming you for anything?"

"The Ladies' Aid and Women's Sewing Circle have both sent me a resolution of sympathy. They're in the mail."

"And I expect the Old Maids' Social Service Club for Gab and Gossip will be sending one, too."

"I'm ashamed to death!"

"Well, you're still kicking, aren't you?"

"You're a big help in time of trouble."

"Look here, Myrtle, ask me to help with something I believe in, will you?"

"You're siding with that boy!"

"Trigger?"

"Robert!"

"Well, it looks like he needs a friend!"

Mrs. Smith looked at him pretty sharp. "Guess I'm Robert's friend, too!"

"Hello!" said George Smith out loud to himself, as surprised as could be. "I thought—"

She interrupted him, "Everybody says I've got to send him away."

"They do, do they!"

"And I don't want to send him away!" Then she got to crying and that made George Smith shuffle round and pat her shoulder.

"Come on, Myrtle, old girl!"

"I'm not an old girl!"

"I didn't know you felt like that!"

He stood back and looked at her, pleased as Punch.

"Well, I like having him around. It may be wicked, but I like it. Besides, there must be a good side to it, because he's a trouble and trouble's good for a person."

"I guess we both like having Trigger around," he said, looking way off somewhere.

"Robert!" she corrected.

"Robert, then!" he agreed for once about it.

"But they're all telling me I have to send him away, because he's an evil influence in the town."

"They can tell it to the moo-cow," George Smith said. "Anyhow, we can't. We've adopted him, haven't we? He belongs to us."

"He's got to have schooling, hasn't he?"

"Gosh!" exclaimed George Smith. "Is that what's worrying you? I thought you had moral scruples!"

"I have!" she said. "He can't go to school here." But she looked hopeful about it. "Can he?"

George Smith shook his head, "I guess you've been hearing about that petition that's going around. It won't do any good. Mr. Woodruff is on his hind legs with righteous wrath and the School Committee's afraid of him."

"The old bear!"

"Hello!" George Smith said. "Well, don't blame him, Myrtle. Mr. Woodruff's cold is permanent and he can't help his growl. Maybe we can get him interested in some other moral issue by next term. Trigger could do it!"

"George Smith!"

"Well, I am only talking to myself."

Mrs. Smith stopped rocking and got up, kissed George Smith smack on the mouth and he put his arms round her and squeezed her, and then they broke apart and both got red in the face.

"Anyhow, I've written to Aunt Clarissa and told her everything and asked her what she wanted to do about it."

"Heck!" said George Smith. "Have you mailed the letter?"

"Yes," Mrs. Smith said. "I thought I ought to act at once while my duty was clear."

George Smith sat down and considered. "Oh, well," he said at last, "Aunt Clarissa won't want to be bothered to do anything about it anyhow."

But George Smith guessed wrong, for that letter had consequences and Aunt Clarissa did do something about it.

XXXII. AUNT CLARISSA

When Aunt Clarissa read Mrs. Smith's letter she packed up and started off for Beechwood. When she got as far as Lock Haven she sent a telegram to say she was coming and that was the first and only answer Mrs. Smith ever had to her letter. When it came, it set things humming, for Lock Haven is only two hours off and two hours wasn't half time enough to get the house ready for a visit from Aunt Clarissa. Mrs. Smith told the boy that brought the telegram to run to the store and tell George Smith to come home right away and help her get ready. When he got home, George Smith found housecleaning nearly finished, and about all he could find to do was to put the dust back in place, and change his neck to a clean collar. Then it was time to go and meet the train.

Trigger was up at the cemetery when the telegram came, and

didn't come back till he got hungry and wanted a piece of the new mince pies. He was in the pantry helping himself, when he heard voices and heard the gate click. He looked out and there was George Smith with Aunt Clarissa. He ducked out into the woodshed, but he had a big piece of mince pie with him. He was glad of that because he made up his mind he wouldn't be on hand for supper. George Smith came out to look for him as soon as he could get away, but Trigger got into an empty barrel and hid, and as soon as George Smith saw he was in the barrel, he chopped some kindlings to show Trigger he understood and then went back in the house.

Next morning Trigger was on the back porch when George Smith came down and they had their dip together as usual. He had Tip with him, because he wanted to see if Tip took to Aunt Clarissa. After the dip, they went into the woodshed to wait for breakfast. George Smith said:

"You don't want to be disappointed, Trigger, if you find you like her. She's not so bad."

She wasn't. When they went in to breakfast there was Aunt Clarissa sitting in the big rocking chair in a calico Mother Hubbard just as if she didn't have any money at all. Tip went right up to her and wagged his tail. Trigger expected she'd say, "Get away, you brute!" or, if she wanted to pretend, "How do you do, little dog?" But she didn't. She just scratched Tip's ears and let him get up in her lap and cuddle down.

She wasn't any bigger than a minute and when she moved it was so quick you couldn't see it. She was just here now and then there. She got to the table when Mrs. Smith said, "Breakfast's ready," as if she had an appetite. She talked like a blue streak all the time and hardly looked at Trigger.

Mrs. Smith said nothing was good or up to snuff, but it would have been better if she'd known Aunt Clarissa was coming. Aunt Clarissa said if it was any better she'd kill herself eating and then they'd have to take her to Calais to bury her, because all her folks were buried there, and that would be a trouble. Mrs. Smith said she hadn't time to prepare a thing, but she had some mince pies on hand, thank goodness, for dessert at dinner, and that relieved her some. George Smith said he guessed they were good pies, because he noticed a big notch out of one of them. George Smith looked as if he didn't mean anything in particular, but Mrs. Smith jerked up suddenly and looked hard at Trigger, but before she could say anything, Aunt Clarissa started to tell about her trip to Beechwood and it sounded funny and interesting all the way.

"Did you come in a box car?" George Smith asked her.

"No, I couldn't," she laughed, with a side look at Trigger,

"That's the trouble with being a woman and especially an old woman—you can't navigate in rough water."

Right after breakfast, Trigger and George Smith left; and Mrs. Smith and Aunt Clarissa did the dishes and then settled down to talk.

"What are we going to do about Robert, Aunt Clarissa?" Mrs. Smith asked.

"Who's Robert?" demanded Aunt Clarissa.

"Why, why—that's his name. That's the name we gave Trigger. Trigger isn't any real name."

"Nonsense!" exclaimed Aunt Clarissa. "If Trigger isn't a real name now, it'll be as real as a turnip by the time Trigger gets through with it. They'll be calling kings and presidents Trigger, when all the Myrtles and Clarissas are just bones in a graveyard. I shouldn't be surprised if Trigger himself'll be the first president to bear the name."

"But, but—" began Mrs. Smith.

"No buts about it," ran on Aunt Clarissa. "As for what to do with him, that's already decided."

"What decided?"

"This town isn't big enough for Trigger. That's clear enough, isn't it? He's too conspicuous and makes other folks envious."

"But," gasped Mrs. Smith, "you can't take him away now?"

"Now's just the time," Aunt Clarissa said firmly. "Good gracious, Myrtle! They won't let him go to school here. He's got to go to school somewhere, hasn't he?"

"Wh-where?" Mrs. Smith asked, in a weak whisper.

"There's just one place for Trigger—Boston, the hub of the universe."

"Boston," Mrs. Smith echoed.

"Yes, Boston! All that's known is known in Boston, and Trigger's got to have a chance to make his own selections."

George Smith came home for lunch on account of Aunt Clarissa, and was told about the plan for Trigger to go to Boston. He looked pretty glum at first. After a while he pulled himself together. "It's a good place for Trigger to go," he said, and added: "There's something to be done first. Trigger's not going to leave because he has to. He's going to leave because

it's the right thing for him to do. I'm going to make that School
Committee take back that vote."

Mrs. Smith gasped: "How you going to do that?"

"I'm going to get a town meeting to do it."

Aunt Clarissa clapped her hands. "Bully for you!" she exclaimed, and added: "Excuse my French!"

Mrs. Smith was dubious. "What about Mr. Woodruff?"

"He can come to the meeting," George Smith told her as
he made for the door, "if he wants to."

Aunt Clarissa turned on Mrs. Smith: "What about you?"

"Me?"

"Don't you think enough of Trigger to tell some of those
women a few things?"

"Yes, I do!"

"Then go and tell them. I'll go with you." Which they proceeded to do with very satisfactory results.

Meanwhile, George Smith got on his high horse and rode
it around the town. He wrote out a petition for a town meeting and in two hours he had five times as many signatures as
he needed to call one. He took it back to the store and put
it on the desk right under Mr. Woodruff's nose.

The Burgess read it and went red in the face with anger.

"Did you circulate this petition, George Smith?"

"I did!"

"What is the purpose of the meeting?"

"To force the School Committee to allow my boy Trigger
to attend school—if he wants to."

The Burgess was so furious he stuttered: "If you d-do this
you may c-consider yourself d-discharged."

"Good!" said George Smith. He took a piece of paper and
wrote on it. "I resign, George Smith," and planted it in front
of Mr. Woodruff. Old Woodruff looked at it and suddenly be-

came old indeed. He settled into his swivel chair and sort of shrank. He couldn't believe what he saw. When he could, he looked up at Gerge Smith and stared at him vacantly for a long time. Then his eyes filled up and the tears began to run slowly down his cheeks.

George Smith's mouth dropped open. He couldn't believe what he saw either. Suddenly he grabbed up his resignation and tore it in two. "Aw, I didn't mean it," he grinned at the Burgess, a little embarrassed. "I guess you didn't mean what you said either."

Mr. Woodruff got up heavily and held out his hand. "I couldn't run the General Store, George Smith, unless you told me how."

George Smith was more embarrassed. "Heck!" he said. "You always have to tell me what to tell you, don't you?" They shook hands.

The Burgess turned away and went across to the safe and looked into it and kept looking.

George Smith turned around and got another surprise.

A man was standing in front of him and he had a muffler wound around his face so that George Smith couldn't see his features. He unwound the muffler and George Smith gasped:

"Mr. England!"

"Yes, and you're George Smith! I know your voice. And I know what you look like, too."

George Smith was so pleased he didn't even look funny. He just grasped the old Englishman's hand and wrung it.

Mr. England looked around quickly as if he was afraid of being seen, then he said:

"I want to give a surprise party and I want you to help me. I want all the gang, the Goosetown gang, to come to my place and find me there. I want to thank them for what they did for me. I want them to see me and I want to see them. And I want to ask you if you'll be kind enough to get as much food as you think the boys can eat and bring it up to the party and help us eat it."

He handed a bill to George Smith. "You see, I still have some of their money left."

"Don't take it, George Smith!" Mr. Woodruff had heard everything. "I want you to charge whatever you take up, and take plenty, to me."

He got his hat and put it on as the other two men watched him. He said to George Smith, "I'm going over to see the members of the School Committee. I think I can promise you that they will rescind that vote." He went down the aisle and out.

Trigger came in then. The old man quickly wound the muffler round his face and left hastily by the front door.

"Who's that?" Trigger's quick eyes looked after Mr. England. "Is that—that isn't?" He looked questioningly at George Smith.

"Whatever you think, you're wrong," George Smith told him.

Trigger had something else on his mind. "You heard about me, George Smith?"

"Quite a lot."

George Smith tried to be funny, but it was hard work. He and Trigger didn't say anything for a long time. George Smith said at last, "I expect you'll be around here for vacations and the like—if you want to."

"I guess I'll want to, George Smith."

Then George Smith told Trigger to call a meeting of the gang up at the shack for that evening. He said it would be a good chance for everybody to tell everybody else anything that anybody wanted to know.